Groove

Also by Bernice L. McFadden

NONFICTION
Firstborn Girls

FICTION
Tisoy
Praise Song for the Butterflies
The Book of Harlan
Gathering of Waters
Glorious
Nowhere Is a Place
Camilla's Roses
Loving Donovan
This Bitter Earth
The Warmest December
Sugar

WRITING AS GENEVA HOLLIDAY
Fever
Heat
Seduction
Lover Man

Groove

A NOVEL

Bernice L. McFadden

Writing as Geneva Holliday

PLUME

An imprint of Penguin Random House LLC
1745 Broadway, New York, NY 10019
penguinrandomhouse.com

First published in trade paperback in the United States by Broadway Books,
a division of Random House, Inc.

Second American edition published in the United States by Plume,
an imprint of Penguin Random House LLC, in 2025.

Copyright © 2005 by Geneva Holliday
Penguin Random House values and supports copyright. Copyright fuels creativity, encourages diverse voices, promotes free speech, and creates a vibrant culture. Thank you for buying an authorized edition of this book and for complying with copyright laws by not reproducing, scanning, or distributing any part of it in any form without permission. You are supporting writers and allowing Penguin Random House to continue to publish books for every reader. Please note that no part of this book may be used or reproduced in any manner for the purpose of training artificial intelligence technologies or systems.

PLUME and the P colophon are registered trademarks of
Penguin Random House LLC.

Book design by Diahann Sturge

LIBRARY OF CONGRESS CATALOGING-IN-PUBLICATION DATA

Names: Holliday, Geneva author
Title: Groove: a novel / Bernice L. McFadden writing as Geneva Holliday.
Description: Second American edition. | New York, NY: Plume,
an imprint of Penguin Random House LLC, 2025.
Identifiers: LCCN 2025021103 (print) | LCCN 2025021104 (ebook) |
ISBN 9780593472828 paperback | ISBN 9780593472835 ebook
Subjects: LCSH: African American women—Fiction |
New York (N.Y.)—Fiction | Summer—Fiction |
LCGFT: Romance fiction | Novels | Fiction
Classification: LCC PS3608.O4847 G76 2025 (print) |
LCC PS3608.O4847 (ebook) | DDC 813/.6—dc23/eng/20250625
LC record available at https://lccn.loc.gov/2025021103
LC ebook record available at https://lccn.loc.gov/2025021104

Printed in the United States of America
1st Printing

The authorized representative in the EU for product safety and compliance is
Penguin Random House Ireland, Morrison Chambers, 32 Nassau Street,
Dublin D02 YH68, Ireland, https://eu-contact.penguin.ie.

For Elton, who showed me that Death by Chocolate can be a bitterly, sweet demise...

Groove

The end of a bizarro summer, 2002

Now how we all ended up in the Brooklyn Hospital emergency room two days before Labor Day is a long, interesting, funny story that started back in April of that year.

spring

Geneva Holliday

In my bed that April night, my mind was everywhere but where it should have been, which was on my ex-husband's tongue as it slid across my stomach and down my side.

Instead, my mind was on how hard my life was. How hard it was in so many different ways. Hard like a stone when you're black, female, and a single mother holding a GED instead of a high school diploma.

I wasn't thinking about how good it felt when he pushed his fingers through my hair and moved his tongue in circles around my navel. No, my mind was on the fact that I had missed three weeks of Calorie Counters meetings and how in that time I had stopped counting points, calories, carbs, and everything else.

Now my size-sixteen skirts and pants were giving my size-eighteen hips hell! Every morning it was an out-and-out fight. And I was steadily losing. Not the weight, of course. And on top of it, my Calorie Counters sponsor, Nadine Crawford—a former soda-guzzling, pound cake–eating accountant and mother of three, who'd joined the program three years earlier, had shed half her body weight, and was currently a size six and Calorie Counters' biggest cheerleader—was now calling my house every other day like a goddamn bill collector, talking about "When are you coming back, Geneva?" and "I'm here for you" and "Let's get together for an eight-point lunch and talk about it." I know I should have followed my first mind and joined Weight Watchers!

My mind was everywhere but in that bedroom where it should have been.

It was on my two-decade-old secondhand Coldspot refrigerator that was humming so loud, it sounded as if any moment it would hack up something green, cough, and drop dead.

If that was to happen, it would take Housing a whole month to get me another crappy refrigerator in this apartment, and then how would I keep the milk cold for my sixteen-year-old son's morning cereal?

And he was another problem—my son, Eric Jr., who we all lovingly refer to as "Little Eric."

Little Eric hasn't been little since he was ten years old, and now he's a sophomore in high school, towering over me at a staggering six feet, and that boy still has years of growth ahead of him. Just trying to keep him in sneakers is going to send me to the poor house.

He was a good kid, even though I knew he was sampling weed. I mean, do these kids think we weren't kids once too? Do they think we were all born big?

The other day he strolled into the house, smelling like he'd been rolling in a field of reefer. I snatched him by his collar and dragged him through the living room and into the kitchen where the light is better and looked him in his eyes and asked him if he'd been smoking. Of course he lied and blinked those big brown eyes at me and said, "Look at my eyes, Ma—they ain't even red or nothing. I was just hanging out with these guys that was smoking it, but I didn't."

I said, "Fool, I know Visine gets the red out, but it don't take the scent out of your clothes or off your breath!" And with that I popped him upside his head and sent him on his way. I told him that if he came back in my house smelling like a pothead, I was going to call the police on him my damn self!

"*Ohhhhhhhh*," I moan, just so Eric can feel like he's doing all of the right things even though my mind has skipped over to my best friend, Crystal.

Not only is she my best friend but she has been on many occasions a godsend as well.

I've had some rough times, and Crystal has always been there. Like the time when I was still on welfare and I had just collected my money and food stamps for the month and was on my way downtown to buy Eric, who was just about four years old then, a new pair of shoes. I hadn't even stepped off the bus good when two young boys rushed toward me, ripped my pocketbook from my hands, and then took off across Union Square.

I didn't even have a token to get home. It was Crystal that I called, and she left her job and came downtown and got me and then took me to the supermarket and filled up my refrigerator and cupboards with food. When I collected again the following month, she wouldn't even let me pay her back.

Crystal is also the one who saved me from the cosmetics counter at Macy's and got me a job as a receptionist at the Ain't I A Woman Foundation. Ten dollars an hour is certainly better than seven-fifty and standing on your feet for eight to ten hours a day. Much better, and I will be forever grateful to her.

But lately Crystal just hasn't been herself. Something is bothering her; I see the sadness lurking behind that phony smile she walks around with all day.

I keep asking her what's wrong, but she just says, "Nothing."

I guess she'll tell me in her own good time.

That feel good, baby?"

"*Ooooooooooooooooooh* yeah, baby, real good."

Okay, now where was I?

Oh yes, my mind being on everything outside of this here bedroom.

Well, I've also been thinking about Chevy. That's another friend of mine, who is just . . . just—I don't know—just *crazy* is the best way to describe her. Crazy and a chameleon. You can never tell what Chevy was going to look like the next time you met up with her. She could be sporting a long weave, short weave, hazel contacts, red weave, blue contacts, blond Afro puffs, green contacts. Who knows!

Dr. Phil said that a person who needs to change her appearance as many times as Chevy does is unhappy with herself.

I believe that. But what I want to know is, what does it say when that same person can always find money for a new pair of La Blanca stilettos or a slinky thong from La Perla but ain't never got enough money to pay her light bill or rent?

She's making at least twice my hourly rate, for chrissakes! And don't have chick nor child to worry about. Not a dog, goldfish, or hamster, just her! As my mother says, "When she eats, her whole family has eaten."

Crazy is all I can think to call her. Oh yeah, and *selfish* is another word that fits too. It's all about Chevy, all of the time.

You want it, baby, you want it?"

"*Ooooooooooh* yeah, baby, I want it *reaaaaaaaaaaal* bad."

Now finally, there's Noah.

A dead ringer for Howard Hewett, except fairer-complexioned. A successful merchandising manager for the high-end casual clothing company VQ, and a Cancerian, so he can be a moody something.

When we were younger, Noah was the best double Dutch jumper in our building and could corn braid better than any of us. The highlight of his year was the Miss America beauty pageant, which we had to watch with him. Afterward he'd reenact the last fifteen minutes of the pageant—the surprise on the winner's face, the tears, the halfhearted hugs she shared with the losers—then he'd plop a lampshade on his head and tie a bedsheet around his neck and prance back and forth across the living room, demonstrating the proper way the new Miss America should have strutted down the catwalk.

Do you see where I'm going with this?

We've known Noah was gay since forever and have always accepted him. His Jamaican mother, on the other hand, is still in denial and even to this day still tries to fix Noah up on dates with her friends' daughters.

Noah is about the only one that I'm not really worried about. He seems happy with his career and has met some new man who lives in England, so he's always flying back and forth to London to be with him.

Yeah, I think that Noah should be the least of my worries right about now.

Now me; besides the war with my weight and a pack-a-day cigarette habit, I guess I don't have any real pressing concerns. Well, not that living in the projects is a great joy, but at least I'm not on the streets.

I'm thinking about going back to school. College. To major in what, I have no clue, but I think a college degree is something I should have. Well, I know it's something I need if I don't want to be a receptionist forever. And besides, maybe it will motivate that son of mine to do the right thing with his life.

Okay, enough of that, Geneva—try to concentrate on all of the kisses Eric is covering your body with, I tell myself, and I try, but my mind won't stay put. It keeps straying to the load of clothes that needs to be washed, the pile of unopened bills sitting on the kitchen table, and that goddamn pervert with the chiseled good looks and expensive suit who flashed me on the C train this morning when I was on my way to work.

"Turn over," Eric says, and I do and so do my thoughts.

He enters me from behind and I grip the headboard, not because it feels good—it does, though—but to hold on tight to try to keep it from banging too hard against the wall. Little Eric should have been asleep hours ago, but I don't want to take any chances.

Eric stops, his body shudders, and he withdraws. This is his control method. It's been the same for years. Our sex life should have ended when I caught him cheating, moved out of our Queens apartment, and signed the divorce papers, but it didn't. It went on through all of it and still goes on.

Why? I don't know. Stupid, I guess. Or just plain horny.

"Where are you, Geneva?" Eric coos.

"I'm here, baby, I'm here," I assure him and push my behind up into his chest.

He starts kissing my back while his hands massage my shoulders.

He begins to ease his penis back inside me. "You like it? You like it, baby?" he whispers in my ear.

"Uh-huh," I say, and in my mind I start to separate the white clothes from the dark, flip through the mountain of mail on my kitchen table, and clip coupons.

Eric's body trembles with excitement and then he whispers, "You want me to put it in your ass?"

My mind comes to a sudden and complete halt.

I've allowed him there only twice in my life, and both

times we were still Mr. and Mrs. and I was really in love then. So in love that all I wanted to do was please him. But now I just wanted to be pleased and had no desire to have my asshole stretched out of shape. And besides, anal sex is notorious for leaving one unable to control the passing of air, if you know what I mean.

"Uh-uh," I say and start to turn back over and onto my back.

"Oh, c'mon, please?" he begs and gives me that puppy-dog look of his.

"Uh-uh," I say again and shake my head from side to side.

After the day I had I thought some sexual healing was in order, but my mind won't let me concentrate on it, which means I'm dry as a bone down between my legs. Really and truly, all I want to do is just have a beer, maybe some chips, and a couple of spoonfuls of ice cream.

"Turn back over," Eric presses. "I won't put it in your ass."

Now Eric is one who cannot be trusted. He's a liar, cheater, and all-around crooked cop. Oh yeah, he's one of New York's finest. And I do mean *fine*! Six foot four and copper brown. He'd been working out a lot lately and so was cut and as solid as a rock.

"You know, Eric, I don't think I want to do this," I say as I clamp my legs closed and reach for the sheet.

Eric looks surprised. His erect penis looks even more astonished than he does.

"What?" He half laughs.

"I said I don't think I want to do this," I say again as I

catch hold of the sheet and try to pull it up and over my naked body.

"You're fucking kidding me, right, Geneva?" His rock-hard dick gives me an accusing look. "What the fuck am I supposed to do about this?" he says, indicating his stiff member with his index finger.

"Whatever you do when you're alone," I say and try not to smile. "I'm just not here. I'm sorry."

Eric looks down at his penis and then back at me.

I could tell he was having a conversation with it in his mind. His dick was his best friend, and any woman who had ever been with him knew it.

Suddenly his features softened and a mischievous smile spread across his face.

"How about a little licky-licky, then?" he says and sticks his long pink tongue out at me.

I think about it for a minute. If I let him eat me out, it would release some tension. No effort on my part. It seems like I win all the way around. But then I remember who I'm dealing with and say, "What do I have to do to you?"

"Suck my dick, of course," he says proudly and thrusts his hips toward my face.

"Nah," I say and pull the sheet up to my chin.

"You're so fucking selfish," he hisses and sticks his lips out like a two-year-old.

"Then leave."

"Aw, c'mon, Geneva." He laughs.

"Nope."

Eric lets out a long sigh and looks around the bedroom for a moment. "Okay. You win."

Wow, I think, this is a first.

He pulls the sheet away from my body and gently separates my legs before moving into "eating" position.

Eric loves to eat pussy; always has. It's like a delicacy for him.

He begins by teasing my clitoris, rolling his tongue across it and then darting it in and out of my hole, bringing me to the point of orgasm seven or eight times before I finally scream, "Please, please!" when I know I can't take much more.

"Okay, baby, okay," he pants and takes a deep breath before moving in for the kill.

"Motherfucker, motherfucker!"

The firecrackers go off behind my eyes and bells ring in my head, and how it is that my behind and the heels of my feet are able to levitate above the sheets for a moment is anyone's guess, but they do.

That's how Eric makes me come: cussing, screaming, and levitating, which is why even after all of the low-down shit he's done to me and the half-ass child support he pays I'm still fucking him.

I don't have any excuse and won't even try to make one up. All I know is, a good dick is hard to find and an orgasm that can shoot you to the moon and back is even more elusive.

After my body stops shaking and I begin to feel uncomfortable in the wet spot, he lifts his head off my thigh, looks up at me, and asks, "You sure you don't want me to fuck you?"

"N-no." I can hardly speak, and I lock my hands

around his head and guide his mouth as far away from my vagina as possible.

Even if I wanted to fuck, I wouldn't allow it—shit, my pussy might explode!

Eric looks up at me and smiles. "I am good, ain't I?" he gloats and moves up beside me.

All I can do is shake my head in agreement and turn over onto my side.

Eric kisses my shoulder and then tries to put his arms around me, but I don't want that part of it. That tenderness belonged to us a long, long time ago. What we do now is primitive and carnal and that's the way I want it to remain.

"What's up with you?" he says and sucks his teeth in disgust.

"Shouldn't you go home to your wife now?" I say before punching the pillow and readying myself for dreamland.

Chevy

There is power in the pussy.

All pussy—not just mine, all of ours.

I tell you, if those boys on Wall Street would take pussy public and trade it on the OTC board, it would blow pork bellies, gold, and everything else right out of the water!

Well, that's my Chevy-osophy, anyway.

My name is Chevanese . . . but most poor people can't pronounce that, so I just tell them to call me Chevy. Like the car—only think of me as a Mercedes coupe!

I'm a talker and a taker.

I don't give unless I know that it will benefit me in the end. I'm not talking nickel-and-dime shit either. You gotta be big-time or you get none of my time!

Don't even think about stepping to me with a five-figure income. I need a six-figure nigga or better—you know what I'm talking about?

Someone who can pay to be the boss. Or at least afford to have me make him think he is. I ain't no woman you can walk all over. I tell 'em straight out: I might suck your dick, but I ain't about to kiss your ass!

Ain't nothing free in this world. Food cost, gas cost—shoot, and I cost too.

Too many of y'all chickenheads out there, giving it away for a Coke and a smile.

My mama told me I had a fortune down between my legs, and my mama ain't never told me a lie.

I'm sorry, what was that?

What about love?

Pullllleeeeeeeeze. What about it?

Love is like religion: it's a crutch for people who don't have the looks or the smarts to make it in this kick-ass world. Besides, I tried it in my twenties and it just didn't work for me. I'm not what you would call a committed type of sista. I have a short attention span when it comes to men. You know, I can be digging a guy, but if another one comes along with more bank for my bang, I'm there.

I'm also a mistress of illusion. I like to change up my appearance. Ladies, don't you get bored looking in the mirror and seeing the same old person every single fucking day?

Well, I certainly do.

I like to dazzle myself and whoever it is I'm dating at the time. Well, usually I'm dating about three or four mofos at any given moment.

That's the way you gotta do it, ladies, 'cause there is no perfect man, but if you get three or four okay guys, you can certainly build one. Every man has a purpose.

Lean in close and let me school you.

You have to have one that takes you to expensive restaurants. Another that will buy you clothes. Another that will pay your bills. Another that will keep you in hairdos and acrylic nails. And then there's the sugar daddy who's popping Viagra like mints and still can't keep it up for more than five minutes. He's the one who wants to have a beautiful woman on his arm in Monaco, Madrid, London, and St. Barts. Yeah, I got one of those too.

What about the one to love me, you ask?

We back to that love shit again?

I love me, my mama loves me—what I need a man to love me for? All I need from a man is his money!

Reality?

Well, whose reality are we speaking about, yours or mine? My reality is get yours and move on to the next fool and get some more!

Take this place, for example: Tuesday night, Café Aubette. Wall-to-wall black people, everybody styling and profiling. Most of them look real good, but then some of them . . . well, over there, for instance. Yeah, yeah, that table full of tired-looking bitches with their twenty-five-dollar weaves and Lee Press On Nails.

Oh my God, do you see that? Sister-girl's tracks are showing! And she grinning all up in that waiter's face—he's probably cracking up laughing on the inside!

Readers, should I tell her?

If I tell her *that*, then I would have to go on and tell her about the pink and green nail polish. What kind of fucked-up colors are those?

Hey, girlfriends, I have to let you know that AKA colors do not a French manicure make!

Oh, and do you see that outfit? Lord have mercy—a

hot pink glitter tube top, faded black capri pants, and Payless pumps. That outfit ain't fit to be worn outside!

I'm looking down at a lot of shoes and I see that Star Jones done got a lot of people tripping on some bullshit. Cheap shoes are just a prelude to corns, hammertoes, and bunions. Believe me when I tell you.

Now you see, the proper way to come up through here looking for a man that got some dollars is the Chevy way.

The three-hundred-dollar weave. Um-hmm, and the silk-wrapped nails. A reasonable length, not the claws these sisters run around here with, making you wonder how in the world they're able to wipe their asses properly.

Oh yeah, don't forget the Tahari suit and Italian leather pumps. You gotta know how to do it right. You come up in here dressed like homegirl over there with those hanging tracks, and you gonna get just what you deserve, which is the brother who works in the mailroom, got five baby mommas, is still living with his mama, and is fronting in the passenger seat of his homeboy's ride.

Simply put, a scrub!

I don't want that.

So that's why I come correct. I ooze class and sophistication and that's what I want in return. Don't come all up in my face talking that "baby, baby" shit to me. Been there, done that when I was a teenager. That shit is for homegirl across the bar. She looks like she's about my age, but she still got that ghetto project mentality. I grew up in the projects and fought long and hard to get out of there and I don't plan on ever going back. Shit, not even to visit.

I'll be the first one to tell ya, I'm all about the Benjamins because I ain't got none of my own. I'm one paycheck away from being put out of my apartment. My credit cards are maxed out and now I just carry them around for show.

I got one ride left on my Metro card. You don't believe me; if I'm lying I'm flying!

But you would never know my real situation just by looking at me. I know how to fake the funk!

Tonight I'll go home and dig for change from between the cushions of my couch. I'm sure I can find enough to get me to work in the morning.

Or I can always give Geneva a call; I know she got a change jar up in her place. And if she holds out on me, I can bum a few dollars from Noah. He's a tightwad, though, and I probably wouldn't be able to get more than five dollars from his cheap ass.

But I can't ask Crystal; I borrowed five thousand from her two weeks ago for some "required" surgery and ain't paid back dime the first.

Crystal

This time next year I'll be thirty-six. The middle of the road, the halfway point between whatever this is and forty. I'm not scared. I've read all the magazine articles. "Forty and Fabulous." "You Know Who You Are When You Reach Forty." "Sex Is Better at Forty."

I'm well prepared.

I hold a BS and a MS from Princeton and Cornell Universities, respectfully. Five foot nine inches, one hundred and thirty-five pounds, honey-colored skin, hazel eyes, and an ass like a racehorse's. I am a prize filly, at least that's what my boyfriend, Kendrick, tells me. And he should know—he rides it well.

I live in a turn-of-the-century building on Central Park West. Funny, I read something once that said people generally die five to ten miles away from where they were born and raised.

Well, I was raised exactly one block away from where I live now. Right on the corner of 90th and Columbus Avenue. Come to think of it, we were all raised there, and we all got out. Well, everyone except Geneva.

So here I am, living a block away from the projects, in a beautiful building with a doorman who refers to me as

Ms. Atkins and is at my service whenever I need extra hands to help with my groceries or Bloomingdale's bags.

I have a two-bedroom, two-thousand-square-foot tenth-floor apartment.

Moët, pâté, and Evian fill my refrigerator the way government cheese fills Geneva's.

I am the director of the Ain't I A Woman Foundation. We assist women who are in abusive relationships. We get them out of their unhappy situations, place them in safe houses, and counsel them until they feel confident enough to reenter society.

I am one of a handful of African-American women holding a top director's position in an old-boy, stuffed-shirt, all-male, all-white private organization.

I know I'm a token and I know I have this job because over the past twenty years a lot of brothers and sisters have been popping up on *Fortune* magazine's wealthiest people list. Black people are pulling some serious bank, and AIW wanted some of that money. Installing me as director guaranteed donations from Oprah Winfrey and Michael Jordan.

I can't say if affirmative action helped me, so I'll just leave that alone. I do know that I worked my ass off to get to this point.

Children?

I used to think about having children all the time. I kept scheduling and rescheduling the year I would finally get pregnant. But something always disrupted my plans: a change in boyfriends, another promotion, the state of the world.

And then I looked up and I was thirty and then thirty-two, and so I just started telling myself that there was no place for a child in my life. I mean, how would I do it? Where does a child fit into traveling around the country and working thirteen-hour days?

Then I turned thirty-three, met Kendrick, and started hearing my biological clock ticking loudly inside my head.

Two years later and it's so loud at times that I can hardly sleep at night.

Kendrick and I have spoken about children in passing. He says he would love to have a baby with me, a little girl. He has a son from a previous relationship. But he says now is not the time. He says we need to enjoy our lives before we settle down and have babies.

I never hear the word *marriage* from him, just *babies*. I assume he means marriage too, just like in that movie *Ghost*, when Demi Moore knew that Patrick Swayze meant "I love you" when all he would say was "Ditto."

So I pushed back my baby-having year and just hope that Kendrick's schedule is open at the same time mine is, because I love him and we're good together—when we are together.

He's been working so hard these past few weeks. Running from one country to another, buying and selling property, initiating plans for new buildings.

There's been very little us time, but I don't complain. I know that being with a successful black man can be lonely sometimes.

Sometimes after he returns from an exceptionally long business trip, he's cranky and wound up so tight he snaps at every little thing. But I understand and work through it with him until he feels more like himself again. And when we do finally get him back to the Kendrick that I know and love, he's got to jet off again.

So that's me. Crystal Atkins. Not bad for a girl who was raised on welfare and ate pork and beans for breakfast, lunch, and dinner.

Not bad at all.

Noah

I have a secret.
And the secret ain't the fact that I'm gay. I came out of the closet when I was fifteen years old. I'm thirty-six now. You do the math.

I'm talking ass-switching, wrist-snapping, eye-rolling, will-cut-you-till-you-bleed-with-my-tongue-trashing, one hundred percent homo and proud of it!

So that's where the dilemma comes in. You see, recently . . . okay, over the past few months, I've found myself in a precarious predicament.

What is it, you ask?

Well, calm down. I'm about to tell you, but I have to whisper it.

I'm on the down low.

What! How can you be? you scream in disbelief.

Well, not the type of down low that you all are familiar with. No, no. I'm not into animals. You and your filthy, filthy minds!

I'm talking about the pum-pum, the punany, the cat, the snatch: you know, pussy!

And you know where there's a pussy, there's a woman attached to it.

So what's wrong with me?

I've been happily homosexual for more than twenty years now, and one day I woke up with a taste for pussy and a craving for titties!

It's disgusting, I know.

It's that damn Beyoncé Knowles who done it to me.

I mean, did you see her in that Sean Paul video or any of the others? She is a sexy bitch! I didn't want to believe that watching her was giving me a hard-on. I mean, I tried to fool myself into thinking that it was whatever man happened to be in the video. But the whole time I was jerking off, it was Beyoncé I was seeing dancing across my mind's eye!

Oh, just talking about it gets me hot!

Is there a group out there for this particular problem?

My therapist says, "Maybe you're not really gay?" But I say, "What the hell do you know?" One hundred and fifty fucking dollars an hour, and that's what he has to offer?

This obsession is taking over my life.

I'm sneaking into straight bars, plying beautiful women with alcohol until they look at me and no longer see my processed hair, glossy lips, or perfectly manicured fingernails.

All of a sudden, their hands are on my thigh or their heads are resting against my shoulder—in any case they're all up in my face, telling me how cute I am and saying, "When you first sat down, I thought you were gay!"

I laugh along and say, "Yeah, I get that a lot."

Up until a few months ago, I'd been able to walk away from the temptation. But one March evening I found myself sitting at Night of the Cookers on Fulton Street, enjoying an apple martini and the live band that was playing that Friday night.

I'd had a ballbuster of a day. Back-to-back meetings with factory presidents who spoke very little English, after which my boss practically got down on his knees and begged me to take this young, hip new designer that *Women's Wear Daily* hailed as the Second Coming to lunch in the hopes that she would come and work for VQ.

WWD may have hailed her as the Second Coming, but they failed to mention that the French talent had no table etiquette whatsoever and had no idea that there was a pecking order where her silverware was concerned, because she used her entrée fork for her salad and her salad fork for her entrée.

Yes, those things bother me.

And finally, my train ride home was disrupted by a lunatic preaching wannabe evangelist who marched up and down the aisle of the car screaming, "All child molesters, fornicators, and gays are going to hell!"

Why do they always group us with child molesters?

Anyway, I needed a drink after having a day like that.

Lost in my thoughts, I didn't hear the woman that had sidled up next to me ask if the stool beside me was taken, and so I was a bit startled when she touched my shoulder.

"Excuse me," she barely uttered above the music, and when I turned to look at her, I almost fell off my stool.

"B-Beyoncé?" I whispered, everything in me going to mush.

"Sorry?" she said, leaning in with a puzzled expression.

Well, at first sight she did look like Beyoncé. The flawless skin and long gold-blond hair that framed a beautiful set of eyes.

I swallowed hard, and my eyes traveled down her body to see if she only resembled Beyoncé in the face. And lo and behold, wrapped snugly in the cream-colored lightweight wool skirt she wore, were Beyoncé thighs, hips, and, best of all—the famed Beyoncé bottom!

A wide grin slowly inched across my face.

"Someone sitting here?" Beyoncé's look-alike inquired.

"N-no," I mumbled, recovered enough to feel embarrassed about my reaction.

I returned my attention to my drink. She ordered a glass of the Shiraz, and for a good ten minutes we said nothing to each other, while I seized every opportunity to snatch glances at her in the wall-length mirror behind the bar.

She was quite magnificent, and so when she drained her glass of wine, I quickly offered to buy her another.

She accepted, seemingly without thought, and we fell into a conversation that took us through two of the band's sets, three apple martinis, and a glass and a half more of Shiraz.

Her name was Merriwether Beacon, and yes, she had been told on a number of occasions that she resembled Beyoncé, but Merriwether considered herself to be better-looking.

Merriwether Beacon would be the beginning of my descent into heterosexual hell.

She asked me to walk her home. "I'm just around the

corner," she purred, and she took my hand before I could even decline.

She lived in a two-bedroom brownstone apartment that sat on the corner of South Oxford and Dekalb and smelled of cheap candles and a long-neglected litter box. This woman had taken shabby chic to a new level. Her furniture didn't even look secondhand; it looked more like third- and fourth-hand.

An invitation for a late-night cup of coffee, which I would learn later as I descended into my addiction was nothing more than a thinly disguised prelude to sex.

I waited anxiously on her overworn green and yellow brocade sofa as she stole off to her bedroom to slip into something more comfortable. While waiting I amused myself by mentally rearranging her furniture, tossing out the pieces that not even Goodwill would take. And that was most everything.

It occurred to me quite quickly that the only thing this Merriwether had going for her was her good looks. As a straight man, I would need a woman who knew how to decorate!

When she came back, she was dressed in a raunchy, crotchless leather and lace one-piece that looked as if she'd painted it on.

Merriwether took a seat at the far end of the couch and then began a slow, catlike, erotic inch-and-crawl across the cushions toward me.

I was scared and excited at the same time, and when her lips closed around my earlobe I heard myself yelp like a bitch in heat.

Her hands were everywhere: in my hair, pinching my nipples through my silk shirt, fumbling with the zipper of my khakis.

I told my hands to push her away, but they were defiant, clamping down on her waist and pulling her closer. Her mouth was suddenly on mine, her tongue pushing at my tightly pinched lips until I lost all feeling in my face and my mouth dropped open. A second later my air was cut off by the yard of tongue she'd stuck down my throat.

Everything seemed to be happening so fast. The room was spinning, and I lay there helpless as she wrangled my zipper down, slipped her hand inside the opening of my red silk boxers, and grabbed hold of my Johnson.

"Damn, baby, for a small guy, you carry a big stick." Merriwether drooled, her eyes sparkling beneath the milky moonlight that spilled into the living room.

Was I supposed to say thank you?

In a flash she'd yanked khakis, boxers, and all down to my knees. I tried to object, but by then she was on her knees, yanking off my shoes and tossing them aside.

"Hey, hey, wait a minute!" I pleaded, but it was no use. She'd gotten to all of the buttons on my shirt and now we wrestled as she tried to get it off me and I tried in vain to keep it on.

She won, and my two-hundred-dollar silk shirt went flying over the arm of the sofa.

In no time, Merriwether had stepped out of her Frederick's of Hollywood getup and demanded that I follow her to the bedroom. I didn't want to, but my Johnson was like a magnet, and he pulled me along helplessly after Merriwether's jiggling behind.

The bed was early IKEA, queen-size. When she tossed me down onto the mattress I could immediately tell that the sheets were less than two hundred count and knew that my body—which I faithfully treated to a ginger salt scrub every other Tuesday—would no doubt go into shock after the chafing from her cheap sheets.

Merriwether went for my nipples like a starving newborn, and just when I was about to tell her that no matter how hard she sucked, they would still be unable to produce milk, she shifted her mouth to my navel and then just above the space where Johnson waited at attention.

Her head popped up, and I looked down to see her staring amusedly up at me. "No hair, huh?"

"I—I like it smooth down there," I uttered.

"I like it too." She moaned as she licked and nibbled her way around Johnson, sending him into a trembling frenzy of excitement.

Me, I kept my hands at my side, and when I thought I would grab hold of her head and force her mouth, I resisted and brought my hands up, shoving them behind my head.

Her mouth closed over my scrotum sack, and I looked around for the cat that was mewing loudly from the corner of the room before I realized that I was making that sound and it was echoing back at me.

My leg bounced rapidly off the thin mattress as Merriwether finished up, rose, and sauntered over to her bureau, where she opened the top drawer and pulled out a box of condoms.

"Do you prefer ribbed, extra-lubricated, colored, or all three?" she asked as she flipped through the box.

"What-whatever suits you," I said, being the gentleman that I am.

It was my last chance, so I looked down at my dick and mentally told him that what we were about to do was wrong and went against everything I'd ever believed in. But that dick of mine just looked back at me and said, "Shut up, fool. I believe in it, so don't block. Put the condom on, 'cause I'm going in!"

What could I do?

I listened to my dick, because he'd been with me from the beginning, and in a relationship that spanned more than three decades, there had been plenty of compromises, plenty of give-and-take.

She was the freakiest sex partner I'd ever had. She had a closetful of sex toys! Vibrating plastic butterflies, leather whips, and even a strap-on penis, which I was thrilled to see, because after I did her from behind, she was able to return the favor!

Merriwether gave, and I took, and took and took until we both exploded. It was the nastiest, funkiest sexual encounter I'd ever experienced.

And in the end, when I exploded, it was Beyoncé's name I screamed out, not Merriwether's.

The disgust at what I'd done came not too long after Johnson had shriveled up and gone off to sleep. I poked him and said, "Hey, wake up. I need to talk."

He just flinched, yawned, and said, "Nah, dawg. A brother's got to get some shut-eye. We'll talk in the morning, during the first piss of the day."

"What happened to the compromise, the give-and-take, the respect?"

"Whatever," he said and retreated further into his foreskin.

Bastard.

So off I went to the bathroom to wash off that female scent and to throw up.

"You okay?" she hollered from the bedroom.

"Yeah, just had some bad fish, I guess," I said.

There was a moment of silence and then she said, "When did you have fish?"

A few minutes ago, stupid! I thought, but I said, "For lunch."

I promised that I would call. But never did.

And then I promised myself that that was the first and last time.

I screamed down at my dick, "No more!" and then two nights later, there I was again at another straight bar, my tongue wagging for another hit of the pum-pum, looking for another unsuspecting victim.

You see my problem?

I need some professional help, and quick. If this goes on any longer, I'm going to get caught. You know everything you do in the dark comes to light sooner or later.

It's so bad that I haven't had the nerve to confide in my girlfriends. Lord only knows how Geneva, Crystal, or Chevy will feel about all of this.

You've met them already. An interesting group of women, don't you think?

They're the Grace to my Will, the hag to my fag.

You know what I'm saying?

But back to me. What the hell am I going to do?

One

"Geneva, you did what?" Crystal was speaking to me from between clenched teeth. "I can't believe you slept with him again. What's wrong with you?"

I was horny, that's what was wrong with me, I wanted to scream.

But instead I just mumbled, "I dunno."

Eric and I had been apart for years. We were only married three years, but right after Little Eric was born it became clear that my husband wasn't interested in playing house or forging a relationship with his son. What he was interested in was sleeping around.

And he was never able to shake that part of himself. He'd been married twice since we split and had had three more children, and still he continued to fuck around.

I was awarded a pittance for child support when we divorced and was told that it would be increased with every pay raise Eric received, but I've never gotten a dime more, and he had made detective by the time Little Eric was ten years old.

Crystal says I should go back down to court. She says that it's not right that Little Eric and I are living in a tiny two-bedroom apartment while Big Eric is living high on the hog in a split-level home in Hempstead, Long Island.

She says I can go back to court and they'll pay me arrears and then maybe I can buy myself some new clothes and put a good chunk away for Little Eric's schooling.

But I can't be taking time off work to run back and forth to court. Crystal doesn't know how the system works, how long they can drag a matter like this out. I don't have the time or the patience.

So I keep it as is and take the extra Eric gives us when he can.

People treat you the way you allow them to. It's true. I had no one to blame but myself. But the sex between us had always been amazing, and I was just too weak to give that up.

"You really need to stop that shit, Geneva. I mean, he's no good for you, or haven't you noticed that yet?" Crystal sucked her teeth and stabbed at her Caesar salad. We were having lunch at Red's restaurant at the South Street Seaport.

What did she know? She was practically perfect. She had her education, a successful career, owned her apartment and a time-share in the Bahamas, and to top it off she had a man who was fine and wealthy!

She had no idea how hard it was for women like me. There was a shortage of men out there, and so a lot of sharing went on. The statistics are astronomical. Shit, I was tempted to tell her that she could be one of us and not even know it. But I just gritted my teeth and said, "I know, Crystal. I just felt like I needed some affection."

Crystal threw me a disgusted look and shook her head.

"Geneva, you act as if there's no other men out here. There are plenty of men out here. Look," she said, pointing across the square, where men in suits and casual wear walked up and down or sat on the benches, talking or eating slices of pizza. "Plenty," she emphasized again and then picked up her water glass.

Yeah, plenty. Plenty of men with hang-ups and diseases and wives and babies. Plenty of men who wanted a model-thin woman. Me, I was enough woman for three men, and not every man out there knew how to appreciate a woman of my girth.

Besides, when I made love to Eric, he made me feel like I was a size six.

"So how's Kendrick?" I asked, tiring of the subject of my dysfunctional life.

Crystal rolled her eyes at me before answering, "Okay, I'll lay off you. He's fine, I guess. He's in London this week on business." The smile that usually accompanied any mention of Kendrick was missing from Crystal's face. "He'll be back on Thursday, I think."

"Oh," I said and picked up a french fry.

Something was wrong with them, I could feel it.

"Have you talked to Chevy?" I asked, changing the subject again.

"Uh-huh, and I'm sure we won't be talking until she has the money she owes me, and you know that may be weeks from now." Crystal's voice was filled with loathing.

"She borrowed money from you again?" I asked, in shock. Chevy seemed to think that Crystal was the Bank of New York. "How much this time?"

"Girl, I'm embarrassed to say," she said as she swirled the ice around in her glass.

"Oh my God, Crystal, how much?" I pushed.

"Well, she said she needed it until she could get her money out of her 401(k)."

"How much?"

"Five thousand."

"Five thousand dollars! Are you crazy! What the hell did Chevy need five thousand dollars for?" I guess I was a bit loud, because the people at the table next to us turned around and gave me a look.

Crystal leaned in and spoke in a dramatic whisper. "She said she needed to get some surgery done."

I looked at Crystal like she had three heads. "And you believe that?"

I may be still screwing my baby's daddy, but even I wasn't stupid enough to believe a lie like that.

"What kind of surgery, and how come her health insurance couldn't cover it?"

"I don't know, Geneva. Please, it's over and done with and I know that I won't see that money anytime soon."

"Or ever," I said and bit into my hamburger.

Two

"Geneva, what plans you got brewing for the weekend?" asked Maria Vasquez, the hefty-hipped Latina human resources temp with long raven-colored tresses.

Maria, unlike me, always had hot weekend plans. In fact, now that I think about it, she had "hot plans" even during the week. According to her she was currently juggling an NFL rookie, an NBA guard, and some major solo artist who she was very tight-lipped about. All she would say is that the world loves his ballads.

"Ah, not much," I said.

"*Girrrrrl*, you really need to start getting out!" she squealed and rapped her half-inch perfectly French-manicured nails on the top of my station.

"Been there, done that. I'm too tired for all of that running around," I said and reached up and snatched my headphones off. "Now, when I was your age . . ." I started and then pressed my index finger against my lip. "What are you, twenty-six, twenty-seven?"

A look of disdain blanketed Maria's face as she dramatically pressed her hand against her heart and said, "Geneva, you insult me—I'm twenty-three!"

I gave her a hard look. I was being kind when I said twenty-six or twenty-seven. I really wanted to call a number closer to thirty. "C'mon now, Maria." I smirked at her.

Maria gave me a wry smile. "That's my story and I'm sticking to it," she said before winking and swaying away.

I shook my head as she waltzed down the hall and disappeared into one of the offices. I looked up at the clock on the wall in front of me and was so happy to see that five o'clock had finally come around that I did a little jig at my desk.

"What exactly do you think you're doing?"

It was Ash Canton. He was the floor manager, but he acted as if he owned the company. We all thought he was a closet homosexual—nothing else could explain his obvious distaste for women. A skinny white boy who at twenty-five was still in the throes of pubescent acne.

"Oh, nothing, Ash. Just celebrating the end of the day," I said and bent to pull my purse from the bottom drawer.

"Well, I suggest you do your celebrating someplace else," he said, glowering at me.

He was my superior, so I had to at least act as if I feared and respected him. But I knew Crystal had my back no matter what.

"Okay, Ash, have a great weekend," I said as I breezed past him and out to the elevator banks.

I almost walked into Chevy when I stepped off the elevator. "What are you doing here?" I said, surprised.

"Oh, um, I came to see Crystal," she said, avoiding my eyes.

I studied her for a moment. Something about her looked a little more different than usual.

"She left a little early today."

"Oh," she said, trying not to smile. "You notice anything new?" she asked and did a full spin.

"Yeah, but it could be anything." I scrutinized her. "New shoes, new hair, new suit?"

"Well, yeah, all of those things. But something else too."

I stood back and looked her up and down for a few more seconds before I caught it. "Are you stuffing your bra?" I asked, laughing and throwing my hands over my mouth.

"Shhhhh!" Chevy scolded and grabbed me by my elbow to lead me outside. We were both giggling by the time we hit the sidewalk.

"I got a boob job!" Chevy exclaimed excitedly.

"What!" I screamed.

Chevy stuck her new size-Cs out. A bike messenger rode by and let out a long, loud whistle. Chevy beamed.

"Oh my God, Chevy, are you crazy?" I asked in disbelief.

"No, I'm sane now. I was crazy to have walked around so long with an A cup."

"Double A," I corrected her and then said, "Is that what you needed the money for?"

"Damn, Crystal can't keep shit to herself!"

I just shook my head. "Girl, you were fine the way you were," I said as we started walking toward the train station.

"No, I wasn't. I was flat—now I'm fine!"

"You know, Crystal would have never lent you that money if she knew what you wanted to use it for."

"I didn't tell her a lie. I told her it was for surgery," Chevy said, trying to wave a cab down.

"Yeah, but you didn't tell her what type."

"What the hell—was I lunch conversation?"

I didn't say anything.

"Anyway, it was an investment. These babies will return twofold in less than a month!" Chevy jiggled her new breasts and then twisted her face in pain. "Ouch. They're still a little sore," she said, cupping them lovingly.

"How do you expect to pay her back?" I asked as I dug in my purse for my Metro card.

"My 401(k)," she said quickly, scanning the streets for a cab. I saw that she was going to stick to that lie.

"You only been with Thomas Cook for eight months. I know you don't have five thousand dollars in your 401(k) plan yet," I said, and then I dropped my voice an octave and said, "If you're even contributing."

"Geneva, how do you know what I got and what I don't got? Not that it's any of your business, but I have been contributing, and I rolled over the money I had in my plan from Hilton Hotels. Okay, Sherlock?"

Another lie.

You would think that as much as Chevy lied she would have become an expert at it. You have to have an excellent memory in order to be a good liar, and Chevy's memory was shot to shit.

She'd forgotten that she told me she used the money she had in her Hilton Hotels 401(k) to put down on the apartment she was living in now.

I had a memory like an elephant's.

"Yeah, okay, Chevy, whatever," I said, turning to her. "We still on for Sunday at Justin's?" I asked.

"Sunday? Oh, that gospel brunch thing?" she said, spotting a cab and throwing her hand up in the air. "I don't know, my money is a little funny," she said as she started toward the curb. "I'll call you tonight and let you know." She jumped into the cab and slammed the door.

Three

"She did WHAT with my money?" I had heard Geneva, but I needed to hear it again in order to believe it.

"She got her boobs done," Geneva repeated.

I moved the phone from my right ear to my left. "I can't believe she did that. I can't believe she did that with my money!"

"Well, she said it's an investment."

"A what? A fucking investment!" I screamed. "You know I am so sick of her and her bullshit. I mean, I thought that she had to have some serious surgery done, not a fucking breast enhancement!" I couldn't believe I'd allowed Chevy to play me for a fool again. "I'm going to call that bitch and give her a piece of my mind!"

"I don't know, Crystal. It's Friday night. Chevy never goes home on a Friday night. She hardly goes home on Monday, Tuesday, Wednesday—"

"That bitch!" I screamed, cutting Geneva's ramblings off. "I'll call her on her cell phone!"

I slammed down the phone and stormed into my bedroom to get my phone book. All I could see was red, and it wasn't getting any better when I dialed Chevy's phone number.

Hello, you've reached Chevanese Cambridge. I'm not available to take your call right now, but please leave me a message and I'll get back to you as soon as possible.

I slammed down the phone and threw myself across the bed. Why the hell was I so bent out of shape over this? Chevy was just the icing on the cake. Kendrick was the real problem; he'd been in England for more than three days and hadn't even called. That's what was picking at me. And he had been so distant with me before he left. I was beginning to think that there might be someone else.

I picked up the phone and called Geneva back.

"Hello?" The voice that answered was deep and sexy.

"Is this the man of the house?" I asked, smiling to myself.

"Um, Aunt Crystal?" the voice came back.

"Yeah, it's me. Are you disappointed it's not one of your little girlfriends?" I asked, laughing.

"Nah, Auntie, nah." Little Eric wasn't little anymore. It seemed like only yesterday that I was carrying him around on my back.

"What you been up to?" I asked.

"Nothing. You know, just working and going to school." There was a lull and then, "Ma told you about the rap group I'm in?" Little Eric sounded excited.

"I don't remember her mentioning it. What's the name of the group?" I said, turning over onto my back. I noticed a crack across my ceiling. I would have to call the building superintendent about it.

"Um, we call ourselves BMF."

"Uh-huh, and what does that stand for?"

"Well, no disrespect or nothing, Auntie, but it means Bad Motherfuckers."

I had to bite the insides of my cheeks to keep from laughing. Little Eric had barely whispered the second word.

"Is that right?" I said, letting amusement fill my voice.

"Yeah. We are the illest underground group around!"

"I believe it," I said. "So, when can I see this ill group perform?"

"Serious? Yo, Auntie, you can come on down to Washington Square Park tomorrow around two. We going to be battling three other groups."

"Battling?" I said, sounding every one of my thirty-something years.

"You know, facing off with each group to see who has the illest rhymes."

"Oh, I see. Yeah, I guess I will be there. You are my only godson, and you're too cute for me to say no."

"Ah, Auntie." I could sense Little Eric blushing through the phone. "Hey, you seen Uncle Noah? I left two messages on his service and nothing."

I sighed. I'd left a few messages of my own on Noah's machine and hadn't heard back either. "No, I think Noah is out of town on business."

"Oh." Little Eric sounded disappointed.

"Okay, boy, put your mama on the phone."

There was a rustling and then the sound of Geneva

fussing about dishes in the sink. "Hey, girl," Geneva said and then said something else to Little Eric. "That boy is going to drive me crazy."

"Yeah, one day, but not today," I said, still counting the cracks on the ceiling.

"Did you get in touch with Chevy?"

"Nope, got her damn voicemail. I'll catch her slick ass tomorrow." I turned onto my stomach and scooted to the edge of the bed so that I could examine the Berber carpet. "What's this Little Eric is telling me—he's in a rap group now?" I asked.

"Oh yeah, that's this week. That boy changes careers like I change underwear. Last month it was basketball, the month before soccer."

"Hmm," I said as I spotted something on my brand-new rug. It looked like powder but it was copper-colored.

"Yeah and catch this," Geneva started and then stopped. When she started speaking again her voice had dropped down to a whisper. "There's three of them, right? Little Eric, that boy David from the third floor, who practically lives here, and a white boy."

Even I was taken aback. "A white boy?" I asked as I closed in on the copper speck.

"Yeah, girl—like bright white! Blond hair and bright blue eyes. White!"

"White people don't rap," I said.

"Well, there is that Eminem boy," Geneva said.

"Em-who? How the hell do you know about these things?"

"Girl, I live with a teenager."

"Umph. You know what, I gotta go—there is something on my carpet."

"The one you brought back from Morocco?"

"The very same. Bye."

"Later, girl."

I hung up and jumped off the bed. That copper thing was bugging the hell out of me and I didn't know why. I mean, it was one little speck; it could have been a piece of anything. But what?

I got down on my knees and picked it up. It was hard. I rolled it around between my fingers; it felt more like chalk. What the hell was copper-colored chalk doing in my house?

Four

"Hello, love." Zhan's voice came to me from across the Atlantic. It was five a.m.

"Hey, baby," my voice cracked back. "How's the weather?" I asked as I rubbed the sleep out of my eyes.

"Fabulous for London." Zhan snickered. "Will you be sleeping with the Merriwether when you get here?"

"What?" I said and sat straight up in the bed. What did he say? How did he know about Merriwether? Oh God, my secret is out. I panicked as I tried to get a lie together in my mind.

"Well, you asked how the weather was and not me." He laughed.

My heart slowed a bit. Oh, *weather*, not Merriwether.

I dropped back down to the bed. "How are you, honey?"

"Anxious for you to get your fine black ass back over here."

"I'm anxious to get there too."

"What time is your flight?"

"Eight o'clock this evening."

"Are you all packed?"

"Almost."

"Well, okay. I'll send a car to pick you up."

"Thanks, sweetie."
"Anything for my man."
"You are too good for me."
"I love you."
"I love you too."
"Have a safe flight."
Click.
Well, that was a wonderful way to start off my morning. After a shower and a strong cup of coffee, I donned a loose pair of water blue linen pants and a matching shirt.

It was a glorious day. The birds were singing, young mothers were pushing baby strollers up and down the sidewalks, there was not a cloud in the sky, and all was well with the world until I stepped out and onto the stoop of my Brooklyn brownstone and looked down to see a woman looking back at me.

"Noah?"

I smiled. "Yes," I said, trying to figure out where I knew this woman from. She looked vaguely familiar. I didn't think for a moment that it was any of the women I'd had trysts with; I never ever brought them back to my place.

"So this is where you live," she said, leaning back on one leg, folding her arms across her chest, and looking me up and down.

"I'm sorry, do I know you?"

She rolled her eyes and did something strange with her lips. "You should know me, nigga—you fucked me a month ago, promised that you'd call, and never did. So now I'm going to have to kill you!"

I let out a high-pitched bitch scream. Who knew my life would end like this?

"Noah, are you okay?"

The woman was up on the stoop now, her eyes swimming with concern. I took a step away from her and looked down at her hands to see if her fingers were curled around a sharp utensil.

"Uh, what?"

"Well, I told you that we met at the Donna Karan show during fashion week last year, and you just went gray."

I blinked at her.

"Gosh, what kind of impression did I leave on you?" She sounded wounded.

I looked wildly around and then back at her. Surely I was going crazy.

"I'm—I'm sorry. I haven't been feeling well lately," I said and wiped at the perspiration on my forehead. "Yes, yes, what's your name again?"

"Swain Jenkins," she said and cautiously presented her hand. I took it and shook it; it was a weak handshake, the kind I've received from the hoity-toity set, who didn't want to shake your hand to begin with.

"Yes, yes, Swain. Nice to see you again," I said, still shaken.

"Same here," she said, looking at me strangely before she started back down the steps.

Me, I just turned around and rushed back into the house.

Five

"Thank you for calling Thomas Cook Travel Group, Mr. Matsumi, and have a nice day," I said in my brightest voice as I ended the call and pressed the red release button on the telephone console.

Mr. Matsumi's PNR glared at me from my computer screen. The dollar amount it was costing him glowed bright green at the bottom of the PNR, and below that his platinum American Express credit card number mocked me.

Mr. Matsumi, a managing director of one of the largest investment banking companies in the country, had just confirmed an African safari trip for him and some of his business associates. They were flying first class from New York to England on British Airways, staying two nights at the Ritz in London and then hopping a Kenyan Airways flight to Kenya, East Africa, where they would spend one night in Nairobi at the famed Nairobi Serena Hotel before chartering a private plane to take them to Nanyuki, where they would spend ten glorious days at the Mount Kenya Safari Club, which straddled the second highest mountain in Africa.

The entire trip was costing him sixty thousand dollars!

All I could do was shake my head at the type of money some people had. Shake my head and try not to stare too long at or think too hard about what I could do with Mr. Matsumi's American Express card number that was just sitting there, seemingly at my disposal.

"Stop it, Chevy girl," I whispered to myself and quickly hit the Enter button on my keyboard, sending Mr. Matsumi's itinerary hurtling through cyberspace and out of my sight.

Lucky for me, I could see the world for next to nothing. Being a senior travel expert had its perks even though the pay was crap.

I yawned and looked around at my coworkers, who were busy at their computers. I peeked over my monitor and could see that my manager was engaged in an intense telephone conversation, so I hit the red "away" button on my telephone but made sure to keep nodding my head and uttering, "Yes, I understand," into my headset as I typed gibberish into my computer.

I was exhausted. Last night I spent three hours at the very high-end Cipriani bar. A cosmopolitan there cost twenty bucks a glass, so you can imagine the clientele: mostly white people with money.

But to my surprise there was a black man sitting at the bar last night. After the color of his skin, I homed right in on the diamond-studded gold Rolex clamped around his left wrist. My eyes scurried up his hand and saw that there was no ring on his fourth finger. Not that that meant anything these days.

He wasn't good-looking at all, which was fine for me. I prefer a man who's not going to spend as much time looking in the mirror as I do, and besides, a not-so-good-looking man always overcompensates when he has a gorgeous woman on his arm.

You know what you generally do when you see a beautiful woman on the arm of a dog? You double look so quickly you give yourself whiplash, and then as you walk away rubbing your neck you wonder how it is a man like that was able to snag a woman like her.

He didn't—she snagged him!

Think about it now . . .

Anyway, this man was blue-black, with thick lips and a nose that spread east to west across his face. Bulging eyes, big pink lips, and a row of scars that looked like teardrops beneath his eyes.

He caught me checking him out and smiled at me. I returned the smile and then turned my attention back to the drink menu, but before I could decide what it was I wanted to order, the bartender set a bubbling glass of champagne down in front of me. "From the gentleman," he said and nodded in brother-man's direction.

I mouthed, "Thank you," lifted the flute, and began to sip daintily from it.

No sooner than I could swallow, he was beside me.

"Hello, my name is Abimbola," he said in a thick Nigerian accent.

"Chevy," I said as I presented my hand.

"A pleasure," he said and bent and kissed the back of my hand. "May I join you?"

I checked out the suit, the shoes, and the platinum link chain around his neck. If he had the cash and good credit to back up the bling, I might be able to forget about how visually unappealing he was.

"Of course, please do."

A bottle of champagne later and he was putting me into a taxi and shoving a hundred-dollar bill into my hand, along with his business card.

"Call me," he said after kissing my hand again.

"Sure," I said.

I sat there staring at the money. My God, this was the easiest hundred I'd ever made. I grinned myself stupid for two blocks and then told the cabdriver to pull over.

I threw a crumpled five-dollar bill at him, got out, and caught the train home.

Shoot, I had other plans for that "found" money!

My personal line began to ring.

I eyed the blinking red light. It could be a friend. But then again, it could be my manager checking to see if I was working. She was a sneaky little bitch.

"Thomas Cook Travel Group, this is Chevy, how may I help you?" I answered with my most professional voice.

"Hey, Chevy girl, this is Noah."

"Hey, Noah, what's up."

"Well," he started, but I had to cut him off.

"If you're calling about the money, I don't have it yet."

"Do you ever?" He laughed. He knew me very well. "No, girl, I'm going to London for two weeks and need you to come by and feed my fish."

"Fish? When did you get fish?"

"A month ago. I told you that, if you would listen to what I was saying and stop cutting me off when I'm trying to—"

"Noah, I met this Nigerian last night, and—"

"You see what I mean?"

"What?"

"It's not always about you."

"Yes it is." I laughed.

"You still have the key and you know the security code, right?"

"Is it still sixty-nine, sixty-nine?"

"Yeah, my favorite sex position in overdrive!"

"Uh-huh. Going back over there to see your man?"

"You know it."

"How's the weather?"

I didn't get an immediate response, and then he said, "Who?" and his voice sounded a little uneven.

"Not a who, a *what*, Noah. The weather. How's the weather?"

"Oh, oh, I got some static going on on my end of the line." He laughed nervously. "The weather is fine."

"You got it bad, boy. That man is plugging you so hard you don't know whether you're going or coming."

"He's definitely got me coming!" Noah laughed, still not quite sounding like himself.

"Well, better you than me."

"Yeah, well, make sure you water the plants and pick up the mail."

"Pick up the mail? Doesn't the postman put the mail through the slot in the front door?"

"Yes."

"So what do you mean by pick up the mail?"

"Just that. Pick it up off the floor, Chevy."

"And put it where?"

"On the glass console in the foyer. Damn, you having a dumb blonde day or something?"

"Fuck you."

"You kiss your mama with that mouth?"

I hung the phone right up on his smart-aleck, queen ass.

Six

I stood staring at the large white paper that screamed NOTICE OF EVICTION for a long moment before I finally snatched it off the door and pushed my key into the lock.

Well, it really couldn't have come at a better time. Noah would be gone for a whole two weeks, so I could crash there and I was sure that after he got back he'd let me stay until I got back on my feet again.

That shouldn't be too long, I thought as my mind skipped back to the Nigerian. He could probably be good for at least a couple grand.

The three men that I had been stringing along for the past six months were slowly but surely starting to catch on to my scheme, and each one was either pulling back or stepping off altogether.

Arthur Friedman, early sixties, a stony-faced, balding, blue-eyed Jewish corporate attorney originally from Riverhead, Long Island. We met last year on an American Airlines flight from Puerto Rico.

We were about twenty minutes into the flight, and I was sitting in coach and not happy at all about that. The flesh of the woman next to me was spilling over the armrest, slowly taking over my space, and to top it off she smelled like mangoes and rum, a sickly combination.

I hit my flight attendant call button and an attractive young brother began his quick approach. He was all smiles, not like the old hens they usually have working those short Caribbean flights.

You've seen them, the flight attendants who look as if they've been flying just as long as there's been flight. They have so much time on the books that they only have to do one flight a week and that flight is usually three hours or less. They don't smile anymore, don't even try, but still insist on wearing that pink lipstick that was made popular by Maybelline back in 1960.

They don't ask you what you'd like to drink, they tell you, and God forbid if you ask for a pillow or a blanket; that's when you get chastised for not wearing the proper "flight attire."

So the brother approaching was a breath of fresh air, and I felt my own face break into a smile.

"Yes, ma'am?" he asked in a cavernous voice that was laced with an unmistakable southern drawl. I felt the hairs on my arms stand at attention. I wasn't sure, but I thought the brother was straight. Not one of the usual flying fairies the airlines employed in droves.

I quickly crossed my legs and tugged my skirt up so as to expose as much of my tan toasted thigh as I could.

"Um," I whispered, and beckoned him closer with my index finger. He was more than happy to get closer to my exposed thigh and my Miracle Bra–cradled breasts, which were busting out of my close-fitting knit top. "I was wondering if there was any room in first class?" I whispered and then looked at his name tag and purred, "Derek."

Derek's smile broadened, and I think he was about to laugh out loud when I opened my purse and slipped my IATA (International Association of Travel Agents) card out of the inside pocket and presented it to him.

Derek's eyes swung from the card to me and then back to the card.

"I know you've got at least one little ole seat up there for me," I said and seductively licked my lips and dragged my free hand up my thigh.

Derek—he couldn't have been older than twenty-two—broke out in a sweat, and I swear I saw some movement in the crotch of his little uniform pants.

"Give me a minute," he croaked and rushed off.

I waited, confident that I would get my way. That's how you have to think—positive!

The mango/rum-smelling orca shifted, and three more inches of her flesh spilled onto me.

Derek came back, composed now and smiling confidently.

Looks like good news, I thought and readied myself to retrieve my Versace knockoff travel case from the overhead.

"Miss Cambridge," he said.

"Yes?" I said hopefully.

"Please gather your belongings and follow me."

BINGO!

Derek placed me in the only available seat in first class,

which happened to be a window seat right next to a snoring, balding man.

I was about to jab the man with my fingernail and wake him up, but then I spotted the watch and the diamond-studded pinky rings—yes, plural—one on each hand, and that made me think better of my action.

"Hello," I whispered softly into his ear as I gently shook his shoulder. His lids fluttered and before me appeared the bluest eyes I'd ever seen. "Sorry to wake you, but I'm just going to slip into the seat beside you." The man started to unbuckle his seat belt, but I said, "Oh, no, please don't. I can get in. I'll just slide by." I then began the most seductive "slide-through" ever performed, thirty thousand feet in the air!

That's how I met and bagged Arthur Friedman.

Up until recently, we've had a standing Thursday night date. He would always show up at my job in his long black limousine, greet me with a kiss (on the cheek), and present me with two dozen white roses. Sometimes if he'd had a really good day or thought that that was the night he was going to get some of my goodies, he'd bring along a little trinket. To date I've received two tennis bracelets, a sapphire anklet, and a bottle of Clive Christian's No. 1 perfume, which retails for eight hundred dollars!

I acted as if all those things blew me away—yeah, I ooh'd and I aah'd, and I even let him touch up under my blouse, but not up under my La Perla bra!

I ain't stupid. These high-powered attorneys get so many things handed to them, who's to say that he actually spent his ducats on those gifts? And besides, he's going to have to dig a whole lot deeper if he expects even a sniff of my coochie!

The limo, the flowers, the fancy restaurants, and little gifts may seem spectacular to some chickenhead, but not to me. Chevanese Cambridge is in it for the big payoff, which is my own home, car, and bank account.

But I hadn't seen or heard from Arthur in over three weeks. He'd changed his cell phone number, and when I called the office, his secretary kept telling me that he was still out of town, but she wouldn't tell me where or when he'd be back.

Now Frederick Smalls, a restaurant owner, is a good-looking Jamaican brother with a good head on his shoulders—and down between his legs, come to think of it.

Frederick is a cash man. He can't be bothered with shopping for gifts or sending flowers; he'd rather just peel off a couple hundred and send me to get whatever it is I want.

Now him I've slept with, just once. But I made the time unforgettable for him, and now he can't wait to get a second chance. But I keep him at bay. Besides, he's got a steady woman and, from what I've heard, a wife and family back in Kingston. But he's the kind of brother who likes to think he's living in Africa, where they can have more than one wife or woman and everybody is fine with it.

Our little thing worked fine because he was so busy running the restaurant, he barely had time to take a piss, so he appreciated a woman who ain't trying to be up under him all the time. A woman that ain't nagging him about spending time together or carrying on about why he didn't call her when he said he would. I'm that woman!

At least, I *was* that woman.

The last two visits I made to the restaurant, Frederick didn't even come out of the kitchen to see me, and after I had a few drinks and something to eat at the bar I actually got a bill!

On top of that, he hadn't returned my phone calls in about a month. That right there told me his time was done.

The last one was a young boy named Hamil. No last name, just Hamil.

Black, barely thirty, with a bank account that was out of this world. He was a hustler and had a bit of thug in him. I have a weakness for thugs. Anyway, he and I met when I had just stepped out of the nail salon and had stopped to admire my reflection in the tinted passenger-side window of this parked Denali, when suddenly the window started to come down and I was met with a beautiful specimen. A young brown-skinned brother, sporting a baldy and the most beautiful hazel eyes I'd ever seen, leaned over and said, "Can I give you a ride, pretty miss?"

I gotta tell you, it took everything in me to turn that brother down. It didn't help that it was freezing cold out and it sure did look toasty and warm inside that truck.

But I'm not crazy: this is NYC, and we got some stone-cold lunatics who look normal and drive fly vehicles.

So I just smiled and said, "Are those your eyes?"

He laughed, showing me two rows of exceptionally white teeth.

"Yeah—are *those* yours?"

I was rocking my blue contacts that day. "Yeah, bought and paid for!" I said, and we laughed together.

To make a long story short, he gave me his business card, I called a week later, and we had dinner soon after that.

Because of Hamil, I'd been front and center at all the hottest concerts that had come through town in the past six months. I'd partied with major celebrities and drunk so much Cristal that it was coming out of my ears.

I ain't gonna lie: I was living the life I'd always wanted to live. I was living like a superstar! And so Hamil was the one I elected to be able to tap this ass whenever he wanted to. And after that I thought I had him in my pocket (or my purse), because Hamil just started paying my rent and utilities, started talking that "we" stuff, and I have to tell you that that kinda talk sounded good, but I know what these men out here are all about, and it ain't no committed relationship, so when he asked me to stop seeing the other men I was dating, I said, "Yeah, sure," and kept right on seeing them, which explained this eviction notice I was holding in my hands.

Oh well, fuck him! Fuck all of them!

Summer was right around the corner: new season, new meat.

I crumpled the notice and tossed it into the trash can.

This studio apartment was too damn small for me to begin with. I'd be much more comfortable at Noah's three-story brownstone. What did a single man need with all that space anyway?

I slipped my little black Anne Klein dress over my head and kicked my pumps off.

I had packing to do.

Nothing really strenuous. I don't own any pots or pans, plates, or cups. Just my clothes and shoes, two towels, two washcloths, two sets of sheets, a shower curtain, and a sofa that has seen better days many, many years ago.

"I won't be taking you," I said to the sofa and patted the tattered arm.

I pulled out the largest of my Louis Vuitton suitcases from beneath the bed and got down to work.

Seven

I had been successfully dodging Crystal and Geneva for two weeks by the time I strolled into Aubette and heard Geneva scream out, "Chevy, where the hell you been hiding!"

I spun around and my eyes fell on Geneva and then Crystal, who was giving me one of her infamous judgmental looks. I took a deep breath and started toward them.

It was almost eight thirty, and Crystal's platinum American Express card was already resting on top of the bill the waiter had left there. If I had shown up ten minutes later we would have missed each other. If I had had the good sense to remove my shades before walking into that damn dark-ass place I would have seen them before they saw me. Damn!

"I been around," I said as I pulled out a chair and sat down.

"Been around where?" Geneva asked as she tugged at the blouse that was too small for her back when she was a hundred and eighty pounds, and now she was a long way from that weight.

"You still doing Calorie Counters?" I asked, allowing my eyes to roll over her.

"Don't change the subject," Crystal said. She was always coming to Geneva's defense. "Your home number is disconnected." And then she leaned in and took a real good look at me and asked, "Do you have a tan?"

"Yes and yes again!" I said with an air of boredom.

"I've been calling your job for two days, Chevy, and all I get is your voice mail. Tomorrow I was going to call the main number. So where you been?"

"What is this, the third fucking degree?"

"We were just worried about you," Geneva said.

I had to soften. "I know, I know. I-I went down to St. Barts for a few days."

Crystal eyed me suspiciously. "St. Barts? You have money for a vacation but not to pay me back?"

"Calm down. It was on the company. A fam trip. You know those trips are free for travel agents."

"Uh-huh."

"But you were supposed to be taking care of Noah's fish while he's in London," Geneva said.

"Oh, it was just two days. Damn, those fish looked like they could use a few days without some food."

"Well, I hope you've been by to feed them since you got back," Geneva said.

Of course I'd fed them. I looked at the little buggers every day. I was living there now, for chrissakes. Of course, Geneva and Crystal didn't know that.

"Yes, yes, they're fine."

"Oh, okay, 'cause you know Noah would kill you if he came home and found those fish dead," Geneva added.

"Yeah, yeah," I said as I surveyed the tall, dark, and handsome possibilities.

"So do you have anything you'd like to share with me?" Crystal asked coolly as she leaned back in her chair.

Geneva's eyes bounced between us, and then she looked down into her empty glass.

"No, no." I feigned stupidity even though I could feel her eyes boring into my boobs.

"Nothing at all. Nothing?" she pressed, and her eyebrows climbed higher on her forehead.

Now I was wishing that I'd worn something other than this short white dress with the plunging neckline.

"Well, I know that Geneva has already told you all about my little surgery," I spat. "She can't hold water," I added, before I thrust my new size-Cs at her.

Crystal just shook her head at me and drained the rest of her apple martini.

"You know, it's a real shame that you're not happy with yourself," she said as she plucked the wedge of green apple from the glass's depths, "and an even bigger shame Geneva and I have to stake out your favorite Tuesday night haunt just to find you."

She popped the apple wedge into her mouth and chewed on it thoughtfully for a moment. "You lied to me about what you needed the money for."

"I didn't lie. I told you I was having surgery. And furthermore, I wasn't avoiding you. I've been busy and I've been away."

Geneva and Crystal just looked at me.

"Okay, so since you're not avoiding me, I guess we could traipse on over to the Citibank and get some money out of the ATM."

I looked at her like she'd lost her mind. She knew I didn't have no damn bank account!

"Look, Crystal, I said I was going to pay you back and I am. Just give me some time," I said, trying to keep the annoyance out of my voice.

Crystal just eyed me.

"So when did you get back, Chevy?" Geneva asked, trying to break the tension she knew was building between us.

"Late last night, girl. Chile, St. Barts is outta this world. You hear me!"

"Oh, really? St. Barts, or the men?" Geneva asked slyly.

"Oh, them too. And they are rich! Rich! Rich!" I almost screamed.

"Of course they are," Crystal said with a little revulsion. I just ignored her.

"Guanahani is amazing. Little pastel-colored cottages overlooking the ocean. Simply divine."

Geneva looked at Crystal again. Crystal's face was as hard as stone.

"So, um, did you meet anyone?" Geneva asked.

"Of course, girl, this Parisian man. About fifty. He was there on business. I told him I was a wealthy widow traveling the world!"

"So we did the wealthy widow act again?" Crystal chimed as the waiter came and collected the bill.

"I haven't used that one in a while, girl." I laughed and caught the waiter by the elbow. "Let me have an apple martini," I told him.

"Oh yes, you have," Geneva reminded me.

"Really?" I had to search my mind. I'd told so many lies that it was becoming harder to keep up with them. "Was it at the Connaught?"

"I don't know, one of those cities," Geneva said.

Poor thing had never been anywhere out of New York.

"The Connaught is a hotel, not a city. London is the city," I said and rolled my eyes. "Look at a fucking atlas sometimes, would ya?"

"Don't let me come across this table and smack those gray contacts out of your head," Geneva threatened.

I sucked my teeth and looked around for the waiter and my drink.

"Chevy, why do you always have to be so damn degrading?" Crystal leaned in and hissed at me.

I just shrugged my shoulders.

I didn't think I was degrading Geneva. I was just telling her what she needed to do so she wouldn't sound so damn ignorant.

The waiter set my drink down on the table before me and then asked, "Should I add this to the bill?"

"Yes, please," I said and waved him away before Crystal could object.

"You know, girl, you got balls the size of grapefruits," she said with a sneer.

"Oh, it's just one little drink, damn. Just add it to the five Gs I owe you."

Geneva laughed under her breath.

I sipped my drink and smacked my lips together before I spoke again.

"You know, Crystal, you and I need to take one of those luxury trips together."

"Yeah, I haven't been on vacation in ages. I think the last real vacation I took was two years ago to Bermuda."

"It's not like you can't afford it or can't get the time off."

"I'm just really busy," she said and signed the credit card receipt the waiter had set down before her.

"Yeah, busy waiting on that boy to take you away or even take you out."

"'Scuse me, he is a man and not a boy, and I do not have to wait on him. If I want to do something and he's not available, I just do it. I'm an independent woman," Crystal snapped.

"Yeah, whatever." I was uninterested in going down Crystal's yellow-brick fantasy road, but I knew she was going to drag me along whether I wanted to go or not.

"Am I at home now?" Crystal barked defensively as she spread her arms out around her. "I'm here, ain't I? And I think being here and not home constitutes out, doesn't it?" she said and looked at Geneva for confirmation. And, of course, Geneva agreed.

"Yeah, but that's only because y'all came out looking for me," I said, waving at the waiter. "Another one, please," I said as I handed him my empty glass.

"I'm not paying for that one, Chevy," Crystal huffed as she gathered herself to leave.

"Didn't ask you to."

"Whatever, Chevy."

Crystal tucked the credit card back inside her wallet. Tossing the wallet down into her handbag, she looked over at Geneva and said, "You ready, girl?"

Geneva yawned. "Bye, Chevy," she said as she and Crystal stood.

"Yeah, bye."

"Look, Chevy, you make sure to call me tomorrow so that we can discuss those," she said, pointing at my new Cs.

I just nodded my head and turned my attention to the crowd.

Crystal threw a ten-dollar tip down onto the table, and then she and Geneva started toward the door.

Grateful they were finally gone, I was able to really relax. I leaned back in the chair so I could enjoy the first drove of nine-o'clock honeys walking through the door.

My, my, was that platinum I was seeing on that brother's wrist?

I crossed my tight long legs, plastered my face with my million-dollar smile, discreetly plucked the ten-dollar bill off the table, and stuffed it down between my new Cs.

It was going to be a good night!

Eight

"So where's Mr. Kendrick tonight?" Geneva asked as we climbed into the back of the taxi.

"Ninetieth and Columbus and then onto Central Park West," I said before settling into the hard leather of the seat.

Where was Kendrick? The last time I heard from him it was Madrid. That was three days ago. We had had a small disagreement before he left. It was something so silly that I couldn't even think of what it was about now. But I do remember that he'd said some hurtful things to me, which was not in character for him. I put it on the stress that he'd been under. I mean, being the second man in charge of an international multimillion-dollar real estate investment company was no walk in the park.

"Oh, he's still out of town on business," I said and turned my head toward the window.

"Oh," Geneva said quietly and leaned back in her seat.

"You know, this love thing isn't always easy," I said, more to myself than to her.

Geneva patted my knee. "Is it ever?" she said and kind of chuckled to take some of the heaviness off the statement.

"Just once can't it be?" I said, turning to her, hoping

that she had an answer for me, but all she did was shrug her shoulders in ignorance.

I turned my attention back to the goings-on outside my window.

"Well, I thought you guys were so happy. What exactly is the problem?" Geneva asked.

Did I know the exact problem? No, I didn't. It was just little things that I couldn't even put my finger on.

But what I threw over my shoulder to Geneva was "It's hard on me, him being out of town so often."

"Yeah, I guess that is difficult," Geneva said sympathetically. "But it's not always going to be like that, Crystal."

What else was it going to be like, and when? It'd been two years, and the only thing that changed was the amount of time we didn't get to be with each other.

Maybe I was just being a brat, a baby, a spoiled little girl—a Chevy!

"Well, you know I'm here for you," Geneva breathed as she patted my knee.

"I know you are." I sighed and then tapped on the plastic protective shield that separated us from the driver. "You can drop me right here on this corner." I dug into my wallet and pulled a ten-dollar bill out of it and handed it to Geneva.

"Why are you getting out here?" Geneva asked.

"Oh, I just need to walk some."

Geneva gave my hand one good squeeze before taking the money and letting go. "Call me later?"

"I will," I said as I climbed out of the cab and pushed the door closed behind me.

Nine

Once on the sidewalk, I felt weighted down with doubt and was sorry that Geneva had even brought up the subject of Kendrick Greene.

In my musings, I almost collided with a couple pushing their newborn daughter in a blue and white old-fashioned baby carriage. I smiled at them and then down at the pink face of the sleeping baby and muttered, "How sweet."

Walking toward my apartment building, I wondered if Kendrick and I would ever have children of our own.

It was times like this that I felt as if it would never happen.

Kendrick Greene was the vice president of Greene Real Estate Investments, one of the oldest black-owned international real estate investment companies in the United States. His grandfather Collins Greene started the company back in 1925, when he purchased a row of brownstones in Harlem and used the rental income to buy beachfront property in his native Barbados. By the time his son, Aldridge, Kendrick's father, had graduated from Howard University and joined the family business, Collins had amassed more than two million dollars' worth of real estate in Manhattan, Brooklyn, and Newark, New Jersey. He'd also purchased land in Antigua, St. Vincent, and Tobago.

Aldridge came in and more than tripled the land holdings in less than five years. He also added hotels to their growing portfolio, and now Kendrick was taking the business to a new level, buying property in war-torn countries that he knew would be revitalized within the next two decades.

Kendrick's mother died from a severe asthma attack when he was just five years old, and the senior Greene never remarried, but he'd had his share of scandalous affairs with high-profile government officials as well as beautiful celebrities.

I understood the attraction; Aldridge was still a good-looking man, even now, when he was just a few years from his seventieth birthday.

Kendrick had inherited his father's business savvy, as well as his good looks.

Standing six foot five, he was a mountain of a man, with sable-colored skin. His forty-two-year-old physique rivaled that of a man half his age. He kept his naturally wavy hair cropped close and sported an impeccably kept mustache and goatee.

He had the ultimate bedroom eyes, and I'd seen many a woman swoon beneath his gaze.

Shit, it still happened to me.

Our first meeting was one for the storybooks.

On a November afternoon two years earlier, it was

raining cats, dogs, and everything else with a tail and four paws, and there I was trying unsuccessfully to catch a cab.

A sudden gust of wind ripped my umbrella from my hands and carried it off into the gray stormy day. My Bloomingdale's bags were soaked and seemed to disintegrate right in my hands. The two new wool sweaters I had just purchased were ruined.

I felt defeated and started crying right there where I stood. A Mercedes sped by and splashed a blanket of dirty water on me, and then I got mad.

I dropped my sweaters to the ground and screamed obscenities at that car, and then I gave the driver the middle finger, with both hands.

The car stopped with a screech and began slowly backing up. I just froze. I had forgotten what city I was living in. I'd forgotten that I was a woman in that city. I'd forgotten that most of the people around me would stand by and let this man in the green Mercedes beat me down while they went about their business.

Chivalry was dead, and now I was next.

The car stopped in front of me and the dark-tinted window came down. The man sitting behind the wheel was strikingly good-looking, and when he finally spoke his voice sounded like silk.

"So sorry, miss. Please forgive me. I didn't realize that there was such a large puddle of water there until I got up on it, and then, well, then it was too late."

"Oh, that's okay," I heard myself say stupidly.

"Can I give you a lift?" he asked, already out of his car

and retrieving the two sweaters that sat soaked and filthy at my feet.

"Oh, I think these are ruined," he said as he held the soggy material in his massive gloved hands. I just stared at him. My hair was hanging in my face and my mascara was making its way down my cheeks in long black lines. I looked a mess, but this man didn't seem to notice.

"Please get in. You're soaked," he said, running over to the passenger side of the car and opening the door. "C'mon, please," he said, and I almost melted right there, because now he was soaked through too and he looked like a little wet puppy dog. I'm a sucker for puppies.

So I started around the car while trying to block out my mother's voice, reminding me not to accept rides from strangers.

I shut the voice out and climbed into the lush leather of the seat. He had a Luther Vandross CD playing, and all I could think was *This man has got it going on*.

I watched him run around the front of the car, sweaters in hand. He started to climb back into the car and then at the last minute turned and dumped them into a nearby garbage can.

"I'll replace those," he said as he pulled out into traffic.

For a long time we didn't say anything. It was just Luther and the sound of the wipers against the windshield. I finally got up the nerve to break the silence.

"I'm sorry I cursed at you," I said meekly.

"No, I'm sorry. I deserved that and more," he said as he maneuvered his car through the yellow sea of taxis. "My name is Kendrick Greene," he said and extended his hand to me. I placed my hand in his and felt the immediate warmth. It seemed to fill my veins with fire, and suddenly it was too warm in the car.

"Nice to meet you," I said in a small voice. "My name is Crystal Atkins." I couldn't even look at him; all of a sudden I became a shy little girl.

"Nice to meet you. So where is home, Crystal Atkins?" I wanted him to say my name again; it sounded so nice coming out of his mouth. His words were touched by an accent. I had to strain to hear it, but it was there.

"Oh, um, one-fifty Central Park West."

"Good, I'm going that way too," he said as he whipped the car through the Central Park thruway.

I was tongue-tied, so I just played with my fingers and tried to push my limp hair back into place without his noticing my effort to do so.

I snatched little glimpses of him, and every time I did my belly tightened and my knees knocked. This brother was having a serious effect on me.

We turned a corner and the traffic came almost to a stop. There were two police cars and four people standing in the middle of the street, screaming at each other. Apparently there had been a fender bender.

Kendrick laughed as we moved past them. It was a full laugh, but not brawny.

"What's so funny?" I asked as I turned to see what he had found so humorous.

"Oh, I was just thinking how funny it is that you

Americans have such wide roads here and so many car accidents, and we island people have small, narrow, winding roads and we have so few."

"How do you know I'm American?" I asked.

"Well, are you?" he said with a cockiness that angered and excited me at the same time.

"Yes, yes I am . . . is that a problem?" The shy little girl in me suddenly disappeared and I had to quickly remind myself that I was not in the office and this was not a board meeting. I didn't have to defend myself for being an African-American woman.

"Why would it be a problem for me? Is it a problem for you?" Kendrick turned his head to get a full view of me, and then he smiled and shook his head.

"No. So, where are you from?" I asked as I slowly climbed down off my high horse.

"Well, I was born in Barbados. That's where my parents are from. But I was raised and schooled here. I spent all of my summers in Barbados, though."

That explained the accent.

"So do you go to Barbados often?" I asked. I felt myself becoming more comfortable.

"As often as I can, which unfortunately is not often enough."

He pulled the car to a stop in front of my building. The rain had started to let up. I didn't want to leave and didn't want the rain to stop; I just wanted to stay there in that Mercedes with that man.

"Well, thank you so much for the ride, and again, I'm

really sorry about . . . well, you know," I said and extended my hand. He took it and for the second time that day my veins filled with fire.

"Well, Ms. Crystal Atkins . . . is it Ms. or Mrs.?"

"Ms.," I said, a little too quickly.

"Well, Ms. Atkins, it's been a pleasure."

He was waiting for me to leave, but I couldn't move. I just sat there, staring stupidly at him, thinking about what I should say next.

"I would really like to repay you properly . . . I mean, um, lunch, perhaps . . . or maybe dinner?" I couldn't believe I was saying it, but I was.

"Tonight?" he said. The word slid slowly from his mouth like warm honey.

"Tonight? Yes, tonight would be fine," I said, already mentally flipping through my closet, looking for just the right dress.

"Eight?" he said.

"Ei-eight . . . yes," I said.

"Okay. Well, I'll see you then."

I walked into my building in a daze. The doorman said hello twice but I didn't hear him; I saw his lips moving but the sound of my heart beating inside my chest drowned out everything.

I entered my apartment and kicked off my shoes. With each step I discarded a piece of wet clothing until finally I was standing naked in front of my closet, grinning like an idiot and trying to figure out what I could wear that would dazzle Kendrick Green.

I called Pam, my hairdresser. "Girl, I got a hair emergency. If you come right now, I'll pay you triple your usual."

"I'll be right there, Ms. Atkins."

I knew that Pam would stop in the middle of a perm, dye, or cut job at her shop on 125th Street to come to my rescue. I had been a faithful client of hers for years and had referred at least a hundred people during that time.

Pam Pam's Doo Shoppe was the hottest black-owned beauty parlor in the city. It wasn't flashy with lots of mirrors or smart decor. But if you wanted your hair fried and dyed correctly, Pam Pam's was the place to go.

I decided on a red suede dress that hugged my hips and dipped low in the back.

Since I had offered to take him to dinner, I figured I would take him to Jezebel or maybe Bamboo, my favorite restaurants.

Pam blew my shoulder-length hair bone straight and arranged it around my face so that it had a slightly wild, unkempt sexy look about it. I sprayed Passion in all the right places and applied just enough makeup. I was ready at seven forty-five.

I had just enough time to decide which coat I was going to wear when the phone rang. It was the doorman. "Ms. Atkins, Mr. Reme is here to see you. Shall I send him up?"

I froze. I had totally forgotten about Steven.

Steven was the man I had been seeing off and on for nearly a year. At first he seemed like he could be the one. He was okay-looking, intelligent, and funny, and he held down a job as a high-powered attorney. But after six months I realized that his hair was receding and his stomach was growing. He began to look like my Uncle Herbert. Not that I'm shallow—I would have been able to overlook the physical if he wasn't so clingy and whiny and if he didn't worship me more than I deserved.

I was still seeing him because I hadn't been able to summon the courage to break up with him, and, besides, I hadn't really had any other suitors.

But Kendrick Greene was in my life now!

"Yes, please send him up."

Steven was short and light-skinned—the complete opposite of what I usually went for in a man. When he came to the door he was dressed in a gray jogging suit that did nothing for him.

"You look fabulous. All of this for me?" he said as he stepped through the door, and the smell of sweat almost knocked me over. He looked at me, his tongue dangling from his mouth like a thirsty dog's.

"I thought we were staying in tonight. Maybe watch a movie, order some pizza, and then, well, you know . . ." he trailed off and reached for me. Oh yeah: he was always, *always* in the mood.

"Actually, Steven, I forgot we had plans," I said. Well, it wasn't a lie. He reached for me again; I could see his penis growing inside his sweatpants. I was disgusted.

His face changed a bit. "What the hell is wrong with you?" He had good instincts.

"I'm going out."

"Where? With whom?"

"A friend, and I'm leaving right now." I clicked the lights off and gently pushed him back into the hall.

"But we have plans," he whined.

"Yes . . . yes, we did, and I'm sorry. I completely forgot, and this thing came up—"

"Oh, really." Steven watched me carefully. "This thing—it got a name?" he asked.

"Steven, I really don't have time to play this game with you right now—"

"Game?" He cut me off in midsentence. He was beginning to get upset. I heard myself speaking to him in the same manner I spoke to young children—a tone he thoroughly enjoyed in the bedroom but found frustrating now.

"What game am I playing? I think you're the one playing a game."

"Whatever" was all I could think to say. I turned my back to him and slipped the key into the lock. I could hear the ringing on the other side of the door, and I realized that I didn't have my coat. I knew it was the doorman calling to let me know that Kendrick was downstairs.

"Damn, I forgot my coat," I said and pushed the door back open. I ran into my bedroom and settled on a long black Andrew Marc leather coat I'd bought myself for Christmas the year before.

When I got back out to the hallway, Steven was still standing there, sulking. He was done with asking me where, why, and what for the moment, but he would badger me for the next thirty days.

We stepped into the elevator together and rode in silence down to the lobby. Kendrick was standing in front of the building, his back to us.

My feet wouldn't move past the lobby desk. "Well, c'mon," Steven said and gently took my elbow. Kendrick turned around at the same moment. I could see him smiling through the thick glass doors, and then his smile vanished.

I looked over at Steven, and he looked as if someone had just driven a stake through his heart.

I can't remember walking across the lobby floor and out the doors, but there we were, the three of us, standing in a cluster in the cold November night.

"Crystal?" Steven said, shooting me a disapproving look.

"Oh, Kendrick Greene, Steven Reme," I said. The two men shook hands. I could tell that Steven was holding his stomach in and poking his chest out.

"Sir. It's a pleasure," Kendrick said in his silky voice. Steven mumbled what I assumed was a greeting.

"Well, Steven, goodbye," I said and gave him the "please go away" look. Kendrick nodded goodbye and we both started toward the car.

The last thing I saw as we pulled away from the curb was Steven standing in front of my building, giving me the finger.

The night went well. We had drinks at Bamboo and dinner at Jezebel. He told me about his real estate business, making sure to throw in that he'd never been married, although he did have a fifteen-year-old son who was living in San Francisco with his Asian mother.

"It was just one of those things," he said with a boyish grin when I made a face at the fact that the woman was something other than black.

He worked hard but he played just as hard. Racquetball, tennis, basketball. He loved to fish and owned a small yacht at the family residence in Florida.

"Enough about me. Tell me about you," he said and flashed that million-dollar smile. I grinned like a twelve-year-old finally being noticed by the school hunk.

I told him a little bit about my job and he seemed to find it very interesting.

"It must be depressing dealing with so many people and their addictions on a daily basis," he said as he picked over his salmon. His face was solemn, and I felt my heart skip a beat. He was sensitive too!

I had to explain to him that I no longer worked one-on-one with the addicts. I was an administrator and in charge of all the counselors nationwide. I studied other treatment programs and altered them to fit the Ain't I A Woman system. I told him that I also put together grant proposals and wooed the Fortune 500 companies for donations.

"I kind of miss being a counselor," I said. "At the end of the day I really felt like I had accomplished something."

"Yes, that sounds like very fulfilling work. And now is it still fulfilling?" he asked, arching his dark bushy eyebrows.

"Well, now I beg, shuffle numbers, attend parties, and

beg some more. No, I guess it's not as fulfilling." It was the first time I'd openly admitted that to anyone.

Kendrick gave me a soft look and then reached over and patted my hand. "Excuse me for a minute, will you?" he said and stood up and did a little bow. "I need to go to the men's room."

I watched him walk away. I wanted to look away—check out the dessert menu or maybe get the waiter's attention for another glass of wine—but my eyes wouldn't let go of Kendrick Greene until he disappeared into the bathroom.

His stride exuded confidence, and I wasn't the only person to notice; quite a few women shot approving glances his way as he swaggered past them.

That just made me want him all the more.

When he returned, his eyes seemed a bit glazed. He must have noticed that I noticed. "I know, I have a sinus problem and I popped a pill. It makes me look like I smoked a spliff," he said with a laugh. I laughed too and resisted the urge to ask him why he couldn't take the pill right there at the table.

"So listen, pretty lady, can I interest you in shaking your groove thang?" he said in a playful voice.

"Dancing?" I said. I couldn't remember the last time I'd gone out dancing. Could I still do it? I pondered the question for a moment, thinking out every embarrassing scenario that could possibly happen to me on a dance floor.

"Well, I don't know . . ."

"What don't you know? Are you tired?"

"No."

"Do you want this evening to end right now?" he asked. He seemed to be daring me to say yes.

"N-no?" I said, not quite understanding his game.

"Well, then, that must mean you want to go dancing. Right?"

"I guess that's what it means." I didn't know if I appreciated the way he'd just handled that.

We ended up at a club called the Pulse on the East Side. The line of people stretched down the block and around the corner. People stood chatting and rubbing their hands together, trying to keep warm while they waited. They were all black except for the standard sprinkling of whites and Asians sporting locs and nipple rings.

We moved past the people and walked right up to the front door.

"Hey, Mr. Greene, how have you been?" the bouncer, a tall black man with a bald head and two diamond studs in his nose, greeted him. As they shook hands, he threw me an approving glance and then smiled.

"Fine, Jim, just fine," Kendrick replied as Jim stepped aside and opened the door for us.

"Who the hell are they?" someone yelled out from the pack of people behind us.

We checked our coats with a woman and then squeezed our way through the bumping and grinding mass of people.

"Is this a Jamaican club?" I yelled above the music to Kendrick.

"This is a Caribbean club—they play music from all the islands," he yelled back over the noise. "In fact, it's white-owned," he added as he raised his hand to get the bartender's attention.

"What's this?" I asked as he handed me a brown bottle.

"Banks Beer, the national beer of Barbados." He tilted his bottle to his lips and drained it in less than thirty seconds. I looked at him and then the bottle. I didn't drink beer and felt I had had too much alcohol that evening already.

Just as I was about to share that piece of information with Kendrick, someone bumped into me and my bottle went flying through the air. It hit the floor with a crash that could not be heard above the thumping music, but some people had seen it coming and jumped out of its path, avoiding the impact.

"Oh, shit," I said and waited for the woman in the sequined red dress whom the beer had splattered on to come storming at me. She didn't—she looked at the large wet stain spreading on the side of her thigh and then at me. She seemed about to say something, but then the DJ changed the song and all the people around her began jumping up and down and waving colorful handkerchiefs in the air. She got caught up in the frenzy and the crowd closed in around her.

I was still recovering when Kendrick grabbed my wrist and dragged me through the crowd and onto the dance floor. If it wasn't for his strong grip, I would have been caught like a fish in the net of people that hardly opened up to let us through.

The dance floor was packed. I couldn't see how another body would be able to fit, but Kendrick made space and began jumping up and down with the rest of the crowd. I stood before him, watching this man and his massive bulk jump up and down and sing along to the words of a song that I couldn't understand. Sweat poured down his face and soaked through his cream silk shirt.

"C'mon, jump!" he screamed over the music. "Jump!"

The floor was alive beneath me. I got up on my toes and gave a little hop, which made Kendrick laugh and grab me around my waist. "Jump, girl, jump!" he said and began lifting me from the floor. I was embarrassed and looked around to see if anyone was watching. No one was paying us any mind; they were all caught up in the music.

I began jumping, small jumps that barely made my behind jiggle, until finally I decided to hell with everything and began jumping so hard and so high that I jumped right out of my stilettos.

Four hours later we stumbled out onto the sidewalk, breathless and soaking wet.

"Did you have a good time?" Kendrick asked as we sat shivering in his Mercedes, waiting for the heat to fill the cold space.

"Wonderful," I said while trying to stifle a yawn. My hair was a damp mop on my head and I didn't even want to think about what my face looked like.

"Don't tell me you're tired," Kendrick teased. I turned a sleepy eye in his direction. Where did this man get his energy from?

"I was going to take you to this other club I know about . . . they are just beginning to really get started," he said as he revved the engine.

"You're not serious, are you?" I asked, fearful that he might be.

"Naw," he said with a laugh. "How about breakfast?"

I heard my bed calling me, but I ignored it.

"Okay," I said as we did fifty down the street.

We ended up at this all-night spot uptown. The place was run-down, but the chicken and waffles we feasted on were out of this world.

The sun was coming up as Kendrick told me a little more about himself.

"My father let me do whatever it was I showed an interest in. Soccer, tennis, football. Piano, guitar, whatever," he said and drained his coffee cup.

"You were a lucky kid. My parents couldn't afford to pay for anything like that. I wasn't even a Girl Scout," I said, surprised at the bitterness in my voice.

When we finally made it to my apartment building, the early-morning dog walkers and joggers were already on the street.

"Ms. Atkins, it was an enchanting evening," Kendrick said before lifting my hand and kissing it. He didn't kiss the back of my hand; he kissed my palm. It was a long, seductive kiss that melted my insides.

"Goodbye, Ms. Atkins. Sleep well."

I could hardly speak. "Goodbye," I whispered in a weak, trembling voice. I fought the urge to invite him up and into my bed. "Goodbye," I said again, a bit louder this time.

He waited until I stepped into the building before pulling

away, and at the sound of his tires screeching against the blacktop, I panicked and realized that he hadn't said he would call me. In fact, he hadn't even asked for my number!

The sleep my body was craving wouldn't allow me to dwell on it for too long. I turned the ringer off on the phone and fell fully dressed into my bed, where I remained until the loud buzzing of the doorbell woke me up at three o'clock.

"Ms. Atkins, you have a package here," the doorman's gruff voice announced over the intercom.

"Would you send it up, please?" I said as my brain pounded inside my skull. A few seconds later I opened the door and was presented with a large gold-wrapped gift box. "Just a minute," I said to the doorman as I went to get my purse. I thanked him after tipping him five dollars for his trouble.

It's not my birthday, I thought as I placed the box on top of the living room table. There was no card attached. I quickly undid the wrapping, being careful not to rip it up. When I lifted the top the first thing I saw was a white silk rose, and beneath it were two cashmere sweaters, one black and one red. I started grinning like an idiot.

I removed the sweaters, and at the bottom of the box was a blue and white Totes umbrella and a white card:

I had a wonderful evening . . . I hope we can do it again—soon.
Thank God for rainy days.

Kendrick

I smiled and did a jig in the middle of my living room. I had fallen in love in less than twenty-four hours.

That was two years ago, and while he still managed to excite me and I believed more than ever that I loved him, I had the nagging feeling that something wasn't quite right, that maybe Kendrick Greene wasn't my soul mate, my black knight in shining armor.

I couldn't shake the feeling, so I just exerted extra effort toward ignoring it.

Ten

"You spoil me so, Zhan," I purred when Zhan kissed the small of my back to let me know that my massage is over.

"Did you enjoy that?" he asked as I turned over on the massage table. I didn't answer, but I gave him a satisfied smile. He bent and gave me a soft kiss on the mouth.

We were in his London flat, which was located on Cheval Place, an exclusive address in the Knightsbridge section of London.

I turned my head and looked out the floor-to-ceiling windows. It had rained every day since I'd gotten there, and today was no exception.

"You know I love touching your body, love," Zhan said and bent to kiss me again.

"You have magic hands," I murmured and eased myself up and onto my elbows. Zhan's penis was rock hard, and so was mine. I bent my head and kissed the tip of his dick.

"Oooooh," he moaned and his hands came up and began to stroke my face.

I thought, I am the luckiest man alive. Fab job, wonderful man, money in the bank. Healthy and good-looking. What more can a man ask for?

A woman!

The voice came out of nowhere, and I jerked my head back. "What did you say?" I asked Zhan, my eyes bulging.

Zhan's hazel eyes were glazed over with pleasure, and he gave me a sexy look. "I didn't say a word," he whispered and tried to guide my head back down to his dick.

My eyes moved around the room. I am going crazy, I thought.

"Baby, I think you're still jet-lagged," he muttered and then moaned as my lips wrapped around the thick head of his member.

Yes, maybe I am, I thought, and swallowed him whole.

Zhan is a late sleeper. But me, I'm up with the sun. I can't spend the whole morning in bed, even if it is with the man I love. So I got up and out, walking the streets of Knightsbridge, enjoying the first part of the day, which was, amazingly, free of rain.

I moved slowly down the cobblestone streets, absent-mindedly twirling my black umbrella as I went.

A spot of tea and a scone will do me just fine, I thought and then laughed to myself at my corny British accent.

I popped into a teahouse and settled myself down at the table closest to the door. A young Indian waiter approached me. "Can I help you, sir?"

"Yes, can I have a cup of black tea and a scone, please?"

"What type of scone would you like, sir?" he asked and pointed to the chalkboard hanging on the wall.

I perused it for a while and then said, "Um, chocolate, please."

"Very good, sir."

And jolly-ho to you too!

I like London, I really do. Well, I don't like the weather, but the restaurants are great and the architecture is out of this world. I just love how the old and the new blend seamlessly together.

Could I live here? Well, maybe some of the time. Six months out of the year to start with, and then I would have to see from there.

If Zhan had his way, I would be living in London already. But I need some more time, and anyway, I still have this little problem of mine to deal with.

"Here you go, sir. Let me know if you need anything else," the waiter said as he set a bamboo tray down before me.

"Thank you."

I sipped my tea and nibbled on my scone as I watched the Londoners go by. I like to people watch, but I really wished I'd brought a newspaper along to read. I didn't know what had been going on in the world. All Zhan and I had been doing was taking long walks, eating, drinking, and making love. The last time I'd watched television was before I boarded the Virgin Atlantic flight to get here.

"Noah?"

The sound of my name snatched me out of my musings and I looked up and into the warm brown eyes of a very good-looking black man.

"Yes?"

"Hey, I thought that was you."

I looked a bit closer. "Oh my God!" I spouted and

jumped up from the table, almost knocking over my pot of tea. "Will Somers!"

Will had been the love of my life, six years earlier.

I leaned in and we hugged. He still had that football physique.

"How have you been?" I asked after we broke our embrace.

"Good, good. Can't complain one bit. And you?"

"Oh, I'm well," I said and blushed a bit. He still had that dazzling smile that made me feel all tingly inside.

"So what are you doing in London?" he asked.

"Do you have a minute?" I asked and pointed to the extra chair.

He eyed it, threw a cautious look over his shoulder, and then shrugged. "Sure, why not? I got a little time," he said and sat down.

What was that about?

"Well, I'm here visiting a friend," I said and signaled for the waiter. "Can I get you something?"

"Oh no, nothing for me," he said, and so I waved the waiter away.

"And you, why are you in London?"

"What friend? Do I know him?"

I threw him a quizzical look. Did he just totally avoid my question?

"Well," I began and leaned back into my chair, "after you broke my heart, I—"

"Shhhh, don't say stuff like that out loud," he said and straightened his back so that his chest puffed out even further.

What was going on here?

"Don't say stuff like what?" I questioned.

Will cleared his throat and threw another nervous look over his shoulder. "Nothing, nothing, man," he said and tried to laugh it away, but I wasn't having it.

"What's wrong with you?" The annoyance in my voice was evident.

"Nothing, man, really," he said as he kept his eyes focused on my scone.

"Okay, if you say so," I said as I snatched at my napkin and began twirling it around my hand. "So why are you here in London?" I probed again.

It took a beat for Will to look me in the eye and another beat for him to answer me, and even then his words came out as a whisper.

"I'm getting married tomorrow."

I laughed. I'd have to see a doctor when I got back home. Surely I was losing my mind.

"Did—did you say 'married'?"

Will just nodded his head.

"To . . . to a man, right?"

He shook his head no, and I clutched my chest in horror. "A woman!" I squealed.

"Shhhh," Will warned me again. "Yes. A woman."

Okay, so it was a sickness. Maybe Will had started out the same way I had. A Beyoncé video, a little craving here, a little pussy there, and then total heterosexuality!

Now I was really scared.

"Are you serious?" I said, feeling a little faint.

"Yes, very," he said, almost sadly.

"But why—" I started, when a woman walked through the door and called his name.

"Will, baby, there you are."

Will abruptly stood up. "Hey, sweetheart," he said as he caught her by the waist and planted a big wet one on her lips.

Was this show for me?

"Wow," she said, a little more than dazzled.

I couldn't really see her face. Will's height and massive-size body blocked most of her from my view.

"Who's this?" I heard her ask.

For a moment I didn't think Will was going to turn around and introduce me. I thought he would just whisk her off her feet like Superman and leap into the sky. Anything not to have to introduce his wife-to-be to his ex–gay lover.

"Oh, baby, this is an old coworker of mine," he started before he even turned around.

I tried to put on the most nonchalant face that I could muster so that when he stepped aside and his fiancée's eyes met mine she would be none the wiser.

"Noah Bodison," he said, finally turning around and moving aside, "this is my fiancée—"

"Merriwether Beacon," I whispered in astonishment.

Will stopped short and his head swiveled in surprise. "Do you two know each other?"

Yes, we knew each other very well.

"I-I," I started, in total shock.

Merriwether didn't miss a beat. She smiled sweetly and approached me with open arms. I stood without knowing

I had. "What a small, small world we live in," she sang as she embraced me.

She pressed those size-D tits against my chest and the movie that was us less than six months ago clicked on and began to play in my head. I immediately recalled the stink of our X-rated sex and the cheap scent of her dime-store candles.

"It's so nice to see you again, Noah."

"I . . . I" was all I could say, still not knowing where we were going to go with this.

Will gave us both a quizzical look.

She turned to him and said, "Baby, Noah and I were on the same plane a few months ago." I just stared. "Oh, Lord, Noah, where were we headed?" She looked at me for an answer.

Was I going to play a part in her evil doings? Who had made it her business to turn the homosexuals of the world straight, and, more important, who had granted her the powers to do so?

"Boston?" I squeaked.

Will's eyes swung between Merriwether and me.

"Not Boston, silly. I haven't been to Boston in years." She laughed, but I didn't miss the evil eye she tossed me. "It was Chicago. Yes, yes, it was Chicago." She laughed again and moved toward Will's side and wrapped her arm around his waist. "Noah and I sat together on that flight, and we talked all the way to Chicago."

"Yes, yes, we did." I nodded like some kind of machine.

"Oh, he was a pleasure to fly with, and *fuh-nee*," she said, slapping her thigh.

Will seemed to relax a bit. "Yeah, he is very funny," he said, giving me a wry smile with a hidden meaning that I didn't miss.

"Well, it was nice seeing you again, Noah," Merriwether said before turning to her fiancé. "Will and I have a lot to do before the day is over." She looked at Will and grinned and then back at me. "Did he tell you that we're getting married tomorrow?"

"Oh yes, he did. Congratulations," I said tightly.

"Thank you." She beamed.

"Yeah, thanks, man, and hey, it was nice seeing you again," Will said and extended his fist toward me.

What the hell was I supposed to do with that?

Slowly my right hand balled into a tight fist and came up and over the table. I leaned forward a bit so that our fists kissed—I mean, bumped—and then they were gone. Will threw a "Take care man" over his shoulder as they strolled through the door.

Merriwether Beacon—hmm, I mused as I sat back down and looked suspiciously around me. I wonder how many more of her kind are out there?

Eleven

It was Saturday morning, barely eight o'clock, and I was up. Little Eric was in the living room, watching MTV, and Jay-Z was so loud, I thought that if I opened my eyes he would be rapping right over me.

I pulled the pillow over my head and told myself I was not really going to get up, walk out into the living room, and crack my child over his head with the remote.

"Eric!" I yelled at the top of my lungs so loud that my ears began to hurt.

He didn't answer. I knew he heard me but ignored me just the same. "Eric!" I yelled again as I sat up in bed and placed my feet on the cold linoleum floor.

The sun was bright and there were already children in the playground below my window. The weather report called for temperatures in the high eighties. I sighed and looked at the broken air conditioner sitting in the window across the room.

I stood up and stretched. I had so much to do. The clothes needed to be washed, the kitchen floor needed to be scrubbed and waxed, and the refrigerator was desperately in need of a good cleaning-out and defrosting.

But none of that could happen until I'd had a cigarette,

a cup of coffee, and my Saturday morning free of MTV. So I charged like a bull out of my bedroom and into the living room, where I stood glaring at Eric's neck, hoping he would feel the darts my eyes were throwing there. But he was oblivious.

"Eric!"

My son jumped and whipped his head around on his long thick neck and grinned. "Hey, Mom."

I released a heavy sigh before I spoke again. "Turn that mess down. Don't you have any consideration?" I asked, knowing full well he didn't.

"Sorry," he said, and the volume on the television dropped two levels.

"Is that room of yours clean?" I asked as I walked into the kitchen.

There was a bowl sitting on the card table that served as a dining table. The bowl was half filled with cloudy milk, where four lone Cheerios floated at the top.

I snatched up bowl and all and deposited it into the sink.

"I asked a question, boy."

He mumbled something.

"What?"

"I said I'm going to get to it in a minute."

I gritted my teeth and felt for my pack of cigarettes on top of the refrigerator. Finding them, I flipped the top open and peered in.

I knew I had eight cigarettes left in the pack before I went to sleep; now there were five.

"You been stealing my cigarettes?"

"No, Mother."

I knew he had. I wasn't crazy. I loved him, but I'd sure been counting the days until I put his narrow ass on the bus to be rid of him for the summer.

I hurriedly slipped a cigarette between my lips. Leaning over the stove, I lit it on the burner, singeing my eyelashes. "Shit," I mumbled as I batted my eyes with my hands.

I wanted a cup of coffee so bad, but I had none in the house. I didn't have much of anything in the house. I would have to go food shopping today too.

I smoked for a while as I looked around the apartment and wondered why I didn't hear the tornado that had come through and wrecked my place last night.

With that thought, the phone rang.

"Hello?"

"Geneva, it's Nadine."

I twisted my face up and thought that I really needed to pay the extra five dollars a month for caller ID.

"Oh, hello, Nadine," I barely responded through gritted teeth.

"I've been trying to reach you for days now," she sang in her birdlike soprano.

"Yeah, I been real busy," I said and took a long drag of my cigarette.

"Well, you haven't been to a meeting in almost a month."

Like I didn't know that. "Yeah, it's been about that long."

"Well, when do you think you'll be coming back?"

"I really couldn't say right now."

"Well, in order for the program to work, you have to work the program, Geneva."

"Yeah, yeah, I know."

"Have you at least been keeping up with the point system?"

"Uh-huh," I said as I used my index finger to remove a piece of tobacco from the tip of my tongue.

"Well, that's good." Nadine sounded relieved. "So, can I look for you at the afternoon meeting today?"

"Sure." She could look for me, but I wouldn't be there.

"Oh, goody! Can't wait to see you, Geneva!"

"Same here," I said and hung up the phone.

I was going to have to change my number.

I looked down at my gut hanging over the waistband of the boxer shorts I slept in and was immediately angry and disgusted with myself.

"Turn that mess off and help me clean this place up," I yelled at Eric as I snubbed the cigarette out into the green glass ashtray.

Well, I had to take it out on someone, didn't I?

Eric just kept bopping his head and snapping his fingers, so I jumped up and marched over to the coffee table and grabbed the remote and clicked the television off.

"Get up and start cleaning, boy!"

Eric made a face and slowly lifted himself from the couch. "Dang. When I get rich, I'm gonna have a maid to do all of this!"

"And I want the bathroom spotless!" I yelled at his back as I began to remove the week's debris from the coffee table.

In no time, Eric was back on the couch, surfing through channels.

I looked at him like he had four heads. "What are you doing?"

"What? I straightened up the room."

"You did, that quick?" I laughed and looked at the closed door of the bedroom.

"Yep," he spouted and tried to look around me.

"What about the bathroom?"

"I just cleaned it last week. How dirty could it really be?"

I felt the blood boiling in my head, and my heart began to run a race in my chest.

"Get your behind up and clean that goddamn bathroom before I put these size-tens up your ass!" I screamed at the top of my lungs.

Eric gave me a bored look and got up and headed toward the bathroom. He mumbled as he went and I had to remind him who was boss and say, "Don't get your teeth knocked out, boy!"

The phone rang before I could say much more.

"Hello?"

"Hey, Geneva." A voice came across the phone line in disconnected syllables.

"H-hello?"

"It's Noah."

"Noah?"

"The one and only."

"Hey, how was your trip?"

"Very interesting," he said.

"Where are you now?" I asked as I swung the refrigerator door open to see what was inside. Nothing.

"I'm on my way home from the airport. How's Little Eric? I got his messages about his upcoming performance. Did I miss it? I'm all turned around with the dates."

"No, you didn't miss it. He's going to be so thrilled that you'll be able to be there."

Noah sighed. "Oh, good. So, catch me up. What did I miss?"

"Oh, plenty!" I laughed, eased down into one of the kitchen chairs, and prepared myself to dish the dirt. "Chevy borrowed money from Crystal to get a boob job."

"Get the hell out of here!"

"Noah, I am dead serious!"

"Ms. Drama is always up to her tricks."

"She sure is."

"Well, I guess I'll get to see her new additions up close and personal when I get home."

"Yeah, I guess so."

"I meant to call her while I was in London, but you know Zhan had me tied up for the entire time."

"Literally?" I laughed.

"Only some of the time!"

"Well, you wouldn't have been able to reach her anyway."

"Don't tell me her phone is cut off again."

"Yep."

"That child is so trifling!"

"But yet you still trust her with your home and your fish. I see you still haven't learned your lesson."

"What are you talking about?"

"Remember the last time you went away and left her in charge? Didn't she almost burn down the house?"

"Yeah, but, see, I went on after that and got that sprinkler system installed."

"That damn Chevy, always costing us money." I laughed and stood up again to look in the refrigerator.

"Baby, wasn't nothing in there the first time you looked," Noah said.

"What? How do you know I'm looking in the fridge?"

"Well, you ain't chomping in my ear, so either you looking for something to chomp on or there ain't nothing there!"

"Fuck you, Noah."

"Wouldn't you love to."

We laughed until the signal went dead.

Twelve

I was still laughing when my taxi pulled up to my three-story brownstone on Stuyvesant Avenue in Brooklyn. I could see, before I even stepped out of the cab, a week's worth of mail spilling out the brass mail slot of my mahogany door and the browning petals of my potted yellow and white petunias.

"Shit."

Hadn't I asked Chevy to take care of this for me? Water the plants, collect the mail, and feed the fish. Was it so fucking hard to do?

I shuddered at what I would find floating at the top of the fish tank.

Geneva was right. Chevy was like some type of high-maintenance, unruly stepchild. Always between jobs, apartments, and only God knew how many men.

"Keep the change," I said as I shoved a fifty-dollar bill at the turban-wearing cabdriver.

I stepped out onto the sidewalk, barely skirting a little girl on her roller skates. "Hello, Mr. Noah!" She beamed and waved at me as she struggled down the sidewalk.

"Hey, baby. You be careful now."

Stevie Wonder was blaring from my open parlor-floor

windows. And as angry as I was, I found my head bopping to the music as I fumbled for my keys.

I slowly opened the door and was met by the pungent scent of marijuana.

Stevie was louder inside, and I could hear Chevy singing off-key to "Sir Duke." I walked into the entry hall and dropped my suitcase to the floor. Turning right and into the parlor, I expected to be greeted by my reflection in the nine-foot pier mirror on the wall, but instead my eyes collided with Chevy, who was spinning awkwardly toward me, one hand gripped tightly around a forty-ounce bottle of Old English beer while the other clung to a lit joint.

"What the hell are you doing?" I screamed over the music as I watched beer splatter across the shiny wood of my parquet floors.

As I surveyed the room, I saw that she'd practically turned my home into her very own walk-in closet. There were pieces of her clothing everywhere. A bra across the arm of the sofa, a pair of gym shorts on the ottoman, and a mountain of sandals and stilettos piled in the corner of the room.

Chevy stumbled over to the wall and pressed her shoulder against it to steady herself as she waited for the world to stop spinning. I marched over to the stereo and pressed the off switch.

"Hey, Noah! You're back!" she screamed as if the music was still blaring.

"Yes, I am. And you're high."

I looked around for something to clean up the mess

Chevy had made on the floor, but there was nothing available that I was willing to sacrifice.

"You know I don't allow drugs in my house," I said tightly.

"*Suuuuuure* you don't. Where the hell do you think I got it from?"

I balled my fists and pressed them into my hips and said, "You went into my private stash?"

Chevy just grinned wickedly and held the joint up to my face.

There was never any shame in Ms. Drama's game. I walked toward her and plucked the joint from her pinched fingers, put it to my lips, and puffed.

Passing it back to her, I walked through the cream-colored living room and into the family room to examine the damage.

The family room was intact, thank God, and the soft sage-colored walls and large, inviting silk floor pillows reminded me that I was severely jet-lagged and needed sleep.

I walked over to the fish tank, and the colorful tropical fish rushed the glass, pleading with their eyes for me to feed them.

"They're starving!" I yelled at Chevy, who was in the midst of a drunken Electric Slide.

"How can you tell?" She burped and then turned the forty up to her lips. "I fed them," she whined after she burped again and took another puff of the joint.

"Liar."

"They're still alive, aren't they?"

"Barely," I said and gave her the finger.

Chevy, finally exhausted, plopped down onto the living room couch and threw her legs over the ottoman.

I spied her clothing everywhere and said, "Chevy, did you move in or something?"

"No," Chevy sang back to me as she pulled herself up from the couch and strutted up the stairs toward the bedrooms.

I followed her, ready to give her the best piece of my mind, but she ran into the bathroom and locked the door. I could hear her giggling madly.

"You really shouldn't do drugs if you can't handle it," I screamed through the locked door. "You gotta come out sometime."

In my room now. My sanctuary. No television here. Just my king-size sleigh bed, a wine-colored comfortable chair with matching ottoman. Nightstands piled high with books. Wall fountain. "Ahhh."

All I wanted was to get a shower, some Thai food, a glass of Chardonnay, and some sleep.

I stripped down to my boxers and walked down the hall to the extra bedroom, where my treadmill, a small library, and a pull-out sofa were. But as I walked in, it seemed that the room's contents had grown to include three large suitcases, a duffle bag, dozens of boxes of shoes, and black Hefty bags bulging with clothes.

I was heated and charged back out of the room and down the hall to the bathroom. I'd have to get her out of here in less than thirty days or before she started receiving mail. After that, the law would see her as a tenant and

I'd have to evict her, and that could take six months or more.

"Bitch, you did move in!" I said as I banged heavily on the door. "Chevanese Cambridge, you better open this goddamn door now!"

I could break it down, but I'd just had these new oak doors hung two months ago.

"Chevy!" I screamed again. "I ain't playing with you, girl. Don't let me have to get a locksmith, 'cause I will!"

Nothing.

"I want you out of here tomorrow!"

Still nothing.

I panicked. Maybe she'd fallen and hit her head on the toilet and was bleeding to death. "Chevy?" I gave the door a gentle rat-a-tat-tat.

I pressed my ear against the door and listened.

Snoring.

Was I hearing right?

I dropped down onto my knees and peered through the one-inch space between the door and the floor. Chevy was seated on the floor, her back resting against the tub, the joint burned down to a roach and resting alongside the half-empty beer bottle.

Her legs were stretched wide open and, good God, she wasn't wearing any drawers. Damn. I just couldn't seem to get away from pussy.

Thirteen

"Where are you, at the gym?" I asked Crystal as I haphazardly cradled the phone between my face and my shoulder.

"Naw, girl, I could not get with that waiting-on-line-for-a-machine shit, so I just bought me a treadmill. Didn't I tell you?"

"Nope."

"Oh. Well, I called to invite you over for a girls' thing tonight. I meant to mention it at work yesterday, but I got so busy I forgot to. I know you don't have any hot plans. Or do you?"

"Maybe. Let me just go get my planner out and see," I said as I snatched up the *TV Guide* and loudly flipped through the pages. "Oh dear, it looks like I was supposed to have dinner with Denzel Washington this evening. Well, it would be the third time this week. I guess I could cancel for you," I said in my best Elizabeth Taylor voice.

"Yeah, well, you do that." Crystal laughed. "Let's say about eight."

"That should be fine."

"Um, do you know where Little Eric is?"

"He said he was going to play basketball, why?"

"Where?"

"The court right downstairs."

"Really?"

"Why?"

"Well, you ain't heard it from me, but I saw him headed over to the park."

"What park?"

"Central Park."

"When was this?" I asked, already feeling my good mood changing for the worse.

"Just a few minutes before I called. In fact, seeing him is what reminded me to call you."

"Was he by himself?"

"No, he had some little light-skinned chick with him who had on a pair of shorts that was so small her butt cheeks was playing peek-a-boo."

I sucked air and bit down hard on the inside of my cheeks.

"Geneva?"

"His ass was supposed to be keeping an eye on the damn laundry!" I screamed. "I gotta go," I barked and slammed the phone down.

I grabbed my keys off the kitchen table. Too angry to wait for the elevator, I took the stairs two at a time down to the basement of the tenement where the laundry room was.

It was Saturday, the big wash and dry day, and the laundry room stayed packed until at least four or five in the afternoon. If you had sense, you didn't leave your clothes, not even for a minute, because you could return and find them removed from the washer or the dryer and thrown onto the floor or, worse yet, gone.

I walked into the laundry room and came face-to-face with at least twenty other women who practically mirrored myself. Rags tied around their heads, breasts swaying lazily beneath the yellowed and thin material of the old clothes they wore.

I nodded at the women I knew and then began my search, which took me to five dryers before I stumbled upon Little Eric's football jerseys, jeans, and T-shirts in the sixth one.

Now I just had to find my sheets, towels, and washcloths.

I rounded the corner and was ready to inspect the second line of dryers when I spotted blue ducks and yellow daffodils lying in the middle of the floor in a wet heap.

Someone had tossed my shit out of the washing machine and onto the floor!

"Ten, nine, eight—" I counted.

Doing laundry on Saturday was like going to war.

I propped my hands on my hips and heard the music from Clint Eastwood's *The Good, the Bad, and the Ugly* in my ears.

"Seven, six, five—"

I snatched at a black Hefty bag that rested on top of one of the washing machines. It wasn't mine, but in the laundry room, all was fair in washing and drying.

I slowly picked up my linens and noticed that one or more people had actually trampled across my sheets. How foul is that?

My rage flared.

"Four, three, two, one."

By the time I got back to my apartment, I'd counted backward from ten at least five times.

I have something for Little Eric's sorry ass, I thought as I went to the clothesline that extended from the kitchen window to the bathroom window and hung the filthiest sheet, pillowcase, towel, and washcloth on the line.

Still not satisfied, still boiling with anger, I stormed back out of the apartment, determined to find my son and commit murder.

I marched up 90th Street and past Crystal's building, across Central Park West Drive, and straight into the park.

Forgetting that I had my Saturday morning cleaning clothes on, I charged ahead, oblivious to the heat and the swinging of my large breasts that were practically visible through the thin material of my T-shirt.

After about ten minutes, the sun beaming on my neck, I moved to the grassy, tree-lined edges along the concrete pathway.

The heat made my scalp feel as if a million fleas were attacking it, and I became even angrier.

My mama was right; children drive you crazy.

I gave some people evil looks and yelled, "And what?" when they stared too long. I knew I looked homeless.

I almost laughed in spite of my anger when I imagined what it was they must have been seeing.

"This is what teenagers turn you into!" I screamed and made a face at an Asian woman struggling to get out of my path.

After about twenty minutes, I was out of breath and dehydrated, and so I staggered into the children's park and sat as close to the sprinkler as I could without actually stepping into it. Even though I really, really wanted to. I wiped at my sweat, thinking that it must be the hottest spring on record.

Nearby, a mother tended to her daughter's bruised knee, lovingly placing a Band-Aid over the child's scrape.

I smiled, reminiscing on those carefree, innocent days when my biggest worry with Little Eric was a bruised knee, runny nose, or fever. Those times seemed very far away now.

The woman sat back, sensed me staring, and turned toward me, and the smile she was wearing froze before cracking and falling away. She could not scoot her behind across the bench fast enough before snatching her daughter's hand and declaring, "Come on, Chelsea. It's time to go."

Fuck you too, I thought as I watched them rush off.

Suddenly I felt beaten and was reminded just how hard my life was. Shit, I didn't have a chance to grow up and here I was trying to raise a man.

If I had money, things would be different. I'd be living in a house in the suburbs somewhere and my son wouldn't have to go to the building laundry because we'd have our own washer and dryer right inside the house!

I was doing the best I could, but it was times like this that I didn't think my best was good enough.

I slowly raised myself off the bench and started toward home, and suddenly I was reminded that I had to have been doing a halfway decent job, because my baby ain't ever been profiled on any news station's breaking bulletin—knock on wood.

The sound of a bouncing basketball snatched my attention; suddenly reenergized, I turned around and followed the sound eagerly, like a hound dog sniffing out a fox.

I prayed for my son as I rounded the fence and headed toward the swarm of young black men. I prayed that he wasn't there, because if he was, I could already picture the headline:

Mother Pummels Son to Death with Basketball in Fit of Rage over Abandoned Laundry

It wasn't him. Just a whole bunch of young black males who could have been him and probably had mamas looking much like myself out hunting them down too.

Back at the apartment door, I heard the last few rings of the telephone, but whoever it was would have to call back, because I couldn't get the key in the lock good.

Walking back into the apartment was like entering a sauna. The afternoon sun radiated through the windows, and I could swear I saw smoke rising off the coffee table.

The linens I'd hung on the line were already dry, and I retrieved them and started toward Eric's room.

"I got something for his trifling ass," I muttered as I fitted the filthy sheet onto Eric's bed. "Since he couldn't see fit to do what I wanted"—I shoved his pillow into the dirty case—"then he can sleep on this filth!" I laughed wickedly. "Let's see how he likes this!"

I smelled to high heaven, and so went into my room and stripped out of my clothes. On the way to the bathroom, I caught sight of my body in my bureau mirror. "Ugh!" I said as I took a long gander at my flabby stomach and cellulite-packed thighs. I moaned and quickly streaked to the bathroom to further disgust myself by stepping on the scale.

The needle shook at two hundred and thirty pounds.

"Why, why, why!" I cried and pinched at the tire around my waist. "Go away!" I screamed. "Abracadabra, be gone!" I closed my eyes and demanded. But when I opened them again, the tire was still there.

"Shit," I muttered, "it never works."

Fourteen

I stood staring out the window and thought that I saw a woman who looked suspiciously like Geneva dashing into the park, but I couldn't be sure. But I was more than positive that Geneva wouldn't leave the house looking like that.

I busied myself with things around the apartment, keeping a close eye on the park's entrance, and when an hour had passed, I called Geneva's number. After I'd let it ring for some time, I decided to go into the park in search of Little Eric myself. I gathered my keys and cell phone and headed out the door.

I jogged down to the park and headed toward the basketball court. Halfway there, I saw a face that looked a bit familiar. A young golden-looking boy emerged from a cluster of trembling bushes.

Trembling?

His eyes were bloodshot and he had a stupid-looking grin on his face.

"Hey, Miss Crystal," he said and gave me a wave before walking a crooked line past me. My feet slowed to a stop and I stared at his back before a name attached itself to his face and I lifted a slow hand and said, "Hey, Andrew."

The heavy scent of marijuana trailed behind him and hit me square in the face. I looked at the bushes and then at the cop on horseback, who was smiling down at me.

Somehow I knew Eric was behind those bushes, so I smiled sweetly and bent down to adjust the laces of my sneakers, which were perfectly tied and knotted. Once the officer was far enough away, I gingerly rounded the bushes.

It was dark there beneath that cluster of green, but I had no problem making out the red T-shirt Eric had on, or the bared breasts of the young woman his hands were happily kneading.

"Touch my dick," I heard my sixteen-year-old godson demand, and was stunned stupid by the request. My lips froze up and my tongue was left wagging behind my teeth.

"Okay, Daddy, like this?" the heffa crooned.

Daddy?

I couldn't believe what I was hearing, and I leaped under the bushes like some type of ninja teen sex averter. "You nasty little ho!" I screeched, grabbing Eric's hand and tugging him toward me.

"What the—" Eric started and snatched his hand away from me before he turned his head, looked me full in the face, and said unbelievingly, "Auntie Crystal?"

His face immediately swam with a mixture of surprise and embarrassment as he hurriedly tried to shove his stiff penis back down into his basketball shorts.

"Auntie who?" the girl hooted like an owl as she casually pulled the bright pink cami top down over her taut breasts.

"Crystal. Auntie Crystal," I said, using every bit of my director's voice. "You, young lady, should be ashamed of yourself."

The girl just smirked. I didn't faze her one bit.

"I—" Eric started, and I snapped, "Shut up and let's go."

The girl didn't move; she just sat there throwing me dirty looks.

"Ain't you got somebody else to do?" I used my street voice now and saw from the change in her expression that I was finally speaking her language.

The little ho swung her eyes between Eric and me, and then she pursed her lips and said, "You got my number. You call me when you ready for some of this." And with that she tapped her crotch.

My mouth fell right open.

"What, what-what . . ." I sounded like an idiot, I know, but that's all I could say.

This new generation was bold and brash and didn't have a problem expressing their sexuality. Unlike mine—we took the safe route and got mind-fucked by reading the dirty parts in Jackie Collins and Harold Robbins novels over and over again, putting ourselves in the vixens' place and fantasizing that we were the ones being seduced.

Today, these kids didn't need dirty novels: they had cable television, condom drives at school, and free rein of their residences, because the nine-to-five working hours were a thing of the past. And realistically, if you included travel time, a parent could be out of the home eleven to twelve hours a day.

That's a lot of time for a teenager with raging hormones and nothing constructive to do.

This was the case with my godson.

"What you want with that?" I asked, pointing at the girl's retreating back, even though I knew full well what the answer was.

Eric just shrugged his shoulders and kicked at the dirt.

"I hope you're protecting yourself. You know, there are a lot worse things out here than getting a girl pregnant."

Eric stared at the ground.

"Do you hear me?"

"Yes," he mumbled.

"Do you know that your mother is somewhere out here looking for you?" I said sternly and folded my hands across my chest. "You were supposed to be in the courtyard, weren't you?"

"Yes," he said, still not making eye contact.

"Well, c'mon." I finally brought my tirade to an end and trudged off. "No telling what she's going to do when she gets a hold of you."

Eric strolled behind me but kept quiet.

"It's so easy just to do what your mother asks of you," I said over my shoulder. "Why do you give her such a hard time?" I said, coming to a halt and turning on him.

Once again, Eric just shrugged and stared at the ground.

I eyed him for a moment and then moved toward him, patting him on the back. "Okay, okay," I cooed. "I know being a teenager is hard. I was one too once upon a time, if you can believe that." I laughed as we moved toward the park entrance.

Once we were upstairs, I wasted no time calling Geneva. "Hello?"

"Yeah, Geneva, just wanted you to know that Little Eric is here with me," I said as I swung the door to the freezer open and peered inside.

"Really," Geneva said with an air of calmness that was chilling.

"Um, yeah."

"Well, you better keep him there, because if he comes here, I'm going to have to kill him."

Click.

I just stood staring at the phone. My heart was beating hard inside my chest, and something told me that at that very moment, Geneva might actually act on her threat.

I slowly placed the phone back onto its cradle and then turned and pulled a box of frozen turkey burgers from the freezer.

"What did she say?" Eric asked. His eyes told me that he feared the worst.

"Oh, she said good—she was worried," I lied.

"Oh." He looked meekly down at the floor. He knew his mother better than I did, so he knew that that wasn't what she'd said at all.

Two turkey burgers later, Eric didn't look close to full.

"Do you want me to make you another one?" I asked. I was amazed at how much his stomach was able to hold.

Eric's mouth was full, so he just nodded his head yes.

So I plugged the cord of the George Foreman grill back into the wall socket and went to the freezer to pull out another burger.

He was lucky I even had turkey burgers. The only reason they were in the house was because Kendrick liked them.

The thought of him paralyzed me for a moment, and I just stood there staring at the ice trays.

"Auntie, you okay?" Eric's voice floated from behind.

"Yeah, yeah, just lost in thought." I laughed and pulled out the box of burgers.

After burger number three, Eric finally seemed to be full and pulled himself up from the table and strolled into the living room, leaving me staring at his empty plate and half-empty glass of soda. "'Scuse me, sir," I yelled from the kitchen.

"Yeah?" His head peeked back around the doorway of the kitchen.

"You forgetting something?" I said and placed my hands on my hips.

"What?"

"You ain't got no maids around here," I said and nodded at the table.

"Oh."

He blushed and came back in to retrieve his used wares. I playfully popped him upside his head as he passed.

Back in the living room, Eric snatched the remote control from the coffee table, flopped down hard onto the couch, and swung his leg over the arm.

My look said it all, and Eric cleared his throat and promptly removed his leg.

His eyes wandered around the room. "You got a phat crib, Auntie."

"What?" I am always dumbfounded by the street lingo these kids speak today.

He laughed. "That means you got a nice place."

"It's 'you have' a nice place, not 'you got,'" I corrected him. "What are they teaching you in school?"

Eric ignored the question. "I wish we could live in a place like this." He sighed, standing up and perusing his surroundings. His face turned a little melancholy and then something began to brew beneath that.

"You know, we ain't got nothing. She got that little piece of job, that *you* got for her—"

"She?" I said, flabbergasted at the loose term he was using for the woman who had brought him into the world.

". . . answering phones for a living—huh, that's only one step up from McDonald's as far as I'm concerned . . ."

My eyes were bulging. Where is all of this coming from? I thought.

". . . she can't even get a decent-ass apartment for us. Here we are, living in the PJs, roaches walking around like they pay rent, fridge about to die, water always cold, elevators always broken—I gotta be looking over my shoulder every time I go in and out so's I don't get jumped!"

He slammed his fist into his open palm and I jumped at the loud smacking sound it made.

"All she say is, one day we gonna move. One day? I say what day, because I been hearing that line my entire life!"

I found my voice then and tried to defend my friend who'd given up everything so that her son could have the best life she knew how to give him. "Now wait a minute, Eric. You know your mother—"

"She is so whack, I swear! We were the only people in our building that ain't have no CD player! She was still spinning albums on a turntable and shit."

"All right now, watch your—"

"Until you gave her that CD player for Christmas. You wasted your money. That thing is collecting dust because she says that CDs are too expensive. But I tell you what, she got money for her damn beer and cigarettes—she got plenty of money for that!"

"Eric, I think you need to just calm down and—"

"I bet you don't eat chicken five days out of the week. But you know who does? We do!"

Eric laughed, threw his head back, and hollered. I was convinced the boy was losing it.

"Eric, you don't understand how diff—"

"Chicken and corned beef hash. You know, there's probably a hundred different ways to make corned beef hash, but do you know how many ways she knows how to make it?"

Eric looked at me as if he actually expected me to guess the answer to his ridiculous question. I opened my mouth and he cut me off, like I knew he would.

"Two! She knows two recipes for corned beef hash!" Eric yelled, holding two long fingers up before me.

"'I'm saving money for our future,' that's another line she likes to run. Well, damn, she's been saving forever. I say can we dip into the savings, Ma, so that I can finally get a pair of sneakers that wasn't played out the year before!"

"It's not about the clothes—it's about the person—"

"My mother ain't shit, and my daddy worse than that!"

I don't remember getting up, but all of a sudden I was in his face and my hand was pulling back from his cheek and Eric was standing there staring at me in utter amazement.

The fury that churned in his face exploded, and he lifted a balled fist into the air and aimed it at my mouth.

I braced myself for the blow by cringing and squeezing my eyes shut, but thankfully his fist ended up against the wall.

My eyes were still closed when I heard him rush out the front door.

When I finally opened my eyes and looked at the place on the wall he'd hit, there was a smudged bloodstain looking back at me.

Fifteen

I'd just pulled on my sweatpants when I heard the front door open.

"Eric?" I called and peeked around the door.

"Yeah," he barked and started toward his bedroom.

"Where you been?" I asked as I shot out of the room, stopping him in his tracks. He just stared at me. He was pulling air through his nose like a bull.

"What's wrong with you?" My voice softened. He looked so upset.

"Nothing. I'm a'ight," he mumbled and stepped around me. I let him go.

"Well, where you been?" I gently inquired again.

"I went to the park to play ball," he said before shutting the door to his room.

I just shook my head. Mothering was such hard work; you had to know when to push and when to pull back. This was a time I had to pull back. I could fuss at him about his responsibility later on.

"Well, I'm headed out to the grocery store."

I waited for a response, but none came.

I moved back into my bedroom, opened the closet door, and looked down at the one pair of sneakers I owned.

The white was gray with age and dirt, so I opted for a worn pair of pink and yellow striped flip-flops. "I'm just going to the grocery store," I told myself as I pulled my hair into a tight ponytail.

Always look your best. You never know who you might meet. I could hear my mother's voice in my head.

"Shut up," I mumbled to the air. "At least I have on clean underwear."

"What the hell!" Eric bellowed through the wall.

My heart jumped, and I rushed from the bedroom in a panic. "What's wrong?" I was yelling when we nearly collided in the living room. I was clutching my chest and Eric was clutching the filthy sheet.

"Ma, this sheet is gross. It's covered with all kinds of sh—I mean, gunk."

I looked him squarely in the eye. "Yeah, it is. Maybe next time you'll do what you're supposed to do," I said and snatched my pocketbook off the table and waltzed out the door.

Sixteen

I couldn't believe Noah left me sleeping on the bathroom floor. What kind of friend was he? Now my damn neck was all stiff. I actually woke up with my lips pressed against the toilet bowl—yuck!

God himself only knew what it was I'd been dreaming about. I have to leave that chronic alone.

Once I'd brushed the toilet out of my mouth, showered, and slipped into some tight dark blue Calvins, a white linen halter, and red stiletto slides, I was almost ready to hit the streets.

I was meeting Crystal and Geneva for lunch.

I had to touch up the dark circles under my eyes with some concealer and of course decide what it was I was going to do with this hair of mine. It was time for a new weave. But I didn't have five hundred dollars. And as I said before, my male money pots were drying up faster than the Sahara after a sun shower.

I walked into my room and dug through some boxes in search of one of my wigs. Pulling out an all-time favorite, I moved back into the bathroom where the light was best and fit it on.

"Perfect!"

Once out of the bathroom, I stopped at Noah's bedroom door.

"Noah?" I called and knocked softly on the door. "Noah?" I jiggled the knob but the door was locked. "Noah!" I screamed and gave the door one good kick.

"What, bitch!"

"Oh, so you're awake."

"Now I am. What do you want?"

"Why is the door locked?" I asked and jiggled the knob again.

"'Cause I locked it. Now go away. I'm very tired."

"I'm on my way up to the city."

"So, go the fuck on already."

"Did you forget that you're supposed to be coming too?"

"What?"

"Crystal is having us all over for lunch today."

"Damn, that's today?"

"Did I stutter?"

"Look, don't be working my last nerve early in the morning, Miss Thang."

"Early? It's eleven o'clock."

"What? Oh, shit, I'll be there later. You go on ahead."

Once downstairs, I thought about coffee. But the coffee machine looked so complicated. I just stood there and stared at the sleek black plastic and pristine clean glass. I am so not domesticated. I thought that maybe I'll go back upstairs and have Noah do it for me. I would get cussed out, but in the end he would do it.

I looked at the clock. I could skip the coffee; in another hour it'd be time for lunch.

As I turned to move into the living room, I passed the wall phone, hesitated, and then decided yeah, I was going to go on ahead and call this Negro for the umpteenth time.

I'd called Mr. Abimbola exactly five times. The first three times I got his voice mail but opted not to leave a message. The fourth time I was able to snag him, and we had a delightful conversation—he spoke mostly about what he owned and what else he wanted to acquire before he turned fifty, but more important, what it was he would and could do for me if I'd just give him the chance!

He currently had a loft in Chelsea and a house in West Chester, Pennsylvania, and of course he had a spread in his hometown of Lagos, Nigeria, and an apartment in his home away from home, London.

He'd gone to school in Texas and earned a business degree from Texas State.

"And what kind of business are you in?" I'd asked. He'd just chuckled and said, "Well, let's just say I'm in the import and export business."

I didn't venture to ask what his product was, but I had a general idea that whatever it was he was importing and exporting, the government hadn't placed its stamp of approval on it.

I'd been holding off giving him my number, but seeing that my other prospects were steadily fading, I thought it was time to reel in someone new. And besides, Mr. Abimbola seemed to be meeting all of my criteria: rich, rich, and possibly stinking filthy rich!

I lifted the receiver and dialed.

You have reached Abimbola. I am unable to take this call. Please leave your name and number after the tone.

I began in my sexiest voice: "Abimbola, this is Chevy. I hope you're well. Would love to see you. You can call me at . . ."

I double-checked to make sure my Nokia was charged up, dropped it back down into my Coach bag, and stepped out the door and into the beautiful May morning.

Strolling up Stuyvesant Avenue toward Fulton Street, I took the time to really admire the majestic brownstone and limestone homes and thought about what a great investment Noah had made.

Ten years ago no one wanted to live in Bedford-Stuyvesant. Crack addicts, pimps, pushers, and prostitutes owned the corners on Fulton Street, as well as the park. The district school, Boys and Girls High, was one of the worst high schools in the city.

Back then brownstones here sold for a smile and a song, but now white people had taken an interest in the neighborhood, white people and the upper-crust blacks who had been priced out of Harlem.

They were all here now.

Noah purchased his brownstone for just $130,000. That was back in 1995. He'd spent another $80,000 renovating it, and now it was worth just under a million dollars.

Damn.

I remember when he started looking for a house. We were both living in Chelsea then. He was just a salesman for Barneys and I was working for the Carlton Hotel as a reservations agent. He had some money put away. Me, I had nothing, but I had good credit back then.

"We can do this together." He'd beamed when we sat down to pore over the real estate section of the *Daily News*.

I didn't mind going to the open houses with him. I enjoyed seeing how people live, but really and truly, I didn't have any interest in owning property. Didn't think it was important. Of course, now that I know better my credit is fucked up and I can't afford the prices.

I rounded the corner and descended the steps of the Utica Avenue train station.

In less than forty minutes, I was strolling down Broadway. It was just a little after noon and my stomach was growling. Even though I was hungry, I'd stopped to stare at the sexiest stilettos I'd seen in a long time.

The toe of the shoe was so pointy, I could stab someone with it. The heel was long and as slender as a cigarette, and the straps laced up to the knee!

I was in love!

But I didn't have any money for shoes. Not today. But they wouldn't be here next week. I knew they wouldn't, and this ain't the type of store that deals in layaway.

I walked away and then came back. My mouth was salivating. My heart was pumping blood to my brain so fast, I felt faint.

I pressed my forehead against the window and stared.

The saleswoman inside was laughing at me. Pointing me out to her coworkers.

I walked away and then I came back again.

Fuck it. I went in.

They were even more beautiful on my feet. Shit, I had to have these shoes. I needed these shoes. These shoes wanted to come home with me.

Okay, okay, let's see, I got $120 on me, I got about $60 left on my credit card . . . is it hot in here or is it me? *Concentrate!* Okay, that's cool. Oh, the tax. Shit!

Think, think.

MasterCard should allow me to go over my limit by a couple of dollars. Well, wait a minute now. Did I even pay them last month?

Fuck it. A try beats a give-up any day of the week.

"They look beautiful on you," the svelte woman with the dark hair, green eyes, and Italian accent said.

"Yes, they do, don't they," I agreed as I twisted my foot this way and that in the mirror to catch all angles.

"Would you like to wear them out, or should I wrap them up for you?"

"Wrap them up!"

I handed over all the cash in my wallet, the change at the bottom of my purse, a mint—oops, I took that back—and finally I slid my MasterCard across the counter.

The saleswoman picked up the card, studied it for a moment, and then looked up at me. We both took a deep breath, and I thought she was saying a Hail Mary in her head right along with me as she swiped the card through the machine.

Green numbers rolled across the screen and then the word CONNECTING.

The woman and I exchanged looks and I fought the urge to cross my fingers, eyes, and toes.

CONNECTING

CONNECTING

CONNECTING

I think I'm going to go mad.

PROCESSING

Okay, okay, here we go.

I had the bag in my hands. If the right response didn't come up, I could always make a break for it. There was a security guard at the door, but he was overweight and by the time I hit the corner he'd just be stepping over the threshold.

But then there was Miss Italiano. She looked like a jogger. Probably one of those marathon bitches. She might be able to catch me. But could she fight?

I sized her up.

PROCESSING

What's taking so damn long? And why is she looking at me like that? Why isn't the air conditioning on? It's like a hundred fucking degrees in here.

PROCESSING

Oh, God, please. Please let me have these shoes. If you let me have them, I'll—

APPROVED

"Yeah!" I squealed.

Seventeen

I was talking to my neighbor when Chevy came up behind me and placed her hands over my eyes.

"Guess who?" she said in her best child voice.

"Chevy," I said dryly.

The neighbor threw an amused look at Chevy, said goodbye, and moved away from us.

I turned around and my eyes fell on someone who barely resembled Chevy. I squinted and would have second-guessed myself, but then I saw the shopping bag in her hand. That was a dead giveaway. It was Chevy.

Today she wore a wet and wavy platinum blond wig that hung in long, synthetic Goldilocks tresses down her back. I could barely keep my mouth closed. The wig did nothing for her dark brown complexion, which was getting closer to mahogany with every sunny day. And if the hair wasn't ridiculous enough, the pink lipstick was a little too pink for her. Okay, a *lot* too pink.

Chevy was excellent at putting an outfit together, but some days she was really bad with cosmetics. Okay, most days.

"You look like a clown," I blurted out.

"Oh, so you're jealous as usual," she said and did a little spin for me. "Don't hate me."

"Did you hear me say you look like a clown?" I asked as she strolled off toward my apartment building.

"I thought we might walk over to Merchants and have some drinks," I said, halting her in her tracks.

"I thought we were hanging out at your house." Chevy swung around and batted her fake eyelashes at me.

I knew what that meant. It meant she didn't have a dime to her name. Chevy never gave up an opportunity to be out and to be seen.

"Yeah, that was the plan, but I changed my mind," I said coolly.

Chevy looked down at her watch. "Well, I can just stay for one drink," she said and her voice wavered a bit.

"You don't have any money, do you, Chevy?" I shook my head and eyed the bag she was carrying.

"Oh, this—I'm returning this." She chuckled and swung the bag behind her back. "It's just that my money is a little funny right now."

"No, your money is hilarious all of the time."

Once upstairs, I ordered up some Italian food and called the liquor store and had them send up three bottles of Moët.

When the food and champagne arrived, Chevy pulled the bottles from the bags, and her eyes lit up. "Oooh, Moët—white label, but still not bad. What are we celebrating?"

"Life," I chirped happily.

Normally I drank champagne only on special occasions, but more and more I was coming to realize that every day I opened my eyes was a special occasion.

"Okay," Chevy said, already working at getting one of the bottles uncorked.

What happened earlier in the day was still weighing heavily on my mind, and every time I walked past the wall Eric had hit I started to shake. To think that he had even considered hitting me really messed with my mind, and, try as I might, I couldn't shake the last vision I had of him, wild-eyed and crazed.

"Chevy, I've got to tell you something."

Chevy was reaching into the cabinet, retrieving two champagne glasses. "All right," she mumbled absentmindedly as she held the glasses up to the light to check for spots.

The thing about confiding in Chevy was that half the time she barely heard what it was you were saying, unless of course it directly affected her and had nothing to do with how much she owed you emotionally or financially.

So I guess she was a good person to get stuff off your chest with, if you didn't require any constructive input or a timely resolution to your problem.

I went ahead and shared with her what went down between Eric and me earlier that afternoon. I told her how it was wrenching at my insides and how I hoped this wasn't a preamble to violence against women.

Chevy must have been somewhat listening between the moments she alternated popping grapes into her mouth and sipping champagne, because one of her eyebrows climbed when I mentioned the "violence against women" part, which was followed by a long sucking sound, a typical Caribbean indication of disgust. Although Chevy didn't advertise her Caribbean background, she was a full-blooded Antiguan and had the papers to prove it.

Just as I finished my story, the buzzer sounded.

"That's probably Geneva," I said and pressed the button. "Yes."

The doorman's voice crackled back, "Ms. Atkins, Mr. Bodison is here for you."

"Thank you, send him up, please," I said and moved back into the kitchen to finish spooning the gnocchi into the bowl.

A few seconds later there was a soft knocking at the door and Chevy moved to answer it. She peered through the peephole. "Oh, it's my roomie."

"Your what?" I asked.

She swung the door open and in walked Noah, dressed in a powder blue linen shirt and faded blue jeans.

I blinked. "Roomie?" I said stupidly.

Noah walked over to me and gave me a big hug. It seemed like we hadn't seen each other in ages.

It was as if the two men I loved the most in my life were the ones I saw the least. I hugged him back as hard as I could and planted a big wet kiss on his face.

"I missed you!"

"Missed you too, baby," he said, giving me one last squeeze before breaking our embrace.

"You look good." I beamed.

"You look better," he said and gave me a sly once-over.

"Well, thank you," I said and reached for my glass of champagne. "Now what's all this roomie stuff?"

"Oh, you didn't know?" Noah's eyes popped with surprise as he stepped around me to examine the eats.

"You two are living together now?" I managed to choke out as I swallowed.

"Yep," Chevy said and took a seat at the table.

"Against my will, of course. You know I would never allow Ms. Drama to move into my space."

"Since when?" I asked, turning to Noah.

"Well, let's see, she's been there since I was in London. That was two weeks ago—I came back today, so I guess she's been squatting for about fifteen days."

I turned back to Chevy. "You got evicted again?"

"You know that place was much too small for me. And anyway, my lease was up."

"You got evicted again," Noah and I said blandly.

"Whatever," Chevy breathed, waving her hand at us.

The intercom blared again.

"Yeah?" Chevy pressed the button and asked.

"It's me." Geneva's voice came back.

"Who, the doorman?" Chevy covered her mouth and snickered.

"Stop acting like a child," I warned.

"I don't know where he's at. It's Geneva—let me up."

"I'm sorry, I didn't catch that. Who?"

"Stop it!" I screamed and slammed the spoon down onto the counter.

"C'mon, Chevy, let her up," Noah coaxed and reached for more gnocchi.

"They'll be all gone before anyone else can have some," I teased and slapped his hand away.

"It's GE-NEE-VA!"

"She down there looking all stupid, I know she is." Chevy bent over and laughed.

"Grow up," Noah ordered and moved to the intercom, pressing the in button.

A few minutes later Geneva knocked at the door.

"Hey, lady." Noah greeted Geneva with a hug and a kiss.

"Hey yourself," she said and stood back to get a good look at him. "You look different."

"Do I?"

"Yeah." Geneva walked past him and into the kitchen. "Hey, ladies."

"Hey, girl," I said and blew her a kiss.

Chevy scrutinized Geneva for a moment and then said, "What the hell is wrong with your hair?"

"Well, hello to you too," Geneva said sarcastically and then subconsciously ran her hand over her normal pulled-back do. "Ain't nothing wrong with my hair. What the hell is wrong with *your* hair?"

"I told her she looked like a clown," I piped up.

Geneva laughed and Chevy flipped us the bird with both hands.

"Don't Noah look different?" Geneva posed the question to me.

"Hmm—yeah, a little. Now that you mention it."

"Must be all that protein he's ingesting!" Chevy shouted and slapped the table a few times.

"Ms. Drama, please don't get me started up in here. I was going to try and behave myself today, but you're gonna make me get on you about that hair and that lipstick," Noah sang in a falsetto.

"Are you in love or something?" Geneva pushed.

"You mean with someone besides himself?" Chevy laughed.

Noah gave her a hard look. "Now you confusing me with you," he retorted. He let off two snaps in her face and strutted back toward the bowl of gnocchi. "Must be all that chronic she's smoking."

Geneva and I both turned to Chevy and said, "Pot?"

"No, the album," Chevy mocked us. "And anyway, I got it out of Noah's stash."

Now we looked expectantly at Noah, who turned casually toward her and convincingly said, "You're a liar."

Chevy's jaw dropped. She knew that no matter what she said, we would take Noah's word over hers any day.

"So what if I smoke a little pot here and there?"

"In the middle of the day?" Geneva shook her head pitifully.

"Sound like a problem," I added for effect.

"Rehab may be the next step," Noah threw in, trying hard to keep a straight face.

"Whatever." Chevy snorted and jumped up from the table.

"What you getting ready to do, whoop my ass?" Noah threw at her with a laugh.

Chevy cocked her head in thought. "I probably could if I wanted to," she said and put up her fists like a boxer.

We all burst out laughing.

"Oh, you're all so funny, aren't you?" Chevy jeered, snatching up the bottle of champagne and refilling her glass.

"Oooh, poor baby—you can dish it out but you can't take it, huh?" I teased and lifted my own glass of champagne.

"Well, maybe not," she said slyly as she ran her finger along the rim of her glass. "But I would expect to be knocked down by a man if I laid my hands on him. You know all about that, don't you, Crystal?"

"What?" I laughed, totally missing the point.

"Did you tell Geneva that you slapped the shit out of Eric today?"

"Eric who?" Geneva said, and now all eyes were on me.

Shit. The one time this bitch decided to listen.

Eighteen

Well, I hate to be made fun of. Everybody all up in my business, coming down on me like I was a little kid. Shoot, I'm a grown-ass woman!

Anyway, it got worse before it got better.

"*My* Eric?" Geneva said, pressing her palm into her chest. "My *son*, Eric?" she said, unbelieving.

Crystal just stood there with her mouth open and her face as red as a beet.

"What'd you do, Miss Girl?" Noah asked Crystal, his eyelids flapping anxiously.

"I—I" was all Crystal could manage.

"Yes, *your* Eric," I said, feeling nothing but mean.

"Shut up, Chevy," Noah tossed at me.

"Well," Geneva said and took a step toward Crystal. She was seething, and I could see Crystal's eyes looking around for something to protect herself with. I guess Noah saw it too, because he moved between them and placed his hands on Geneva's shoulders.

"Calm down, Mama Bear," he cooed and tried to push her a few paces backward. But that Geneva is a big ole girl, and Noah is a petite thing. His little nudge didn't even budge her.

Geneva shrugged his hands off her shoulders. "What did you do to Eric?" she barked.

Crystal still hadn't found her tongue, so I helped her out. "She smacked the taste out of his mouth, that's what she did!"

"Chevy!" Crystal and Noah screamed at me in disbelief.

"But she did!" I whined.

With one shove Geneva sent Noah flying into the table, and in no time she was up in Crystal's face, huffing and puffing and turning all sorts of red. "Is that true, Crystal? You slapped my son?"

Crystal did something with her mouth but she didn't cower; in fact, she seemed to stand a bit taller.

"Yes, I did, Geneva," she said with an even voice. "He was disrespecting you and I wasn't having it. I know you didn't raise him that way, and so I did what I knew you'd do and I slapped the shit out of him."

Oh, God, she was using the "it takes a village" bullshit.

Well, all Noah and I could do was brace ourselves for the slap that Geneva would lay across Crystal's face, taking her head clean off her neck, but it didn't happen.

Geneva, who had just a second ago been all puffed up like a fighting cock, was suddenly slowly deflating. The anger in her eyes was evaporating and her face softened.

"Why didn't you tell me?" she said.

"I had every intention to, but Chevy beat me to it," Crystal said, and now the spotlight was back on me again.

I just can't seem to win.

summer

Nineteen

Kendrick sat very still. He was afraid to move, afraid he would start shaking his leg again or tapping his pencil against the glass-top conference table he was seated at.

He hadn't noticed when he was doing all of those things, but everybody else attending the meeting had, and he looked up to find a dozen pairs of eyes staring intently at him.

"Too much caffeine, Kenny?" his father, Aldridge Greene, admonished.

"No, sir, please continue," Kendrick answered swiftly.

Aldridge Greene sat at the far end of the table, directly across from his son. Their eyes met briefly before Aldridge began again to discuss his plans for the next quarter.

"As I was saying," Aldridge continued, "our progress in the South African market is going quite well. Mbeki has proven to be open and willing to allow foreign investment to continue growing under his presidency, and he is being especially kind to Americans."

"Even after all they didn't do for South Africa," Marcia Banks, a senior auditor, mumbled under her breath. The table broke out in uncomfortable laughter at her observation. It was true: the United States had stood by for years, allowing apartheid to ravage the country and the spirits of the black people that lived under that storm. And when things got bad, Uncle Sam cried sanctions. What the hell did sanctions mean to the Afrikaners? Absolutely nothing. Their country was just as economically and environmentally diverse as the United States. They had an underground oil supply that could last for nearly twenty years. The sanctions hurt the United States, hurt the companies that wanted to do business there, and took further advantage of the country's rich resources.

Big business said, *The hell with this! Uncle Sam, you have to do better than sanctions. You've got to put the real pressure on—we're losing money!* So said, so done.

And in the end, who wins? Uncle Sam. So what else is new?

Aldridge, like every other corporate giant, wanted to jump in, make money, and jump out before Mandela passed on or stepped down. They all felt the next president wasn't going to be so kind to Uncle Sam and Mother England. The scars would still be too fresh and the heart too young to forgive and forget. But lo and behold, the second president had been just as cooperative.

"Yes, well, we all know about that," Aldridge put in, "but that's in the past, and we are in the midst of a new beginning. And we all know how much we like new beginnings."

Everyone nodded in agreement.

"So if there's nothing else?" Aldridge looked at all the

faces around the table. "Well, then, have a prosperous day," he said as he pushed himself up from the table.

That's what he always said. "Have a prosperous day"—he didn't care whether an individual in his company had a good or bad day. He just wanted it to be prosperous, and when he said "prosperous" he wasn't referring to the individuals' well-being; he was referring to Greene Investments' corporate and personal bank accounts.

Aldridge Greene's towering figure rose over the black glass table and his reflection wavered there beneath Kendrick's gaze.

"Kendrick, a moment, please," Aldridge said as his son turned to walk out of the boardroom.

Kendrick felt four years old again, sitting across from his father. Where was the cool sophisticated man whom the women loved? Where was the man whom others in the company described as a rainmaker? Where was the man who only last month graced the cover of *Fortune*? He certainly wasn't in that room.

"Kendrick, were we boring you in there today?" Aldridge asked in a cool voice.

"No, sir."

"Well, you seemed very distracted. And I've noticed this not only today but a number of times over the past few weeks." Aldridge lit up a Cuban and inhaled deeply. "Is there something bothering you, something I should know about?"

"I guess I'm just a little tired," Kendrick said as he studied the tops of his Italian leather shoes. He was immediately sorry for his answer.

"Tired? Tired of making money? Tired of being one of the most respected men in Barbados? Next to me, of course. Tell me, son, which exactly are you tired of?"

"I'm tired of you . . . I'm tired of your stoic bullshit. I'm tired of doing all the work and you getting all the praise. I'm tired of being on call, being bound to the end of your leash!"

That's what Kendrick wanted to say, but he knew he wouldn't.

"Dad, I guess I'm just a little physically tired, that's all."

"*Physically* tired?" Aldridge spoke into the lit end of his cigar. "My boy is physically tired. Could it be the bar and club hopping? You cannot stay out all night and then try to run a company during the day. You're forty-two years old and the vice president of a multimillion-dollar company. For chrissakes, start acting like it."

The spies. Oh, Aldridge had people everywhere, watching all of his children, watching to see that they stayed on the straight and narrow. He intended to make sure they avoided anything or anybody who could rupture the reputation he and his father before him had worked so hard to construct.

Kendrick just nodded his head and stood to leave.

"Did you ask to be excused?" Aldridge barked, his eyes narrowing.

"Sir, may I be excused?" Kendrick said, looking his father directly in the eye.

Aldridge leaned back into his leather wing chair so far that Kendrick thought he would tilt backward and out through the glass window that made up one side of the room. Or at least he wished he would.

Aldridge grinned, victorious, and then sent Kendrick off with a flick of his hand.

Kendrick walked slowly from his father's office and down the white-walled hall to his own grand office. Kayla, his secretary, was watering the large ficus that stood in the far left corner below a picture of Aldridge.

"Good morning, Mr. Greene," she said sweetly. Kayla had been with Kendrick for three years now. Kendrick liked her; she was dependable and extremely proficient. Only twenty-four, she was worlds above her peers and carried herself as if she were ten years older.

Kendrick greeted her and sat down heavily behind his desk. He stared blankly at the picture of his son on his desk, and then his eyes wandered to Kayla's taut behind wrapped in a pink silk skirt. She felt him staring and bent over a bit more just so he would know she cared.

Kendrick knew Kayla would do more than type and take steno for him; he'd often fantasized about her, but he knew he would never allow it to go any further than a simple daydream. Being intimate with an employee could cost the company millions. He was better off finding a Kayla look-alike from one of the high-end escort services they used when their *special* clients came to town.

Aldridge, on the other hand, had dipped quite a few times into the company pussy jar. Nothing had come of any of his escapades, but Kendrick knew that at some point everyone's luck ran out.

When Kayla left, Kendrick picked up his phone.

"Cassius and Lee. How may I direct your call?" the perky voice answered.

"Cassius, please," Kendrick said in a hushed tone.

"Who may I say is calling, sir?"

"Kendrick."

"Kendrick? Is there a last name, sir?"

Kendrick exhaled heavily. He'd told Cassius to tell that dumb bitch receptionist to have him patched through immediately—minus the damn questions.

"Just Kendrick," he said between clenched teeth.

"Yes, sir . . . one moment, please." There was music and then a clicking sound.

"Cassius here."

"Yeah, Cassius . . . Kendrick here. I—"

"Kendrick Greene. How are—"

"Could we please leave last names out, Cassius?" Kendrick was speaking practically in a whisper.

"You have become extremely paranoid, you know that? We are bug-free here . . . you understand what I'm saying? Now, your lines are a whole different story."

"Can never be too careful," Kendrick said with a nervous laugh. "I need to make a purchase."

There was silence.

"Kendrick, I'm looking at my file here and it seems as though a delivery was made to your office not more than three days ago. Have you depleted your supply already?"

Kendrick bit his lip nervously.

"Whose money am I spending?" Kendrick asked.

"Is it yours? I thought Aldridge was still breathing."

Cassius let out a wicked laugh like only she could. It was a laugh that pierced and humiliated.

Kendrick banged his hand down on the desk, sending his son's picture as well as the Berlin Wall stone paperweight flying off and onto the floor.

"Don't fuck with me, Cassius. I can take my business elsewhere, you know. Let me remind you that you are not the only supplier in town."

"Threats?" Cassius squealed and continued laughing.

Kendrick hated her. He wondered if she treated all of her clients this way.

"Okay, Ken. When and how much?" Cassius was serious again and maintaining a business tone.

"Um, two grand now."

"You got it. Cash, credit, or shall we bill you later?" Cassius asked.

"Cash." Kendrick said and slammed the phone down. He was beginning to feel better already.

An hour and a half later Kayla's voice came through the intercom: "Mr. Greene, a woman named Cassius is here to see you."

"Who?" Kendrick asked. He couldn't believe that Cassius herself had come.

"Cassius?" Kayla repeated slowly. "She said she doesn't have a last name."

"Uh, send her in," Kendrick said.

He stood up and then sat down. He wanted to be in a comfortable position. He wanted to look like a man in control. He crossed his legs and then uncrossed them again. Finally, he just picked up his Waterford pen and tried to look engrossed in the paperwork spread out before him.

Cassius entered the room like the wind. Her signature scent, Poison, filled the room and commanded as much attention as Cassius herself.

"Kendrick." She moved swiftly toward him and extended her hand. Kendrick stood and extended his own hand.

Cassius was beautiful, a knockout, towering six feet tall with sandy brown hair brushed back in a sharp upturned flip that rested on the base of her neck. She wore an orange linen skirt suit that hugged her perfect figure-eight shape.

Cassius was biracial. Her father was a white man and her mother Ethiopian. She was born and raised in Nigeria and then sent to school in London from the age of twelve. Her fair complexion, sexy British accent, and ever-present air of confidence were what drew people to her.

Kendrick took her hand in his and nearly wounded himself on the two-carat diamond on her ring finger. She pulled him toward her, leaned over the desk, and ran her tongue across his lips. "I know how much you like to be licked," she said breathlessly.

Kendrick smiled nervously and all but snatched his hand from hers before stumbling backward and into his chair.

He hated what she did to him. He hated that he wanted her almost as much as he wanted what was in the black attaché case she carried.

The first time Cassius and Kendrick met was at a Lower East Side restaurant. He had been entertaining clients there but found himself unable to take his eyes off the stunning woman who watched him from the bar.

When he was done with dinner and had sent the clients on their way, he doubled back to the restaurant, took a seat next to her, and struck up a conversation.

He was flattered to know that she knew right off who he was. She commented on the articles she'd read and "kept" about him. "I'm a big admirer," she'd said, leaning in and breathing into his cheek. "And I would do anything to be with you. Rich, successful black men turn me on."

Kendrick was stunned and infatuated by her frank, no-nonsense approach.

"I have a suite at the Morgan. My room number is 204—you're more than welcome to spend the night with me," she said as she collected her purse to go.

"Is this a joke?" he'd asked, amused.

"Am I laughing?" Cassius said.

Kendrick, still believing this was all too good to be true, accompanied the woman to her hotel room and had a drink, a hit of Hades (which he had already been casually acquainted with), and the best sex he'd ever had in his life.

Afterward, Cassius slipped him a vial and told him that whenever he needed to make a purchase he should call her.

"Can I call for sex too?" he'd kidded.

"Maybe."

Kendrick didn't think that he would be calling Cassius

for anything but sex. He wasn't a junkie. But three days later, feeling down and out, he plucked her business card from his wallet and made the call.

It quickly became a habit, the drug and Cassius, but as time passed he craved only the Hades. Cassius was just an afterthought and then not a thought at all, because during moments of clarity, Kendrick believed it was Cassius who'd turned him into the addict that he'd become, and he hated her for it.

"So business must be bad," Kendrick said as he watched Cassius take her seat and cross her long legs. Her short skirt rose three more inches when she did, revealing a curvaceous thigh.

"Why would you say that, Kendrick?" Cassius asked, looking genuinely surprised.

"Well, you don't usually make deliveries. What's the matter, did you have to lay off the delivery man?" Kendrick teased.

"Oh, no . . . he is still with us. But you are such a special client that I thought, What the hell? And besides, it's called excellent customer service." She laughed a deep, throaty laugh that both excited and disgusted Kendrick.

"Yes, well, that's very nice of you. I'm sure you're very busy, so if you would just give me what I ordered, we can both get back to work."

"You are quite the rude little boy, aren't you?" Cassius's eyes slanted and she slowly turned her head and looked at the door before turning back to him and whispering, "Does that door lock?" A mischievous grin covered her face.

"Of course it locks," he heard himself say.

"So, we can maybe . . ." Cassius nodded toward the large brown leather sofa.

Kendrick shook his head no, but Cassius had already stood up and started to remove her jacket.

Kendrick watched, his objections stuck in the back of his throat, as Cassius tossed her jacket aside and then removed her blouse and then the cream-colored lace demi-cup bra. That she dropped into his lap.

Her breasts were large and firm, melonlike and just as sweet. He knew that for sure and licked his lips at the memory of it. Her nipples jutted out at him, beckoning to be sucked.

By the time Kendrick was able to will himself to stand, Cassius was wearing nothing but her six-inch Jimmy Choos.

His reasoning slowly coming back to him, he shot a look at the unlocked door and quickly crossed the room to it.

"Put your clothes back on, Cassius," he demanded in a hushed voice.

"No," she said simply as she strutted to the leather sofa on the opposite end of the room and stretched herself across it.

Kendrick eyed her, growing more excited by the moment.

Cassius threw one long leg over the back of the couch, while extending the other across the carpeted floor.

He could see everything—her vaginal lips, her bell. The soft pink flesh insides of her cunt were moist and reminded him of the polished conch shells that dotted the shores of the Bimini Islands.

He licked his lips.

Kendrick's eyes went from Cassius to the attaché case and then back to Cassius.

"C'mon, Kenny baby, you know you want it," she purred as she slid her ring finger up inside herself. A gasp escaped Kendrick when the two-carat diamond ring she was wearing on that same finger disappeared into the polished pink folds of her pussy.

He wanted it, all right—the "it" not necessarily Cassius's cunt—but if he had to fuck her to get what he *really* wanted, then he would. At least I'm not no crackhead, sucking dick for a hit of rock, he told himself.

Kendrick turned the lock on the door, went to his desk, picked up the phone, and said, "Kayla, hold all my calls, and please don't disturb me for anything." He hung up and began to undress.

Twenty

I love men. I love men. I love men. I love men.

That was my new warrior chant against pussy.

I called the cable company and told them that I wanted them to block all the music video channels.

"May I ask the reason, Mr. Bodison?"

"Yeah, 'cause they making me straight!" I screamed into the phone like a lunatic.

I realized that it's not only that damn Beyoncé Knowles: that li'l Jessica Simpson is kinda sexy too. If you like white girls. And I don't. I don't even like girls! Or do I? I don't know, I don't know!

Lord, why are you doing this to me?

I looked back into the mirror and began my warrior chant again:

I love men, I love men, I love men, I love men.

I hadn't been out of the house since the last Saturday night when I went to Langston, a gay nightclub on Atlantic Avenue. I was having a good time. Ran into some friends of mine. We were all drinking, dancing, and just acting the fool. I was feeling so *gay*! I mean the happy kind as well as the homo kind.

Right there on the dance floor, dancing between all the

hardbodies to Sylvester's "You Make Me Feel (Mighty Real)," I felt like the old Noah had finally come back. And then I saw this brother watching me from the other side of the dance floor. He was doing more than watching me: he was salivating, and by the time the DJ started spinning "Love Is the Message," so was I.

He had a body to die for. Muscled arms covered in tattoos. Oh, man, a barrel chest and a neck as big as a trunk. I just wanted to throw myself into his arms!

When I saw him nodding at me, I gave him my sexiest come-hither look. And honey chile, did he come. Just a-strutting!

When he finally made it through the crowd of people, he took my hand and pulled me to him.

Right then and there the DJ announced lovers' hour an hour early. Go figure!

"Fire and Desire" came on and he pressed his body against mine. We clung to each other for that entire song, and the two that came on after that. His dick was as hard as a rock; I still have the bruise on my stomach.

He told me his name was Rick and asked if he could have my telephone number. I said I was kind of involved but wouldn't mind taking his.

Rick walked me to the door and gave me a kiss so passionate, I wanted to throw him down right there and then and do him!

But thoughts of my lover, Zhan, kept me from doing that. And besides, I ain't no ho—don't get it twisted—but I am human, and a little innocent slow grinding on the dance floor does not a cheater make.

So you wags out there, put your tongues right back in your mouth. I tossed that number in the very first trash receptacle I came across.

It was such a beautiful evening, I decided to walk home. I love strolling down the residential streets, admiring the brownstone homes, inside and out. White people are the strangest creatures; they keep the windows of their parlor-floor homes free of window treatments, allowing the world outside to see in. Delicious—I've gotten many decorating ideas by just strolling the neighborhoods.

I'd picked up two new ideas for bookshelves and was seriously considering cutting a hole in my living room ceiling and installing a spiral wrought-iron staircase when it hit me. I had to pee. I mean, really, really badly. You can't be taking any chances pulling your dick out and stealing a piss behind a tree or beside a dumpster anymore. Those good old days are gone. These white cops are looking to bust a black man for anything. And shoot, I'm liable to get shot right away if they catch me holding my dick.

So rather than take a chance, I hurried down the street to Brown Sugar, one of the neighborhood watering holes.

When I stepped through the door, I was immediately hit with a sultry singing voice. I turned to see a short, brown-skinned, buxom woman with a mane of fiery orange hair.

Her octave skills were so impressive that I temporarily forgot my pressing emergency.

Our eyes collided as I moved through the crowd and toward the bathroom. Halfway there, a large meaty hand fell on my shoulder. I turned around and looked up and into the ugliest face I'd ever seen in my life. "My God, you are an ugly motherfucker!"

"What did you say?" the seven-foot-six, three-hundred-pound bouncer asked.

I couldn't believe I'd said it out loud. Sometimes ugliness startles you into verbalizing your thoughts.

I had to think fast and stood on my tippy toes, cupped my hands around my mouth, and yelled into the cauliflower-shaped ear he tilted down at me. "I said my God, it's hot in here!"

"Yeah it is," he said, and his eyes rolled hungrily over me.

Oh my God, he was one of my peoples!

I tell you, we come in all shapes, sizes, and *ugly* nowadays.

"Um, look, little man," he began, his hand still on my shoulder. "The bathroom is for customers only."

My bladder was screaming.

"Of course I'm going to have a beer, but I need to drain the snake," I said.

"Drain the snake"? Where the hell did that come from? Wasn't that a straight expression? Didn't Guido white boys say shit like that?

It was worse than I thought.

"All right, man," Ugly said. "I'll be watching you."

And I knew he meant it.

Now at the bar. My bladder was empty, but my eyes were struggling to stay open. I was exhausted and knew if I had another drop of alcohol I'd fall asleep standing on my feet, so I ordered a club soda with lime.

As I stood sipping, I perused the restaurant. Brown Sugar was packed wall to wall with patrons. To my surprise there were even a few white faces floating among the varied brown hues. And they seemed to know every word to each soulful song the singer belted out.

I found myself singing along too, and once again my eyes found hers and I swear she winked at me. I hurriedly gave her my back and mentally ran my chant through my mind: I love men. I love men. I love men.

I was still mentally chanting when the band announced that they would be taking a fifteen-minute break. Immediately the room was filled with the sound of quick conversation and laughter.

"Hello." A sweet voice came from behind me.

I slowly turned around and came face-to-face with the songstress.

"H-hey."

She squeezed in beside me, expressed her gratitude to some people who approached her with compliments, and then turned back toward me.

She fluffed her hair and her massive bosom jiggled beneath the close-fitting hot pink and red silk dress she wore.

I felt the heat start to build beneath my collar.

"Never seen you here before."

Her voice was deep and husky and seemed to have fingers, because her words stroked my cheek.

I shuddered.

"Um, I come in every now and again," I said, looking

everywhere except at her. My eyes moved to the door and Ugly was standing there, giving me fish lips.

"Really?"

"Uh-huh."

"Well, I'm glad you're here tonight," she breathed and placed her warm hand on my wrist.

Johnson stirred.

"What's your name, honey?" she asked, stroking my hand.

I eased my hand from beneath her touch and finally turned to face her. "Noah," I said, presenting my other hand.

"Candy," she said as she looked deep into my eyes and took both of my hands in hers. They were warm and soft and I immediately wondered if it would feel the same between her thighs.

Damn.

"Um, is that your real name?" I said, clearing my throat and taking back my hands.

"Yes it is, honey. Do you mind if I call you honey, Noah?" Her plump red glossy lips turned up into a devious grin.

Me, I just shrugged my shoulders.

I turned away from her. Johnson was fully awake now, banging on my briefs, begging me to unzip my pants so he could get a look!

"Stop it," I bent my head and whispered.

"Stop what?" Candy said, her face puzzled and amused at the same time. Then she lowered her gaze. "What's going on down there?"

My dick bucked, and I discreetly stuck my hand down into my pocket and tried to adjust it back into an unnoticeable position.

I just grinned like a naughty five-year-old.

Candy sipped from her wineglass for a while, shared a few words with some people, and then turned her attention back to me. I drained my club soda and was eager to be out, but Ugly was still standing at the door, eyeing me, and I looked around for an emergency exit I might be able to escape through.

"Honey, can I get you another drink?" Candy was so close to me now that I could feel the heat rising off her body. I sniffed and my nose was filled with a slightly musky scent. I knew that odor well; she was already creaming her panties, if she even had any on.

Ahhhhhhhhhhhhhh! Let me out now! Johnson was twitching this way and that, determined to bust out. I had to get away from her, and fast.

"No, thank you," I said, turning to leave, but Candy caught me by the elbow.

"Do you have to go so soon?" she whispered into the back of my neck. All of the hair there stood at attention. "Please," she uttered, pulling me backward and spinning me around to face her.

"But—" I started to say.

"You can't go. You have to stay for my next set. I'm going to sing a song just for you." She leaned in close and brushed her button nose against mine. Our lips brushed and she didn't even seem upset when Johnson poked her in a happy place.

"Hmm." She looked down and moaned.

I love men. I love men. I love men.

"Stay right here," she said and started back toward the stage.

I looked down at my erection.

You know, you're going to have to fuck her, Johnson said.

I know. I know.

I love men. I love men. I love . . .

I hadn't left the house since that night.

I'd barely left my bedroom. I called in sick and told my boss that I had a summer flu. I figured, I was going to lick this sickness. So I played gay porn videos all day and night.

"What are you doing in there?" Chevy yelled through the door.

"Leave me alone. I'm sick. Go to work."

"What's wrong with you?"

"Go away!"

"Noah!"

"Leave your rent money on the kitchen table," I said, pulling out the heavy artillery.

I heard Chevy tiptoe away, which is exactly what I knew she'd do.

Twenty-One

"Can I see you in my office, Chevy?" Ms. Fitch, or Ms. Bitch as I like to call her, said as she walked past my desk.

I'd just walked through the door. Okay, yeah, I was a little late. But shit, it was Friday, and so what? Do they realize how much money I generate for them?

"Okay, let me just—"

"Now," she said as she twitched her narrow, stuck-up behind into her office.

I followed.

"Close the door," she said as she peered at me over her wire-rimmed glasses.

She was, what, twenty-six years old? I had her by a good nine years and I had more experience in this business in my pinky finger than she did in her entire lily white body.

I mean, what the fuck, just because she graduated from Johnson and Wales, that made her an instant expert in this business? Not!

How much time did she do in the trenches before they promoted her? Six months, maybe?

Now she was my boss. I tell you, white people are magical!

"Yes?" I said as I sat down, folded my hands, and gave her my best uninterested look.

She blinked her green eyes at me, tugged at the hem of her pin-striped suit jacket, leaned back into her leather chair, and considered me for a moment.

"Yes?" I said again, using my annoyed tone and rolling my eyes for effect.

Ms. Bitch picked up some papers and looked over the black numbers that filled the columns. "It says here, Chevy, that you were 'away' more than twelve hours this week."

"What?" I'd been late a few times that week, but nothing that would add up to twelve hours. Okay, I took an extra half an hour on Thursday to get a manicure and pedicure, but that was it. What was this bitch talking about?

"Your telephone," she said and tapped the paper with her index finger. "All of the phones are computerized. I can see how many calls you take, how long it takes you to service your client, how many calls you make, and how long you put your phone on 'away' during business hours." Her eyes bored into me and her face did something. I leaned in a bit closer. Was she sneering at me?

She never liked me. I was a better dresser than she was. Plus, I was better-looking.

"Well, Ms. Fitch," I said brightly, "as you know, a great majority of my job involves paperwork. And so for me to do it accurately and to Thomas Cook Travel Group specifications, I need to be able to focus my attention on the job at hand, and so, yes, I put my phone on 'away' so that I can do what needs be to done as efficiently as possible."

"Aha," Miss Fitch said and then chuckled a bit. "Well, Chevy, your coworkers have the same responsibilities you do. And none of them needs twelve or more hours a week to look over a PNR, pop it into an envelope, and drop it in the mail basket. So why do you?"

She had me there.

I just shrugged my shoulders.

"On top of that, your lateness has become a real problem."

I yawned.

"If this behavior continues, I'll be forced to write you up, and you already have two warnings in your file. One more and you're gone," she said, a little too happily.

Gone?

I sat straight up. I needed this job, no matter how crappy it was.

"I'll do my best," I said as humbly as I could.

"I hope so, Chevy. All of these things aside, you're a damn good travel agent."

"Thank you." I grinned and then asked, "Is that all?"

"Yes, Chevy," she said without looking at me as she reached for her phone and began dialing a number.

"Have a good day, Ms. Bitch," I muttered under my breath.

"Thank you, Chevy. You too."

Twenty-Two

I'll transfer you," I said into my headset and looked up at the clock that sat directly on the wall in front of me.

It was ten minutes to five and it seemed to me that it had been ten to five for the past half hour.

Little Eric had left for basketball camp that morning. I had to admit, I was already missing him and not at all looking forward to going home to a lonely apartment.

I picked up my pen and began making little hearts across my yellow notepad. I looked at the clock again and it was still ten minutes to five. "Jesus Christ," I griped under my breath as I began drawing link chains between the hearts.

The switchboard began to blink.

"Ain't I A Woman Foundation, how may I help you?"

"Geneva?"

"Yes," I said, not immediately recognizing the voice.

"I looked for you all day last Saturday."

"Nadine?" I uttered in shock. "How did you get my work number?"

"I got it off your application."

"I thought those were confidential," I hissed into my

headset, already feeling the heat of my anger climbing up the back of my neck.

"Well, I have friends in high places," Nadine said with a snicker.

"Look, Nadine," I began. This was the last straw; I was getting ready to tell that bitch where to get off when Ash came slinking up.

"I hope that's not a personal call, Ms. Holliday?"

I just blinked at him and shook my head no. "No, I'm sorry, we already have a long distance carrier," I said quickly into the mouthpiece of my headset and then pressed the release button on the switchboard.

Ashton scrutinized me as he absent-mindedly picked at a ripe red boil on his cheek.

I smirked at him and then bent down to remove my worn pumps from my feet. I opened the bottom drawer of my desk and reached in and pulled out my old, dirty Reeboks.

I really needed a new pair of sneakers, but as long as they weren't to the point where I had to use cardboard at the bottoms, then they would have to do.

"Excuse me." The words came like tiny pinpricks to my scalp.

I slowly raised my head and came face-to-face with Ashton once again. Hadn't he left? The little sneak.

"Ms. Holliday, I believe your hours are from nine to five," he advised sourly.

"Yes, you're correct," I said, trying to keep my tone even.

"So being that your hours are from nine to five, I expect that your job would be your focal point during those hours."

"Yes, yes it is," I repeated like a parrot.

"If that is the case, why are you putting on tennis shoes at ten minutes to five? Is that part of your job description, Ms. Holliday?"

I looked at the clock, and sure enough it was still ten minutes to five. I felt like I was in the Twilight Zone.

"No, it's not in my job description, and yes, my job does end at five," I said in a defeated voice.

"Are you sure about that? Because if you're not, I can always pull your job description from the file so we both can know where we stand."

"No need for that, Ashton."

Ten, nine, eight, seven . . .

Ashton looked me over once more, wriggled his nose like I hadn't washed my ass that morning, and then slinked away.

I really don't know how much more of him I can stand.

I didn't want to mention to Crystal that Ashton was harassing me. It would seem as if I was whining and worse yet, that I couldn't handle myself with a corporate asshole.

So I just kept on with my calming countdown.

Six, five, four . . .

The switchboard light began blinking again. I looked up at the clock. Three minutes to five. Thank God!

"Good evening, Ain't I A Woman Foundation, how may I direct your call?"

"Hey, girl," Crystal's voice rang out.

"Hey," I answered coolly as I leaned over to see if Ashton was lurking somewhere down the hall.

"You up for a drink?" Crystal asked.

"Well, I don't know," I hedged.

It had been a few days since I'd last spent time with her. She'd been in Texas all of last week for a conference, and we'd been playing phone tag for the last few days.

I have to admit that I was still feeling a little sore about what she'd done to Eric. I mean, he was still my son. My child. My baby.

"Aw, c'mon. It's Friday," she wailed like a five-year-old.

"Where's Kendrick?" I said in an icy tone.

She was quiet for a while.

"He's around. But what does that have to do with us?" Crystal sounded wounded.

I felt bad. She didn't really deserve that. Inside I was still in turmoil about what had happened. On one hand, I felt like no matter what Little Eric had done or said, she should have kept her hands to herself. I handle the discipline. But on the other hand, I knew that Crystal had been like a second mother to him. When I was pregnant she'd accompanied me to most of my doctor appointments, and she was the one, not Big Eric, who went to Lamaze classes with me. Not that those classes helped either one of us when it came down to the delivery; we were both screaming and hollering like we didn't have good sense!

And somewhere in my junk drawer there was a letter that I'd signed when Eric was a baby, explaining that I wanted Crystal to have custody of him should something ever happen to me.

So why was this whole thing picking at me so badly?

Crystal hadn't given me the entire story. She said she thought it would be better if Eric told me what had happened, but when I'd pressed him for information he'd just said, "Let it rest, Mom, okay?"

"Well, just one drink. I'm tired," I said, finally caving in.

"Good. Meet you out front in about five minutes."

I shut the switchboard down and changed back into my shoes. Going out drinking with Crystal wasn't something you did in run-down Reeboks. I powdered my face and applied a bit more of the copper-colored lipstick to my lips before snapping off my desk lamp and heading toward the bank of elevators across the floor.

I checked my appearance in the mirrored walls of the elevator before stepping out and into the main lobby.

My thoughts on what it was I would do with myself over the next few weeks while my son was gone, I almost walked into a woman who was standing in the middle of the hallway, digging frantically inside her purse.

"Oh, excuse me," I mumbled and started to walk around her.

"You got an attitude about something?"

I spun around. "Chevy?" I said in disbelief.

"*Chevy?*" Chevy said, mocking my surprise. "Yes, it's me, fool! What's wrong with you?"

"What the hell did you do to your hair . . . your eyebrows?"

Chevy was really spinning out of control. The blond was bad, but this fire engine pinkish red was completely out of order!

"They let you go to work like that?"

"They let *you* come to work like *that*?" Chevy retorted, referring to my wool houndstooth suit. "It is summertime, ain't it?"

She eyed me and then said, "Girl, invest in some clothes, some shoes, and a hairdo other than a damn ponytail."

"Don't start with me, okay?"

"Let's play nice, children." Crystal approached from the bank of elevators across the hall. She gave Chevy a quick once-over and then shook her head in dismay.

She always handled Chevy's eccentricities better than I did.

"You look very nice, Geneva," Crystal said to me, seeing the hurt misting in my eyes. Then she turned to Chevy. "Well, let's see . . ." Crystal placed her hands on her hips and took a step backward. "This is what," she said, waving her index finger at Chevy, "the Lil' Kim look?"

"Screw you," Chevy spat and started off.

We took a table outside Ollie and Pinks, a small upscale barbecue place inside the South Street Seaport.

Crystal was dressed in a beige linen tank dress with a matching jacket the same length as the dress, while Chevy sported a black knit mock-neck sleeveless dress that clung for dear life to her size-eight curves.

Men walked by and gave them both approving smiles while I cooked in my fall wool houndstooth suit and got no looks. Not even pitiful ones.

Oh, well.

The waitress brought apple martinis for them and a Corona Light for me.

"Would you like a glass?" the waitress looked at me and asked.

I shook my head no and took it by the neck. After a few gulps I saw Crystal looking at me with an amused expression, while Chevy's face registered disdain.

"What?" I asked defensively.

Chevy just shook her head.

"Chevy, what's wrong with Noah? I've been trying to call him all week, and either I get his machine or he picks up and gives me some random excuse as to why he can't talk right then."

"I don't know, Crystal—he's been acting real strange lately. I leave for work and he's locked in his room. I come home and he's locked in his room."

"Did he break up with Zhan?" I asked after I took another gulp of my beer. "Remember the last time he went through a breakup? He almost had a nervous breakdown."

We all nodded our heads at the memory.

"Maybe you being in his space is upsetting him," Crystal said and turned her eyes on Chevy.

"It is not. We never even see each other." She waved her hand. "He don't even know I'm there."

"Uh-huh." Crystal gave her an even look.

"So how's work, Chevy?" I asked.

"Next subject, please," Chevy said and winked seductively across the room at a man who had caught her attention.

"Why? You do still have a job, don't you?" Crystal turned expectant eyes on Chevy.

I leaned in and waited for the answer.

"Okay, if I say, 'Beautiful . . . fabulous . . . wonderful,' then can we move on to something else?" Chevy said, all snidelike.

"You got fired, didn't you?" Crystal spouted as she set her glass down on the table.

"Not again, Chevy," I chimed in. "We can't afford it!"

"No, I didn't get fired. But I wish the hell they would fire me so that I could collect unemployment for a few months."

Crystal and I uttered a sigh of relief.

We looked over the menu and threw some small talk around the table. I was just about to ask Crystal about the garlic mussels when Chevy's cell phone rang.

She looked at it and made a face at the number.

"Hello?" She listened for a while before she began to grin. "Well, hello, stranger."

Crystal and I turned to each other. "A man," we said in unison.

"It's been some time. How have you been?" Chevy said as she leaned back into her chair and crossed her legs.

Crystal and I turned our attention back to our menus. We knew from experience that Chevy was going to be a while.

"Dinner, tonight?" She beamed. "Um, I don't know—it's so last minute."

We rolled our eyes at her.

"Asia de Cuba? Yes, I know it. Actually, it's one of my very favorites."

"Very favorites"? We thought we were going to be sick.

"Nine o'clock sounds fine."

We looked down at our watches.

"No, no, you don't have to pick me up. I'll meet you there."

Chevy, giving up a ride? She must have a fever.

"Ta-ta," she said and flipped the phone's face closed.

"'Ta-ta'? Who the hell are you supposed to be, Zsa Zsa Gabor?" Crystal laughed.

"And why didn't you want him to pick you up?" I asked.

"Oh, this is a new one. You know, I got to weed the crazies out before I let them know where I live, and even then I don't like to give out my address."

"So I guess you'll be leaving us now? It's almost seven and you have to get to Brooklyn and slip into something even more fabulous than what you already have on, right?" Crystal's voice was heavy with playful sarcasm.

"You are right!" Chevy said as she jumped up, barely waved goodbye, and dashed away.

Twenty-Three

I was late. What else is new?

It took me some time to get my outfit together. After trying on about ten different dresses, skirts, and pantsuits, I decided on a beautiful cream Ungaro linen halter jumpsuit and a pair of strappy gold high-heeled shoes. Some gold Monet jewelry to complement, a small gold and white clutch bag, an *I Dream of Jeannie*–style ponytail, and I was out the door.

I really didn't have money to spend on a cab from Brooklyn, so I jumped on the train and crossed my fingers, hoping that the NYC transit company would for once in its miserable existence not let me down. But, of course, it did.

We sat between stations for a good ten minutes while the lights blinked on and off and the motorman halfheartedly apologized for the delay.

Once in the city I strolled confidently past gawking men and turned down 37th Street, headed toward Madison Avenue and the Morgans Hotel, where Asia de Cuba was housed.

Once inside, I checked with the maître d'. "Um, reservation for . . . for . . ."

Dammit, I'd forgotten the man's last name. Had I ever even known it?

The maître d' smiled tightly at me and waited.

"Oh," I said and dug into my purse for my wallet. I'd slipped his card behind my driver's license. Pulling it out, I slowly pronounced his name so that I wouldn't butcher it too badly.

"Abimbola Lenguele."

The maître d' looked down at his book and then back at me and smiled. "Yes, Mr. Lenguele hasn't arrived yet. So you can take a seat at the bar," he said, sweeping his hand left and toward the bar area.

I loved this restaurant. The billowy white curtains, seductive lighting, and wood paneling gave it a smoky, sultry feel.

"What can I get you?" the bartender asked.

"Champagne," I said, already light-headed from the atmosphere.

Beautiful people came and went, and before I knew it I was sipping on my second glass of champagne and it was a quarter to ten.

Where the hell was he? Now I was getting mad. No one makes Chevy wait! Who the hell did he think he was? I looked at my watch again. I should just leave. But I'm starving and haven't had anything but a bag of potato chips since noon.

And to make things worse, the bubbles from the champagne were starting a war with the gas in my stomach.

I discreetly rubbed my chest and was able to slip out two small, dainty burps without anyone noticing. But then my stomach began to swell up like a balloon and I knew that the air building inside me wasn't going to be passed through my mouth. If I didn't get up soon and hustle my fine ass off to the ladies' room or outside, I was going to blow a hole the size of Texas out the seat of my jumpsuit.

I jumped up from the stool and quickly negotiated my options.

Outside, or the ladies' room?

Which one was closer?

I could feel the air seeping out even as I stood there trying to look calm.

I looked toward the restroom and watched as four women sashayed through the swinging door. That option was out.

The bartender gave me the "Where do you think you're going?" look.

I clenched my butt cheeks together, dug deep into my purse, pulled out a twenty-dollar bill, and threw it on the bar. "I'll be right back," I mouthed and made my way, as naturally as I could, toward the front door.

The maître d' eyed me suspiciously as I wobbled out and onto the sidewalk. A small crowd was milling in front of the restaurant, so I had to sidestep my way past them, and then . . .

Bllllllllllllllleeeeeeeeeeeeeeeeeeeee!

It was the loudest release of air I had ever been witness to. The legs of my jumpsuit fluttered as if caught in a great wind, and the small group looked around and above in search of the offensive noise. Me, I had my right hand cupped to my ear and my mouth chattering happily away as if I were on my cell phone.

A few more small explosions, and I was done. Whew!

I looked at my watch again. It was ten o'clock, and my anger started a slow, heated climb up my neck. Some people just had no consideration for others!

Just as I made up my mind to start home, a long, sleek black limousine pulled up alongside the curb and Abimbola climbed out.

As unsightly looking in his face as he was, the cream and gold dashiki he was wearing somehow made him not so hard to look at. I felt that we must be linked in some cosmic way, because we had chosen the same colors. This was a very good sign.

He looked left, smiled graciously at the white people who stood outside smoking and gawking at him, and then waltzed into the restaurant.

I did not follow. Who the hell was he to make me wait on him all this time?

I turned on my heel and started down the street, raging inwardly. Once I reached the corner, my stomach grumbled and reminded me that Asia de Cuba had some damn good food. That release of air had opened up an empty pocket in my stomach that needed to be filled.

"Damn," I muttered, spinning around and starting back to the restaurant.

"Chevanese," Abimbola sang when I sashayed up beside him. He stood and took both of my hands in his. "How are you, my beautiful queen?" he said as he bent and kissed me first on one cheek and then the other.

His lips felt like mink. Mink—hmm.

"I'm fine," I said.

"I can see that. More than fine . . . extraordinary," he said, taking a step back to admire me. "You wear white well," he said.

"So do you," I returned, with a big sparkling smile.

The maître d' approached. "Mr. Lenguele, your table is waiting, if you're ready," he said.

"I am at the mercy of the beautiful lady, Marco," Abimbola said, bowing his head at me.

I think I'm melting. That's so unlike me!

"Sure, I'm ready to eat," I said.

"After you, my queen."

I grinned so hard, my cheek muscles screamed.

I don't think a man had ever called me a queen before. I liked it.

Anything else?" Abimbola said as he touched the linen napkin to the corners of his mouth.

I shook my head no and leaned back contentedly in my chair. I couldn't eat another bite and didn't think I could drink another drop, but I don't believe in the wasting of good champagne, so I tipped the crystal flute to my lips and drained its contents.

I'd already been to the ladies' room twice. The champagne was just running through me for some reason.

Now, sitting there, belly full, I reflected on the past

two hours. As always, our conversation was wonderful. Abimbola was truly an interesting man, funny, light-hearted, and full of compliments—which I love.

When I set my flute back down, he was staring intently at me. My head was swimming, and I felt warm all over. I smiled at him and reached into the empty chair for my purse. "Excuse me," I said as I scooted my chair back and stood up. Abimbola rose as well. The room swam around me and I quickly sat back down.

Abimbola frowned, came around to my side of the table, and rested his hand on my shoulder. "Are you okay?" he asked, his voice filled with concern.

I touched my head. "I think I've had a little too much champagne." I giggled.

"Can I help you to the ladies' room?"

I looked up into his eyes. "No, no, thank you. I can make it alone."

"You're sure?"

"Yes," I said and gave my head a good shake before standing up again. The room was still swimming, but not as much this time, and I managed to cross the dining area and make it into the ladies' room without bumping into anything or anyone.

Once inside the stall, I struggled with the clasp of the halter. My fingers didn't want to cooperate, so finally I just pulled it over my head.

I was doing the pee-pee dance, hopping from one foot to the other and willing my urine to stay contained until I got my thong pulled down. After a thirty-second struggle, my will lost out and my bladder burst. I quickly dropped down onto the cold toilet seat, immediately aware and disgusted that I had just exposed my behind to a billion microscopic germs.

Revolted that my bare ass was on a public toilet seat and on top of that I'd pissed through some very expensive silk and lace thongs, I proceeded to remove my shoes. I stood and worked my limbs the best way I could in the small stall in order to slip my jumpsuit off without the white material mopping the floor.

Afterward, I stepped out of my soaking wet thong and tossed it into the sanitary napkin bin on the floor by the toilet.

I needed to wash up. I couldn't go back out there smelling like piss!

I eased the stall door open and peeked out into the restroom. Currently it was empty, but I knew that someone could walk in at any second. And if I'm correct, being nude in a public restroom is considered a "lewd and lascivious" act punishable by law.

I had to risk it.

I dashed out, naked as the day I was born. Rushing to the sink, I quickly snatched up a handful of paper towels, turned on the hot water faucet, and shoved the towels beneath it, all the while keeping my eye on the door. I then pushed the wet towels underneath the soap dispenser and gave it two good whacks with my hand, forcing the creamy liquid soap out and onto the towels.

Luck is on my side, I thought as I was about to grab up some more paper towels, but just as quickly as I'd thought it my luck changed and the door suddenly swung open.

I froze like a deer in headlights. The women who were coming in looked, blinked, and then threw their hands over their eyes in terror before screeching in surprise.

"S-sorry," I managed, dashing back into the stall. "I had an accident," I yelped from behind the door as I quickly tended to myself.

All I heard were whispers laced with revulsion.

Clean, or as clean as I could get, I stepped back into my jumpsuit, slipped my feet back into my sandals, straightened my back, pushed the door back on its hinges, and walked as proudly as I could into the lions' den.

The women, three of them, were huddled together at the sink, where I joined them and said, "Wonderful food here, don't you think?"

They shrank away from me, careful not to make eye contact in the wall-length mirror, as I reapplied my lipstick, flipped my hair, and then washed and dried my hands. I gave myself one last look and then strutted out.

Abimbola was impatiently checking his watch when I returned. "Hello," I said as I reached for my chair. He hurriedly jumped up, ran around to my side of the table, and eased the chair out for me. I thanked him.

Once back in his seat, he shot me an awkward look before uttering, "Are you okay?"

I waved my hand at him. "I know I was gone for a while—you know how these ladies' rooms are: they never have enough stalls, so there's always a line."

Abimbola gave me an unsure smile.

There was a fresh glass of champagne waiting for me.

My mouth watered, but I looked at him and said, "Oh, really, I couldn't."

"Oh, please do. I know how much you like it." He lifted his own glass of cognac up to me in salute.

"To many, many more evenings like this."

"Yes, many, many more," I said and turned the flute up to my lips.

Twenty-Four

I was standing in front of the full-length bathroom mirror, examining my nude body. It was my ritual, twice a day, every day.

I decided, as I reached for the Neutrogena sesame oil, that, yeah, I still looked good.

After dousing my wet body with the oil and then patting myself dry, I walked through the connecting door that led to my bedroom.

I loved being naked. There was something so freeing about it. It's even better being naked after a few martinis, I thought and then laughed out loud.

The phone rang, cutting through Toni Braxton's "Unbreak My Heart," which was playing softly in the background.

"Hello?"

"Sweetheart." Kendrick's sexy voice came across the receiver.

"Well, hell-o, stranger," I replied and stretched myself across my king-size bed. I hadn't seen Kendrick since he'd returned from London or the subsequent trip to Montreal, but he'd sent me three vases of red roses.

"I tried to reach you at the office today, but Kayla said

you were in meetings all day and couldn't be disturbed," I said as I slid one of my legs back and forth across the silk comforter.

"Yeah. It was a long, hard day," Kendrick breathed. "You sound very relaxed, lady. What are you doing?"

"Lying here naked and growing hornier by the minute."

"Oooh, that's a great visual. Tell me more," he purred.

I wasn't one for phone sex. But what the hell, right?

I flipped over and onto my back and used my free hand to play with my nipples. "Well, right now I'm rolling my nipples between my fingers."

"Umm. Does it feel good?" I could hear the change in his voice.

His breathing was becoming labored.

"Oooh yeah, baby. It feels *soooo* good," I said, really getting into blue movie mode.

"Touch yourself," Kendrick whispered, and so I let my hand leave my breasts and move down my body, across my taut stomach and down between my legs.

"Oh," I moaned as my finger brushed my pulsating clitoris before heading down to my hole.

"What, what? Is it wet there?"

"Oh, baby, it's *so* wet there," I crooned.

"Push your finger up inside your cunt," he ordered, panting now.

Shoot, we both were.

So I did. But that's where the magic ended. My finger was no substitute for my man's big black dick, and I told him so.

"I need you here, baby."

"I'm coming," he said and there was a rattling sound as the phone missed the base once, twice, and then finally—eureka—dial tone.

It seemed like only a few minutes had passed before the buzzer sounded.

I jumped up, grabbed my green silk robe resting on the bench at the foot of my bed, and skipped to the intercom.

"Hello?"

"Mr. Greene is here to see you," the doorman announced.

"Send him up!" I said, sure that the excitement in my voice was not lost on the doorman.

When Kendrick walked in he swept me up and into his arms. "I missed you," he murmured as he fumbled with the belt of my robe, frantically trying to undo it.

"Kend—" I tried to talk, but his mouth was on mine before I could utter a word.

He laid me down on the couch and the robe fell open, revealing my still moist nude body.

"You are so beautiful," he said as he kissed me softly on my eyelids, the tip of my nose, and my neck. Slowly he moved down to my breasts and lovingly suckled my nipples.

Then he inched down to my stomach and allowed his tongue to trace half circles there before moving his head low enough so that his lips brushed my pubic hair.

I moaned and squirmed and dug my nails into his shoulders.

When his tongue found my clitoris I thought I would go mad with pleasure.

"P-please," I groaned as he pushed his face deeper.

Finally Kendrick opened his mouth and took in all of my womanhood. I wrapped my legs tightly around his head and bucked. My hands were locked in his hair, and when the thunderous climax shot through me, I screamed his name: *"Kkkkkkkkkendrick!"*

My body was still trembling when Kendrick lifted me and carried me into the bedroom, where he gently placed me down onto the bed.

There I watched him slowly remove his clothes.

When he was finally naked, he mounted me and I curled my arms and legs around his beautiful body.

"Oh, so sweet . . . *sooo* fucking sweet. It's so wet . . . so sweet and wet, Crystal . . . oh, shit shit . . . ohhhh, Crystal." Kendrick moaned into my neck as he expertly moved in and out of me.

My body was still recovering from the first orgasm when I felt another building up. Where I got the strength, I don't know, but suddenly my hips were moving in rhythm with his.

The tempo grew and swelled until my headboard sounded like a beating drum against the wall. Pleasure climbed through me, and then Kendrick's body stiffened and he went into light-speed mode. We were both there, both on the edge of mind-boggling pleasure—one, two, three, and *booooooooooooooooom!*

We came together. Our bodies shuddered and we both

let out a long, pleasurable "Ahhhhhhhhhhhhhhhhhhhh-hhhhhh."

It'd been so long since we were last together that we had to go for another round. This one was shorter, calmer, but just as sweet. Later on, famished, we found ourselves naked in the kitchen, feeding each other Godiva chocolate ice cream straight from the container.

I glanced over at the clock on the stove.

I yawned and spooned another glob of ice cream into Kendrick's mouth. "If I don't get some sleep, I'm going to be puffy-eyed and cranky in the morning." I yawned.

"Okay, baby," he said and pressed cold lips against my forehead.

"So did you get a lot accomplished in London?" I asked as I placed the ice cream back into the freezer and then dropped the spoon into the sink.

Kendrick wrapped his arm around my waist and we started toward the bedroom. "Yeah, I guess. The move to the new office went smoothly. We've installed a new director . . . a woman, you'll be glad to know," he said with a wink. "And I took your suggestion and commissioned that sculptor you liked so much to create a piece for the main lobby area."

"Really!" I squealed.

I loved Akamafula's work. I owned three of his pieces and always received fabulous compliments on them. The brother was seriously talented and the world was finally beginning to realize that.

I'd met him personally at a gallery showing of his work

three years earlier. We even tried to date for a minute, but he was just too eccentric for me. We decided that we would just be friends but weren't even able to sustain that. Not that it bothered me; I still promoted his work and supported him.

By the time Kendrick and I climbed into bed, the small hand on the clock was edging toward two. I curled myself into Kendrick and thanked God a million times before I finally dropped off to sleep.

Twenty-Five

My Friday night ritual consisted of me, a small pepperoni pizza pie, a six-pack of Corona, a pint of ice cream, and a movie rental.

I'd already had four slices of pizza, making my already mammoth-size gut bulge out even further.

Tomorrow, I told myself. I'll go back on my diet tomorrow. Oh, wait a minute, tomorrow is Saturday, I thought. Saturdays aren't good days to start a diet. Maybe Sunday?

No, Sunday is the Lord's day. No room for the diet deities.

Well, Monday it is, I told myself and gulped down my second Corona.

Immediately after I drained the bottle I felt guilty. It seemed as though I worked hard at everything except me. I worked hard at my job, worked hard at keeping my son in school and on the right track, worked hard at keeping my home comfortable, but I always seemed to neglect myself. My feet were in need of a pedicure, and as much as I hated to admit it, Chevy was right: I needed to do something with my hair besides pull it back into a ponytail.

But right now I had no money for those luxuries. I had

to save every penny because I knew within the next few days I would be receiving a letter from my son begging for one thing or another.

I tugged my T-shirt down over my bulge and had to laugh at my circumstances. It's funny, I thought, how all four of us came from the same place, all with parents who hadn't made it out of high school but behaved as if landing a city or government job was as big as hitting the state lottery.

They instilled in us the importance of education. Prayed that we'd all find a way to get into college—and pay for it too. But being black in America had turned them into staunch realists who made sure to drop a copy of the *Chief* on our pillows every Thursday, every city application and federal examination deadline circled in red.

If they had had any dreams, they never commented on them.

Some of us did make it into college. The some of us being Crystal and Noah.

Chevy felt she didn't need college. She believed her brains, beauty, and street smarts would carry her as far as she wanted to go. And so far they'd carried her practically around the world and had gotten her into some pretty interesting social circles along the way.

She was smart and savvy. And Crystal and I both agreed that she could have so much more if she used her powers for good rather than evil.

As for me, I was an average student, more Cs than Bs, but always my teachers would comment on the back of my report card "a joy to be around."

Not that that did anything for my average. But they were also fond of saying "Geneva displays great effort."

And I did. I worked my ass off when I did go to school. I liked school, to tell you the truth, but at fifteen when the cutest boy in the senior class approaches you, takes you by the hand, calls you a "fox," and then says, "You wanna go with me?" all thoughts of education go right out the window. I know that happened for me. All my energy was turned to doing whatever it was I had to do to keep Eric interested in me. Including cutting school and using my lunch money to buy him sappy "I love you" greeting cards, and letting him have me "raw dog" on my childhood bed, on my mother's bed, and, when we had no place else to go, on the top-floor stairwell in the adjoining building.

Needless to say, those reckless sexual acts disqualified me from participating in the race for a college education, as well as the one I'd barely been running for my high school diploma. It was all over the minute the little square box on the plastic stick I pissed on indicated that I was pregnant.

But I persevered. Yeah, I was a single teenage mother on welfare, struggling to make a home for my newborn son in a space that was already overcrowded and slightly dysfunctional. But it seems to me that any family has to have at least a splatter of dysfunction to be considered normal. Whatever that is!

I took GED classes at night while my mother watched Little Eric, and even though she bitched and moaned the whole six months I went, when I passed with flying colors she was the happiest I'd ever seen her.

It's been an uphill battle ever since that day. Taking the

best I could get jobwise meant a three-year stint at the local McDonald's and turns as a cashier girl at a five-and-dime, Key Food, and Foodtown. Finally I landed a job at the Macy's perfume counter and then my present position as a receptionist at AIW.

I've worked hard as hell to get this far, and while this far may be nowhere to some people, it's everywhere to me right now.

I've started thinking seriously about college. At first the thought of going to college scared the hell out of me—I just didn't think I was smart enough. But I've met enough degree-carrying stupid people in my life to change my mind about that!

Ring, ring, ring.

My thoughts were interrupted by the telephone, and I answered with a full mouth.

"Hello?"

"Are you eating pizza?" Nadine's voice floated through the receiver. At first I felt guilt, but that was short-lived. "Bitch, get a life!" I screamed into the phone and slammed it back down onto the base.

Just for that, I snatched another slice of pizza out of the box and greedily inhaled it. That'd show that size-six bitch!

I popped the *Steel Magnolias* videocassette into the VCR and leaned back to watch it for the umpteenth time. It always makes me cry, and I was PMSing so hard that a Hallmark commercial could have sent me over the edge.

I was just at the part where Julia Roberts is going to have her seizure. I clutched the pillow to my chest and held my breath.

Ring, ring, ring.

Don't the phone always ring at the most inopportune times?

It better not be that damn Nadine again, or I swear I'm going to call the cops.

I snatched up the remote and pressed pause before I answered.

"Hello?"

"Hey, it's Eric."

"Hey," I breathed.

"What you doing?"

"Getting ready for a date."

"Liar." He laughed.

"What, you think I don't date?"

"I'm in the neighborhood."

"And?"

"Thought I might come up and see you."

"For what?"

"Well, I got a few dollars I wanted to give you to send to Eric at camp."

"That's your excuse for coming here? You could have dropped it in the mail, or, better yet, sent the check directly to the camp."

"C'mon, girl, stop giving me such a hard time," he said, laughing.

I thought that right about now a warm body was better than a long hard cry, and I said, "Okay, c'mon up." But I told myself that this was the last time.

Twenty-Six

Sometime before ten o'clock that morning I regained my senses, opened my eyes, and found myself splayed out, buck naked in between the silk sheets of a king-size bed. I blinked, thinking this must be a dream, because Noah wouldn't let me use his silk sheets on that godforsaken, backbreaking futon of his.

I tried to look to the left, but that only started my head to hurting, so I looked up and was met by my own disheveled reflection in the mirrored ceiling above me.

Where the fuck was I?

Slowly, carefully, I sat up and looked around. There wasn't much else to the room. A nightstand, empty except for a glass of water. I looked over the edge of the bed and saw that my Kenneth Coles were safe and sound and placed neatly together on the carpeted floor. I turned my head to see that my purse was hanging from the knob of what I assumed was a closet door. And on the chair beside it my pants suit was draped.

Now my head was pounding and the bright morning light that eased through the floor-to-ceiling windows did all but blind me as I tossed the covers to the side, cautiously threw my legs over the edge of the bed, and stood up.

The room swam, and my stomach turned over for a minute. "C'mon, don't puke," I told myself as I tiptoed over to the chair and retrieved my jumpsuit. I then moved back to the bed, sat down, and slipped my shoes on. Up again, I eased my purse from the knob, opened it, and examined the contents.

Everything was there.

I moved to the only other door in the room and pulled it open.

Stepping into a large, open, white-walled space, my feet fell on hardwood floors and the clicking sound of my heels sent an echo as loud as an explosion.

I froze, terrified as I stared at the long sheer white curtains that billowed in the soft summer air flowing through the open windows.

I eased myself up onto the balls of my feet and moved on.

Two large white and blue pinstriped sofas sat in the middle of what was the living area, and an entertainment center covered nearly one half of the wall.

My eyes darted around the room in search of an exit, but I could see nothing but walls, and then my eyes fell on another long hallway.

Holding my breath, I crept forward, as silent as a snake moving through high grass. Halfway down the hall I could see the beginnings of a green and gold granite kitchen counter. The sound of a flushing toilet froze me in my tracks.

There was no way I could cover the distance back to the bedroom in time, so I looked wildly around for a closet to duck into, but there was nothing around but solid white walls.

Shit!

A sound came from behind the kitchen counter, and then I heard a heavy sigh that was distinctly female.

I stood there praying for God to make me invisible.

A woman walked out of the kitchen and into the hallway. Her back was to me, and I held my breath for good measure as I began tiptoeing backward.

Just as I took my fourth step, Abimbola appeared from a door in the hallway.

He was dressed in green bikini briefs and his body looked as if it were chiseled from stone. "Well, good morning, Chevanese," he said with a big broad smile.

The woman swung around, her eyes locking with mine. "Oh, yes, good morning, Chevanese," she said, offering me a sunny smile.

"I'm Cassius," the woman said, walking toward me with her hand extended. She was beautiful—striking. So good-looking that I forgot not knowing where the hell I was and started mentally processing her look so that I could imitate it sometime in the near future. Well, if these two didn't kill me.

I cautiously offered my hand.

"Well," Cassius said as she took my hand in hers, "nice to finally meet you." She leaned in and kissed me on my left cheek and then my right. She smelled rich. I inhaled deeply. I loved that smell.

"Um, s-same here," I stuttered.

Abimbola approached and threw his arms around Cassius's waist. Pulling her into him, he kissed her neck and then looked at me and said, "You were quite ripped last night. You wouldn't . . . or couldn't tell me where you lived, so I brought you here."

My eyes swung from Cassius to Abimbola and then back to Cassius. I must be still sleeping, I thought as I gave my head a vigorous shake.

"Are you okay?" Cassius asked. "Can I get you some black tea, or maybe some coffee?"

"What the fuck is going on here?" I heard myself say.

Cassius made a face, undid Abimbola's arms from her waist, and strolled into the kitchen. Abimbola turned and watched her walk away before turning back to me again.

"You must have put some shit in my drink," I said, pointing an accusing finger at him.

He must have, because I was a woman who knew how to hold my liquor.

"Well, no, it's like I said: you had too much to drink," he repeated and calmly folded his hands across his massive chest. "And just so you know, you removed your clothes yourself." He winked. "I was the perfect gentleman."

I tried to think backward, but there was nothing.

This was too weird.

I started past him and down the hall. In the kitchen I caught sight of Cassius seated at a glass table, sipping from a mug and flipping through the paper. "It was nice meeting you," she said as I moved toward a blue door at the end of the hallway.

"Yeah, likewise," I said sarcastically.

I'd been wrestling with locks for a few seconds when Abimbola moved in behind me and his large hand gently brushed my hand away. "Let me," he breathed as he expertly maneuvered the locks and then turned the doorknob. The door magically sprang open, and I was about to sprint into the hall when I heard him say, "Please, take this money for a taxi."

Money?

I slowly turned around to see a hundred-dollar bill clutched in his hand and waving in my face.

"Thanks," I muttered and snatched it from him before shooting through the hallway door that said EXIT above it in bright red letters.

I took the stairs three at a time until I found myself out on 17th Street. I sucked in air as if I had been holding my breath for hours and willed my heart to stop running a marathon in my chest.

After I caught my breath and the strength in my legs returned, I moved briskly up Seventh Avenue until I hit 34th Street, all the while trying to figure out what had just taken place but mostly trying to remember what had happened after my fourth glass of Cristal last night.

I remember coming out of the bathroom, having another glass of champagne, and then . . . and then nothing. My mind was a total blank. I smacked myself on the forehead. I am so stupid, I thought as I hustled along. I broke one of my own rules: never leave your drink unattended.

But I actually hadn't. I mean, it was a fresh glass.

Yeah, that Negro put something in my drink—one of those date rape drugs.

As the thought of rape entered my head, my feet came to a screeching halt.

Had I been raped? I looked down at my crotch. It didn't feel like anything had been up in there.

Maybe he brought you home for the woman, an ominous voice whispered in my ear.

"Yeah," I said out loud. "Maybe she just ate me out all night," I blurted at a passing woman and her boyfriend.

I shook my head and started walking again. No, no. None of that had happened. It's like he said, I had too much to drink.

But what about the woman? the eerie voice came again.

A sister, a cousin, maybe.

Have you ever seen sisters and brothers behave like that?

Yeah, in that movie *Flowers in the Attic*.

What the hell did I care who she was? I was alive, safe, and unscarred, and, plus, I had money!

Macy's loomed in front of me, and after I looked around to make sure that neither Cassius nor Abimbola was following me I ducked into the entryway and into the store.

Shopping always helped me to think, and I had a hundred dollars to spend. I rolled the money in my hand, but it felt strange. I moved to the beam near the escalator to examine the bill. The way things were going it was probably counterfeit. But when I opened up my hand, I realized that it wasn't just one hundred-dollar bill, but two!

"What the fuck did I do to deserve this?" I said aloud, and the early-morning shoppers eyed me warily and clutched their pocketbooks as they moved past me.

Two hundred dollars? Already I could feel my head clearing.

I jumped on the escalator and yelled: "To the shoe floor, my good man!"

Twenty-Seven

Okay, I think I might have this thing licked! It's been two weeks and I haven't had one woman. Of course, I haven't left my house, and that might have something to do with it.

But now I'm all out of sick days and vacation days and, Lord forgive me, I even used up three bereavement days when I called my superior and told him that my grandmother had died.

Sorry, Grandma!

So today will be my first day back out into the world. I'm confident that between all of the gay porn I've watched combined with the hours of phone sex with Zhan (my phone bill is going to be outrageous!) I'll be back to my old self again.

It was just past nine o'clock and I was sipping some green tea and listening to a morning radio show. I could hear Chevy snoring like a hog in the bedroom above me. I didn't know what she'd been doing, but working wasn't it because she'd been hanging out until dawn and sleeping until noon for two weeks.

I couldn't imagine that she was on vacation, but I had

my own demons to deal with so I hadn't had the time to question her about hers.

Okay, the clock says nine thirty: time to hit the road. I placed my teacup in the sink, turned off the radio, snatched up my keys, and marched out the front door.

"Good morning, Ms. Anderson," I sang to my neighbor, who was walking her border collie past my house. She was a small gray-haired white woman who'd never been seen without her fuchsia lipstick, a hideous color on her and something I think that Chevy would simply adore. Even now, at nine thirty in the morning, her lips were smeared with it even though she was in curlers and a housedress.

"Morning, Noah!" She waved and then smiled to reveal a line of pink across her crooked yellow teeth.

That sight is enough to keep me off "fish" for the rest of my life, I told myself as I bounded up the street toward the train station.

On the subway platform, I was met with wall-to-wall people, indicating that the trains were backed up. What else was new?

Leaning over, I peered down the dark tunnel in search of the train, but the only thing I saw were rats scurrying across the tracks.

I cursed myself for not picking up a newspaper as I began to try to amuse myself by surveying my fellow straphangers.

The neighborhood was changing so quickly: not more than four years ago you wouldn't have seen a white face, and now there must have been at least twenty of them. Blond-, brown-, and auburn-haired men in their Wall Street business attire. College-aged white girls in the low-rise jeans and cropped tops, with long flowing hair. The Utica Avenue train station is beginning to look like the 125th Harlem station, I thought to myself.

What black Brooklyn neighborhood would be next? I wondered.

Bushwick was the most likely candidate.

My eyes roamed from face to face. An old black man leaned up against one of the steel beams, looking at his watch and mumbling to himself; a young mother was wagging her finger in the face of her small child; and, to the horror of a middle-aged woman, two teenage boys played a game of who-can-spit-the-farthest-across-the-tracks.

I laughed to myself before peering down the tunnel again. I sighed and thanked the Lord when I saw the dim yellow headlights of an approaching train coming from the previous station. As I stepped back and prepared myself for the mad rush into the car, my back hit soft, supple breasts and my nose was instantly filled with the scent of Krizia perfume, and before I could even turn around I already knew I was in trouble.

"Excuse me," I said as I swiftly spun around on my heels and came face-to-face with a statuesque brown-skinned woman with locs. She was so beautiful, she was perfection; she was so astonishing that I thought, This is what Venus the goddess of love must look like.

"No problem," she said, barely looking at me. "Is it coming?"

If you want me to! my Johnson piped up, and I could already feel him beginning to stiffen.

"Um, yeah it is," I said as I took in her Coca-Cola-bottle shape. Her breasts were standing at attention and, oh, my, are those nipples I see pushing through the thin material of her blouse? I looked closer. Yep, this beauty was braless!

Stop it!

I turned briskly away from her.

C'mon, man, don't fight it! my penis screamed.

"Shut up!" I hissed at my crotch. The old man leaning on the beam stopped his mumbling and gave me a wary look.

When the train arrived and the door opened I didn't step in but stepped aside and said, "After you," to the goddess Venus, who smiled at me and stepped in. My eyes fell on a behind that was plump and shaped like an apple.

"Goddamn," I heard myself utter as she walked by me.

We jammed in like sardines and somehow I ended up behind the Venus, both of our hands clinging to the same pole.

"I'm sorry," I bent down and whispered in her ear as the train jerked out of the station.

"Sorry for what?" she said, turning sweet eyes on me.

"I'm apologizing early, because I know at some point I might . . . um . . . um . . ." I didn't know quite how to phrase it.

Was it me, or did her smile just move from sweet to seductive?

She wiggled her index finger, indicating for me to bend in closer, so I did.

"Rub up against me?" she whispered and then let out a little giggle.

My head jerked back in surprise, and I stupidly shook it up and down.

"Don't worry, I don't mind," she said and gave me a wink.

I would have thought that I was still in bed, still asleep and dreaming, if it wasn't for the broad smile the old man on the other side of the pole was giving me.

My mouth went dry and I backed my pelvis as far away as I could from her apple-shaped ass, but with each station stop, more people piled in, pushing me closer to my end.

When we hit Jay Street–Borough Hall, the lights went out. White women clutched their purses tighter to their bodies and someone uttered a curse word beneath his breath just as Venus pushed her ass back, closing the one-inch space I had managed to keep between us.

The train pulled off and into the tunnel, throwing us into darkness, and Venus used that opportunity as well as the jostling of the train to her advantage and began rubbing her behind against my dick with expert precision.

Oh, the pleasure!

Sweat trickled down my temples and I found my hand grabbing a hold of her waist, pulling her closer to me.

"The next stop for this train will be Chambers Street," the conductor belted out over the speakers, and a miserable groan went up from the passengers who needed to get off at one of the three stations we were skipping.

But Venus and I, well, we groaned with pleasure! We would have at least three more minutes to ride this erotic wave of bliss.

Just outside Chambers Street, the train came to a sudden halt and Venus and I slowed our feverish humping down to a slow grind that had me seeing stars. I bit down on my lip to keep from hollering out. She had brought me to the point of no return. I felt Johnson jerk and stiffen, and I knew he was going to blow.

Venus must have felt it too, because she grabbed a hold of the hand I had placed on her hip and squeezed.

The train jerked forward and I nearly bit a hole through my lip as I spewed semen all over my brand-spanking-new, just-out-of-the-package Calvin Klein briefs, and Venus, well, she screamed, "Oh fuck!" before letting out a long shuddering breath and then falling limp against me.

There was some giggling, and then a church woman hollered from across the car, "Don't you be using that type of language in public!"

The lights came on and I swear all eyes were on us.

Venus pulled herself upright again and swiped some damp strands of hair from her face.

When we pulled into the Chambers Street stop, she walked off as if nothing at all had happened between us. She didn't even turn around and wave goodbye. Nothing.

I knew now what cheap felt like.

I watched her calmly walk up the stairs and disappear

before the doors slid closed again, and I was left wondering if I'd dreamed the whole thing.

The old man across from me was laughing now, laughing and pointing down at the wet spot seeping through my rust-colored linen pants. I knew then that it wasn't a dream at all, that it was a nightmare instead, one filled with women and seedy encounters.

One from which there seemed to be no hope of ever waking up.

Twenty-Eight

"Is she traveling?" I asked the woman who'd answered Chevy's private line.

"No, I told you, she no longer works here," she said again, through clenched teeth.

"Yes, yes, you did say that—"

"Twice," the woman snapped, and then I heard a click and a dial tone.

I stared at the phone for a while before dropping it back onto its base.

Something very strange was happening over there in Brooklyn. I couldn't get a hold of Noah or Chevy. They both lived in the same damn house, yet no one ever answered the phone.

I finally called Noah's office and his assistant told me that he'd taken a leave of absence.

Yes, something very strange was happening in Brooklyn.

I picked up the phone and buzzed Geneva.

"Yessum, Missus Atkins," she said with a snicker.

"Stop being so silly," I chastised her, even though I couldn't help but smile. "You up for taking a trip with me to Brooklyn tonight?"

There was silence.

"Hellllllllloooo?"

"Brooklyn, why there?"

"Because I can't reach Noah or Chevy, and I think something is wrong."

"Aw, Crystal, Brooklyn is so far away," she whined.

"Stop it. It is not—it's right over the bridge," I reminded her.

"Yeah, well, maybe so, but it's a goddamn world away!"

"Geneva!"

"And the people there are weird."

"They are not!"

"Yes, they are. People get mugged in Brooklyn. It's all those damn trees, dirt roads, and farmland!"

"What are we, back in the eighteen hundreds now?"

Geneva laughed.

"So will you come with me?"

"Sure, just let me go home and get my Glock first!"

"I'll see you after work." I laughed and put down the phone.

Three hours later, Geneva and I were on the A train headed toward Brooklyn. We'd been to Noah's house maybe six times since he bought it, and just the thought of that made me feel ashamed.

"It shouldn't take something like this to get us to Noah's house," I said to Geneva as the train streaked through the tunnel.

"Uh-huh," she mumbled between bites of her Scooter sweet pie.

"I didn't even know they still made those," I said as I watched her tongue pick the cake out of the corners of her mouth.

"Yep, they still make them," she said as she devoured the sweet pie.

"I guess your diet is history, huh?"

Geneva's face went flat and she turned slanted eyes on me. "No!" she bellowed, and some passengers looked up from their books at us.

"Shh, I just asked a question—you don't have to get so defensive and loud," I whispered.

"Whatever," she mumbled.

I'd hurt her feelings, so I patted her knee and said, "This is kind of like a trip, huh?" It was corny, I know.

"A trip?" Geneva spouted, spraying bits of Scooter Pie in my face. "Sorry," she uttered as she attempted to wipe away the crumbs she'd just covered me with.

I pushed her hand back, completing the job myself, and said, "Well, it's like an adventure, you and me on the A train to Brooklyn. It's exciting!"

Geneva gave me a crooked look. "A train ride to Brooklyn is exciting now? Girl, you're not getting out as much as I thought you were." She laughed.

I smirked at her. "I guess what I'm trying to say, Ms. Geneva," I said from between pursed lips, "is that I'm glad you decided to come with me."

Geneva eyed me for a moment, and then her face softened. "You know I wouldn't let you come here alone. We're girls, and that's what girls do for each other."

Out on Fulton Street now, we tried hard to get our bearings among the rush hour crowd that had exited the station with us.

"Um, 'scuse me, sir, which way is Stuyvesant Avenue?" I asked a young, good-looking man with a baseball cap who was walking by. His head jerked at the word *sir*, and then a broad smile spread across his face. He nodded toward the corner and said, "That way, Ma," before giving me an appreciative look and walking on.

"Ma?" I looked at Geneva for guidance.

"Oh, that's their word for girl, lady, chick," she said nonchalantly.

"Oh," I mumbled and we started in the direction his chin had indicated.

Halfway down Stuyvesant Avenue I realized that I didn't have the address with me. "Do you know the house number?" I asked Geneva, who gave me a comical look and shrugged her shoulders before saying, "Lost in Brooklyn."

"Is everything a joke to you?" I asked, frustrated more with myself than with her.

"Just call Noah and ask him," Geneva muttered as she dug into her pocketbook in search of her pack of cigarettes.

"How many times do I have to tell you that neither one of them has been answering the phone, so what sense would it make to call now?"

"What about the cell phones?"

"They're not answering those either," I said, and then I thought about it and said, "Well, Noah's not answering his and Chevy's is temporarily disconnected."

Geneva gave me a blank look, popped the cigarette between her lips, and lit it with her green Bic lighter. "Oh," she breathed as she cocked off a plume of smoke.

We walked on as I tried hard to remember what Noah's brownstone looked like, but they all seemed to look the same.

Frustrated, I pulled my cell phone from my purse and dialed Noah's number. It rang just once and then his outgoing message came on.

"Noah, Geneva and I are in Brooklyn, right on Stuyvesant Avenue, and I can't remember your house number, so if you're there, please pick up."

I waited for the sound of his voice, but all I got was the beeping sound telling me that the machine had finished recording my message and disconnected me.

I turned and looked at Geneva, who dropped her cigarette butt to the ground and stubbed it out with the toe of her beat-up Reebok.

"Back to civilization, then?" she said snidely.

I didn't even answer her; I just huffed and started back up the street.

Twenty-Nine

Monday morning found me unable to keep my eyes open as I sat listening to the counselors complain about the lack of security in the various rehab houses the Ain't I A Woman Foundation sponsored throughout various inner-city communities.

My head had started pounding as soon as I sat down and switched on my computer, and that had been around eight o'clock. Now, after two hours and two Tylenols, the marching band that had been rehearsing inside my head was giving a concert, with encores.

"It's not fair, Ms. Atkins," a slight, dark-skinned girl with long braids named Camika complained.

She looked every bit of the part of a gutter rat, with her electric blue fingernails and powder blue mascara, but was far from it. She'd grown up in Baldwin, Long Island, and had graduated summa cum laude from Barnard. She was the perfect reminder that one really should never judge a book by its cover. "Our houses have two security officers for sixty in-house residents. That's not enough. Have you seen the reports on the violence we've had over the past ninety days?" she continued.

I nodded my head yes.

"We need more security personnel—there's no way around it."

"One woman was sodomized by a resident, another was beaten and cut up in a stairwell. Ain't I A Woman shelters are experiencing real problems in Houston, Chicago, and Los Angeles, but Detroit is the worst," Cameron, a tall wiry white boy with red hair, quietly interjected. He was the junior director and though he looked only twenty-two he was actually thirty and studying for his doctorate.

I looked across the mahogany table at the dozen or so faces that looked back at me representing a variety of ethnicities, all eager to give back to communities that most of them had never even set foot in until they came to work for this organization.

I remember when I was in their shoes: young, eager, and ready to link hands in solidarity with others who wanted to see homelessness, disease, war, and anything else we thought destructive and inhumane obliterated.

Now I was just a paper-shuffling delegator with a fancy title and a fat paycheck. Was I really making a difference sitting behind my desk? I didn't think so.

"Ms. Atkins?"

I blinked and came out of my daydream. The band in my head had actually taken a break, but the tension in my neck told me that it would be a short one.

I looked at the faces once again and tried to put together

something that wouldn't send them away too disappointed and disillusioned with life.

I straightened my back and dove into the same old bullshit I'd been spouting since I'd assumed my position.

"Like I told you before, AIW has been strapped financially the past year. Donations are down and unfortunately we have had to cut services in some places, and security hire is one of them," I said in the most apologetic voice I could muster. "The new budget is currently being prepared, and I promise you that we are working on trying to increase funds for security personnel," I lied and abruptly stood up, signifying that this meeting was at an end.

I turned my back on a lot of angry faces and could have sworn I heard "bitch" thrown at my back as I walked through the doorway and out into the hall.

Back in my office, I settled myself down behind my desk, allowing the cool blues and warm whites of the room's decor to work their soothing magic on me.

The spearmint tea my secretary brought in for me had succeeded in quieting the pain in my head but did nothing for my mind, which was locked on Chevy and Noah.

I was becoming very concerned about them and could have kicked myself for not having emergency contacts for them. Chevy's mother was living somewhere in Phoenix, remarried, so her last name was a mystery to me. Noah's mother was right in Queens but had changed her telephone number two years ago. I'd never gotten the new one from Noah, and Mrs. Bodison's paranoia prevented her from being listed in the telephone directory.

I didn't want to sound like some crazed, irrational friend, but if neither one of them contacted me soon, I would have to call the police.

I turned to my computer monitor and stared at the seventy-six emails that awaited my attention. My eyes roamed to my desk clock, which indicated that noon was just around the corner.

I would try to knock out as many emails as possible and take lunch at one.

Problems, problems, and more problems. I answered each email feverishly, eager to be done with them. Then I opened one from Sweet Cheeks.

Sweetie,

I'm sorry that I have been AWOL—but I am going through something that has me upside down and inside out. I'm sorry that I have not returned your emails or telephone calls, but I am working through some issues at the moment and need some time alone.

Will call as soon as I find some footing.

Smooches,
Noah

P.S. By the way, Chevy is alive, well, and unemployed. I think there is a new man in her life.

I read the email five times, but the relief I felt was short-lived and replaced by anger. We're all supposed to be best friends, I thought to myself. Anything that affected them, affected me, and vice versa, or so I thought.

I felt hurt and tossed aside. I hit the delete button, switched off my computer, grabbed my bag, and headed out to lunch.

Thirty

Wednesday, hump day for sure. I was lying there, basking in the afterglow of what I thought was the best sex I'd ever had, and it was all a dream.

I thought I must have a ghost in the apartment, or maybe it was the late-night cheesesteak hoagie, fried chicken wings, french fries, and double-thick chocolate milkshake I had at around eleven last night. Whatever it was, I am in heaven and wanting some more, but I can't seem to get back to sleep. I need to find my way back into the dreamworld where that good-looking buck of a man had my legs up on his shoulders and his head down between my legs while his tongue—which was as long as a human arm—was up inside me, touching places I didn't know existed!

And after that he bathed me! BATHED ME!

Not a shower, not a soak in the tub, but a real sensual bath complete with bubbles, silky oils, a soft sponge, his magical hands, and Jill Scott crooning in the background.

This man, this god, lifted my big ole ass out of the bed. Lifted me! And carried me to a clawfoot tub that was six feet long and four feet wide and lowered me into water that was the perfect temperature and felt like silk.

"Ease back, baby," he whispered. "Make room," he

said, and so I did by spreading my legs wide enough for his massive body to slip comfortably in between them.

He climbed in, his dark skin already glistening as he plunged his hand beneath the water and slowly searched for the sponge. His fingers, feather soft, brushed against my thighs and then the silky wet hairs of my pussy as he hunted, finally locating the sponge.

"Lean back," he whispered, and I did, and he lifted the sponge into the air and squeezed it until every last drop of water beaded on my breasts and pooled in the space beneath my throat. He bent his head and licked me dry.

It went on like that forever, until he said, "May I?"

And I heard myself say, "Yes, you may."

Slowly he moved himself over me so that we lined up almost perfectly. He kissed me deeply, and I found myself unable to resist the sweet taste of his probing tongue.

We kissed for a long time, while his hands caressed my breasts and toyed with the lobes of my ears.

When his penis brushed against my thigh, it created music beneath the warm, sudsy water.

"Please," I muttered and gripped his waist, pulling him closer.

He slid into me then, and I arched my back to accommodate him.

We moved in perfect harmony and I heard myself whisper in his ear, "I love you."

And he whispered back, "I love you more."

And that's when some fucking drunk in a Cadillac jumped the curb outside my window and slammed into the streetlamp, dragging me from the best wet dream I'd had in years!

Damn!

My eyes flew open and I saw the cracked ceiling of my bedroom and heard the static drawl of my television. I knew it was all a dream and could have cried right there from the disappointment.

"Shit!" I mumbled to myself as I climbed out of bed, slipped my feet into my worn slippers, and padded out to the kitchen. I clicked on the light and swung open the freezer door to examine what I had left to munch on. Well, there were my good friends Ben and Jerry, and, look, they'd brought Rocky Road along with them!

I plucked the pint of ice cream from the freezer shelf, grabbed a spoon, and settled myself down at the kitchen table and began to eat. The container was only half full, so in six bites everything was gone.

I tossed the container aside and reached for my pack of Newports. Lighting one, I inhaled deeply as I stared through the darkness and tried to recall my dream lover.

Thirty-One

The shrill sound of the phone snatched me from my sleep, and I grabbed it up in the middle of the third ring. "Hello?" I managed to gurgle as my heart beat wildly in my chest.

Kendrick was beside me and promptly turned over, grabbing the pillow and throwing it over his face.

"Hello?" I whispered again when only clicking sounds came out of the receiver.

Someone was on the other end, babbling frantically. "Who is this?"

"It's Chevy!" Chevy screamed.

"Chevy?" I said stupidly as I looked at the fluorescent green numbers on the clock on my nightstand. It was 3:15 a.m.

"Where are you?" I said, shocked to finally hear from her and even more surprised to hear from her at this hour of the morning.

"Jail!" Chevy screamed back.

Kendrick and I walked into the lobby of the 100th Precinct at three fifty a.m. I was amazed at the amount of activity that was going on in the precinct at that hour.

Kendrick sat down heavily on a bench situated directly across from the main desk, yawned loudly, and then leaned his back against the wall.

"Excuse me, I'm here for Chevy—I mean, Chevanese Cambridge," I said to the aging Hispanic officer behind the desk.

"What's the name again?" the officer said without looking up. I inhaled deeply and stared at the shiny bald spot on the top of his head.

"Chevanese. C-H-E-"

"Last name," the man curtly cut me off.

"Cambridge," I replied and then looked over my shoulder to see Kendrick walking through a door marked MEN.

"When was the perp brought in?"

"Um, a few hours ago, I guess."

The police officer, head still bent, turned his body toward the monitor of his computer terminal and typed in Chevy's last name.

"Cambridge, Henry," the cop said, still not looking up.

"No, Chevanese. C-H—" I started again.

The cop cut me off again. "Cambridge, Pauline."

"No, no, I said her name is—"

"Cambridge, Martin."

I could feel my anger building. I dragged my hands down my face, trying hard to keep myself together. "Her name is—"

"Cambridge, Chevanese," the cop said and finally looked up at me, offering me a wry smile revealing the black space that sat where a front tooth should have been.

I always assumed that the city had a good dental plan,

I thought. "Yes, yes, that's her," I said with a heavy sigh of relief.

"You here to bail her out?" he asked, one gray eyebrow climbing his forehead.

"Yes."

"Three hundred and seventy-five dollars."

I blinked a few times and then dug into my purse and pulled out my checkbook. "Who do I make it out to?" I said through clenched teeth.

"The Department of Corrections," he said and grinned. "You her sister?"

"No," I said as I quickly scribbled the amount across the check.

"Friend?"

"Not for much longer." I shoved the check at him.

The cop hit a button on his keyboard, and a printer I couldn't see started somewhere beneath his desk. He reached down, produced two printed copies, signed and stamped both, handed me one, and then swiveled around in his chair and called to a young black cop who was seated at a desk, bent over and engrossed in a conversation on his cell phone. "Franklin!" he yelled, holding the paper out to him. "Go on down and bring this one up."

Franklin gave him a blank look and then said something into the phone before flipping the cover closed, standing up and retrieving the paper, and walking off.

A few minutes later he was back, with Chevy following close behind.

Chevy's face looked drawn. In the three weeks since I'd

last seen her, it seemed to me that she'd lost a few pounds. The one good thing was that she looked almost normal in some respects. Her weave was perfect as usual, and a respectable color. And her eyes were the pretty brown God had blessed her with.

"Whew—let's go, girl," she said after she collected her belongings and brushed past me, heading out the door into the early-morning darkness.

I was dumbfounded. Chevy had the balls of a bull. She wakes me out of my sleep in the middle of the night, has me pay close to four hundred dollars of my hard-earned money to get her sorry ass out of jail, and then just saunters past me with a "Whew—let's go, girl"? Like all of this was nothing but a chicken wing—without even a "Thank you, dog"?

I flew behind her, catching her on the last step.

"What the fuck was that?" I screamed at her back, with my hands on my hips.

"What?" Chevy asked, stepping down onto the sidewalk and turning to me.

"What?" I repeated, astonished. "What the fuck, you can't say 'thank you'? You just walked by me like it was my duty to leave my bed and come out in the wee hours of the morning to bail your ass out!"

Chevy gave me the "Well, ain't it?" look, and I swear my hand twitched at my side. I wanted to slap her into next year!

"Look, Chevy, I ain't your babysitter. We are all grownups here, and you have got to learn to take care of yourself and stop leaning on me and the rest of us. Romper Room is closed!" I screamed. I was so angry and riled up that my whole body shook.

Chevy just smirked at me.

"Why the fuck did they arrest you, anyway?"

Chevy looked around for a minute before folding her arms across her chest. When she did speak, her voice came out low. "I jumped the turnstile," she said quietly, and her face went crimson with embarrassment.

"You did what?" I was stunned. Had she fallen that far? She didn't even have a dollar fifty to ride the train?

"I'm sure you know by now that I no longer have a job." She spoke to the night air around us, her eyes fastening onto the streetlamp to our left.

"Yes, yes, but c'mon, Chevy, you know you could have called me." I felt like shit. Now here I was ranting and raving, and this woman didn't have a dime to her name. It was true: most of us were just one paycheck away from being homeless, and Chevy was proof of that.

"God, Chevy, I'm so sorry," I said, feeling all of my insides turn to mush. I stepped forward and hugged my crazy, dysfunctional friend.

"Yeah, thanks," she said, her arms stiff at her sides.

Kendrick pulled the car up to the curb and honked the horn once. "She need a ride home?" he yelled from the open window.

I looked at Chevy. "C'mon, let us take you home," I said, grabbing her hand and leading her toward the car.

"No, no. I can't let you take me all the way to Brooklyn. You've done too much for me already," she said and pulled her hand from mine.

"It's no problem at all. At this hour we'll be there and back in no time," I urged.

"No. And anyway, I really need some time alone to think."

I could certainly understand that. So I dug into my purse, pulled out my wallet, and gave her all of the money I had. "Here, take this. It should be about a hundred or so dollars there," I said, holding the money out to her.

Chevy eyed it and then sighed and shook her head no.

"Please, take it," I said, pushing the money closer to her. "Take it and I'll call you tomorrow and we can talk about what's going on with you."

Chevy's hand finally came up and took the money from me. "Okay," she whispered sadly.

She was breaking my heart. I'd never seen Chevy look so dejected. "Call me tomorrow, okay?" I pressed.

"Yeah, okay, and thanks," she said before turning and walking away.

I watched her move down the sidewalk and take the first corner.

Something was missing. A friendly hug between sister-friends . . . something.

Thirty-Two

Crystal climbed into the car and turned to face a wide-eyed Kendrick. His body seemed to be twitching with some invisible energy.

Crystal cocked her head. "What's wrong with you?" she said.

"Nothing," Kendrick answered and flashed her his million-dollar smile. He turned the music on and began bopping his head to the beat that banged out of the speakers.

"I just want to go home," she said as she leaned her head back into the leather headrest.

"Home it is!" Kendrick yelled and gunned the car down the street.

After dropping Crystal off at her place, Kendrick went home, stripped himself naked, and stood in the middle of his apartment. Well, it used to be his: now it belonged to Chase Manhattan Bank, which had foreclosed on it two days earlier, giving him thirty days to vacate.

Long gone were the expensive pieces of art that had once graced the walls, the sculptures that once stood on marble podiums throughout the 2,800-square-foot loft, the big-screen television, the leather sectional, the ten-thousand-dollar entertainment center, and the four-poster Kenyan mahogany bed.

It was all gone, sold off piece by piece in order to sustain his drug habit.

People automatically assumed that because he was the vice president of a multimillion-dollar real estate company, he too had millions of dollars, but that wasn't the case. His father, Aldridge Greene, simply employed his son. Kendrick was salaried, just like the goddamn cleaning women!

Aldridge had always assured him that there was a trust fund in his name, and of course Kendrick would inherit the company upon his father's death, but for now, his $300,000-a-year position as vice president would have to suffice, because as Aldridge had put it, "You may be in your forties, but your mind is still that of an adolescent!"

People don't realize how quickly you could party and sniff three hundred grand away. Shoot, he personally knew some former multimillionaires who'd done it.

The car he drove belonged to the company, and he had exactly ten dollars and twenty-six cents left in his checking account. His credit cards were maxed out due to all of the cash advances he'd taken out, and his savings and mutual bond accounts had been emptied and closed three months earlier.

He was flat broke and homeless now.

When would it stop?

A casual habit had grown in just two years to an addiction. He needed the drug in the same way he needed air to breathe. Kendrick felt as if he couldn't live without it.

He opened his hand to expose a small vial of Hades—deadlier than heroin and more addictive than cocaine. Kendrick had a $1,500-a-day habit that was climbing. One vial of the copper-colored dust cost five hundred dollars. It was the drug of the super rich.

Some dude named Musa had turned him on to the narcotic twenty-six months earlier, while Kendrick was in Dubai on business. Prior to that Kendrick had been a casual drug user. A little cocaine, amphetamines, and some marijuana here and there.

But Hades made him feel like the man he was expected to be. The second man in charge of a multimillion-dollar company. Hades made Kendrick feel invincible. It kept him going through eight meetings with six different companies over a four-day period. It kept him cool while he negotiated with Mexican investors in an outdoor café underneath the searing Acapulco sun. It kept him on his toes when dealing with the Nigerians.

Kendrick needed it just to be in the presence of his father, Aldridge Greene. He couldn't stand tall or look directly into his father's eyes without a hit of it.

But now the money was gone. So there he stood in an empty apartment: one vial left and a new day dawning.

What was he going to do?

Thirty-Three

There is something definitely wrong with me, I thought as I sat watching the sun rise over the New York City skyline. Crystal's money still clutched in my hand, I chastised myself about being a bad friend.

I stood up, looked quickly around me, and then gingerly dug my hand down behind the waistband of my slacks and into my panties, where I had the roll of money Abimbola had given me earlier in the evening, tucked safely and securely down between my legs.

"Three thousand dollars," he'd said when he handed it to me. "One run, that's all I need. One run from here to California."

"You want me to be a mule?" I said, astonished by the proposal, but more astonished by the amount of money he was going to pay me to do it.

"Yes, if that's the term you'd like to use," he'd said coolly.

"You'll receive three thousand dollars more when you deliver the goods in California," Cassius interjected between sips of her champagne.

We were at a small Greenwich Village Italian restaurant.

A cozy little place that had expensive food and a sultry ambiance.

I'd learned that Cassius was his second wife and business partner. His first wife was in Lagos with their three children, and he was currently on the lookout for a third.

"Oh, that's nice" was all I thought to say on that subject.

"I—I don't know if I can do that," I said, still clutching the money in my hands. "The airport has those drug-sniffing dogs."

Abimbola bent his neck left and right, cracking it loudly. Cassius's right hand went up immediately and began to massage his neck.

"Only for the international flights," he said.

I rolled the money between the palms of my hands. Six thousand dollars could buy a new fall wardrobe. "How would I carry it?"

Cassius and Abimbola looked at each other and then back to me. "Inside of you, of course." Cassius spoke to me in a tone usually reserved for a potty-training two-year-old.

"Inside of me?"

"Yes. We'll fill condoms with the stuff, and you'll swallow them."

My eyes bulged.

"Of course, you'll have an enema before you do so," Cassius added.

"Y'all are crazy," I whispered, still holding on to the money.

"And if this trip goes well, you can make more for us,

if you'd like," Abimbola said, before he picked up his fork and jabbed at his penne pasta.

"I didn't say I was going to make *this* trip!" I snapped at him and leaned back into my chair.

What a waste of words and breath. Abimbola had me pegged from the time he saw me. Poor little black girl trying to play rich. Hanging out at the bar at the Cipriani, scoping out fresh meat and old money. He knew I wouldn't say no, even when I was sure I would.

"Let me think about it," I said and waved my hand at the waiter to bring me another glass of wine.

And he'd let me walk out of that restaurant with the money. "Good faith money," he'd said as he and Cassius climbed into their chauffeured limousine.

Yes, he'd offered me a ride, but I told him I needed time alone, time to think. The exact same thing I later told Crystal.

But when I left him, I strolled the streets of Greenwich Village, gazing at the beautifully dressed windows of my favorite expensive boutiques, mentally picking out what it was I would come back the next day to purchase.

It wasn't really late, but it was dark, and this was New York City, and I did dress in a manner that made me a target for purse snatchers and muggers, so I strolled into the twenty-four-hour Duane Reade drugstore and purchased a travel-size package of Kotex. Next, I walked into Starbucks, snatched a plastic knife from the commissary table, and waited at least ten minutes on line for the ladies' restroom.

Once inside, I removed one of the sanitary napkins from the package, used the plastic knife to slit it lengthwise, and then slid the three grand between the two halves before tucking it safe and sound down between my legs.

Hey, I grew up in the hood—I knew what I had to do to keep my money safe.

Back out on the sidewalk, I was confident that, short of a rapist approaching me, my money was safe.

That's when I realized that all I had left in my wallet was seventy-five cents. Not even enough to buy a Metro card. There was no way I was going down between my legs to get some money, and besides, transit wouldn't take a bill larger than a twenty.

So I was left with no other choice but to jump the turnstile.

I looked around the lonely station and saw that there was an old blind white man with dark shades sitting on the bench to my left, his Seeing Eye dog curled up and sleeping at his feet.

To my right was a young, thug-looking black boy who was carefully scanning his surroundings the same way I was as he prepared himself to take a piss against the wall.

That was it, except for the rats that scurried up and down the tracks and the token booth clerk, and she was too engrossed in her telephone conversation to pay me any mind.

So I jumped!

My feet had barely hit the platform when a heavy hand came down on my shoulder.

"Shit!"

It was the young thug.

"What are you doing!" I screamed, thinking I was being mugged.

"*Helllllp!*" I shrieked as I balled up my fist and swung at his jaw.

Suddenly there was another hand on me and I turned to see that it was the old blind man, and up close I realized that he was wasn't old or blind. And his Seeing Eye dog wasn't a Seeing Eye dog at all but a vicious German shepherd whose jaws were tearing at the cuff of my slacks.

"Police!" the young thug screamed as he ducked my fist.

"What?"

Both men dug into the tops of their shirts and pulled out badges connected to silver link chains that hung around their necks.

They ran my information and it came up that I had warrants. No surprise to me. I knew they were there. Two, in fact. One for running a red light back in 1992 when I rented a silver Mustang for my birthday weekend. That was back when I was living large and really foul. I'd gotten a boyfriend of mine to rent the car for me; of course, he didn't know that my license had expired. When I ran the light at Broadway and 86th Street, the police officers confiscated the car, wrote me a ticket, and told me that I needed to appear in traffic court the next day. Of course, I didn't go, and I never saw that boyfriend again.

The second warrant was for shoplifting. That was a big misunderstanding; I just forgot I had that four-hundred-dollar dress in my hand when I started out the door. It was an honest mistake—really, it was. I was looking for the perfect dress to go to some high-caliber Upper East Side party with this German plastic surgeon I'd met and I'd been in the store so long that I'd gotten really warm, and so I removed my jacket and slung it over my arm so I could be more comfortable. I had three or four dresses in my arms by then, and when none of them actually tickled my fancy I returned them all back to the rack, except one, the one that was the same color as my jacket.

Believe me, I didn't realize I still had the dress when I stepped out that door.

They booked me, and my mother came and bailed me out. Once again I was given a court date but never showed up for it.

How Thomas Cook had missed those two blemishes on my record must have had something to do with all the praying I did when I handed in the job application!

Thirty-Four

"Why you calling me and telling me lies?" I whispered into my headset.

"I'm telling you, it's the truth," Crystal whispered back to me from her office two floors up.

"Arrested, for jumping the turnstile?" I said again, for the umpteenth time.

"Yes," Crystal breathed.

"Don't they just write you a ticket and send you on your way?"

"I wouldn't know, Geneva. I've never jumped the turnstile."

"Well, Eric did once, and they just wrote him a ticket."

"Really? I didn't know about that."

"Well, it's not like he got on the honor roll, if you know what I mean."

"I hear you."

"She's got to be lying."

"You think so?"

"Chevy? C'mon, you know she'd rather tell a whole lie than a quarter of the truth!"

"Yeah, I suppose so."

"So does Noah know?"

"Who knows? He's going through his own shit. I got an email from him."

"Really? What he say?"

"Just wanted us to know that he was still alive, but going through something."

"You think him and Zhan broke up?"

"I dunno—he didn't say."

"Oh."

We were silent for a while.

"We're going to have to get together and have a coming-to-Jesus session with Chevy," Crystal said.

"Like an intervention?"

"Yeah, something—anything to get this girl back on track."

"She ain't never been on track," I reminded Crystal.

"True," Crystal said wistfully.

"So are we going to go back to Brooklyn?" I asked.

"We might have to, 'cause I don't think I'm going to be able to get her to come to us."

Thirty-Five

Just as I reached the entrance of my apartment building, Kendrick pulled up to the curb and honked the horn. I turned to meet the glowing smile of the man I loved, and all the dark thoughts of Chevy that had clouded my mind all day disappeared.

"Well, hello," I said, pleasantly surprised.

"Hey, baby," Kendrick answered as he leaned over and opened the passenger door. "How about dinner?" he added.

As tired as I was, I should have taken my ass upstairs and straight to bed, but knowing our busy schedules and the lack of time we seemed to have for each other lately, I jumped at the opportunity. And besides, I needed to talk to someone other than Geneva about what was going on with Chevy and Noah.

"Sure," I said as I hopped into the car and threw my Gucci handbag into the backseat.

We ended up at Eugene's, a favorite restaurant and lounge in Chelsea, which we both loved. My mouth was already watering for the goose pâté.

The intimate setting and warm lighting always seemed to put me at ease, and as the waiter pulled my chair out for me I could already feel the tension of the day slipping away.

"A bottle of Veuve Clicquot '95," Kendrick said as he unfolded his cloth napkin.

"Ooooh, are we celebrating something?" I asked as I perused the menu.

"Well, maybe, if you say yes." He grinned and folded his hands beneath his chin.

"Yes"?

Oh my God, was he going to pop the question? Our conversations never turned to marriage, even though I mused every chance I could on how it would be. What kind of wedding would I have, and where?

The Caribbean, definitely the Caribbean. On a private white sandy beach, with a steel band playing "Here Comes the Bride."

My heart fluttered in my chest, and I could barely look him straight in the eye when I asked, "Well, let's see—what's the question?"

"I've been thinking, baby," Kendrick began as he reached over and took my hand in his. I could hardly breathe and was so nervous that spots of perspiration were seeping through my blouse.

"Yes?" I croaked.

"That we should take the next step." He said it so seriously, I felt my head spin. Already my eyes were filling with water and I squeezed his hand in mine.

"Oh, Kendrick," I moaned. "Yes . . . I—I'm ready," I said in a quivering voice.

"Good." Kendrick smiled. "I've started the renovations on my apartment, and I thought I would be able to deal with the dust and noise, but it's really aggravating my sinus condition."

Okay, I thought. Okay. Where's the ring? Why isn't he on his knee? Well, I really don't necessarily need him to be on his knee. But where's the ring, and why the hell is he talking about renovations and sinuses?

"So I figured this would be a good time for me to move in with you. Kind of see if we can live together first before doing anything we might both regret."

What?

My smile slowly faded and the tears of joy that were brimming in my eyes quickly turned to those of disappointment.

"Live together"? "Regret"?

"I—I don't understand," I said stupidly as I slowly retrieved my hand.

"Oh, sure, I could stay in a hotel," he continued as if my face wasn't cracked and lying in pieces on my bread plate, "even rent another apartment. But this is the perfect opportunity to see if we're really a match made in heaven." He winked.

I was speechless.

"So what do you think, darling?" he said as the waiter stood over us and eased the cork from the bottle.

I thought I was worth more to you than that. I thought

shacking up was for people in their early twenties who were too young to commit to any one person. What I thought was *This is some bullshit!*

But "Of course" is what I said as the waiter filled my glass flute with the bubbling champagne.

Thirty-Six

"Oh?" is all I could think to say when Crystal called me that night and shared Kendrick's indecent proposal.

I was stretched across the couch, Ben & Jerry's in one hand, a plate of chicken wings resting on my belly, and a half-finished glass of cherry Kool-Aid on the floor beside me.

I had my Tae Bo tape in the VCR—muted, of course—as I watched Billy Blanks kick and punch his way to good health.

"Well, maybe this is a good thing," I said. "It's important to get used to each other before taking the next step."

"Maybe," Crystal said in a faraway voice.

"When is he moving in?"

"Tomorrow."

"Oh," I said as I removed the plate from my stomach and pulled myself up and into a sitting position. "So have you heard from Chevy yet?"

"No, still no word. I thought we'd try to get over there on Friday."

"You'll have the address this time, won't you?" I said, using my Ben-&-Jerry's-carton-free hand to imitate Bobby and punch at the air.

"Yes, ma'am," Crystal snapped, and then, "Lemme go—I gotta go take a run and clear my mind."
"Yeah, okay. I'm going to get up and do some Tae Bo."
"Really? That's great, Geneva."
"Uh-huh, bye."
"Bye."
I punched the air a few more times and then lay back down and finished my Rocky Road.

Thirty-Seven

I looked like a bum. A vagabond. A freaking homeless person! My process was long overdue to be reprocessed: I had naps the size of tumbleweeds growing beneath my waves. And I had a five o'clock shadow that was five days' thick.

I'd been locked up in the house for days now.

Chevy and I had bumped into each other a handful of times, but I didn't bother to ask what was going on with her and she did the same for me.

But something was happening, because she'd been quiet. So quiet I hardly even knew when she was there, and that's not like Chevy.

She's so loud and flamboyant, if she weren't a black heterosexual female I would swear she was a flamboyant gay man!

Whatever.

I had my own problems, and to top it off, Zhan was flying in on Labor Day. I told him that I had the flu and that I thought it would be best if he'd hold off on coming, but that only made him change his flight in order to get to me sooner.

I was spending all of my time on the Internet, in search

of some type of support group that could help me with this problem of mine, and I'd finally found one.

Homosexuals with Heterosexual Tendencies. HHT.

They're a small group that meets twice a week on the Upper West Side. I'd called and spoken to someone named Bob. Not his real name: "We believe in anonymity here at HHT," Bob had said in a calm and even voice. "What name would you like to go by, friend?"

I racked my brain for a few seconds. "Um, um . . . Wayne?"

"Wayne it is, then," Bob said. "We have group sessions—they usually last for two hours and the cost is one hundred and seventy-five dollars per session."

"Wh-what?" I stammered, thinking about the hit my bank account was going to take.

"Yes, well, while you may think the cost of these sessions is high, especially because you're sharing your time with others, I want you to reflect on the benefits involved." Bob took a breath and then sipped something from a cup. In my mind I'd already put together a visual of him. White, thin, neat. Pinky finger at attention as he sipped.

"We have members who have conquered their heterosexual issues, and they can impart knowledge on newcomers that can make a newcomer's road to recovery an easier journey."

"Well, if they're recovered, why are they still plunking down one hundred and seventy-five dollars a session?"

"Well," Bob began, and then stopped to sip. "Just like alcoholics, gamblers, and other addictive peoples, you have to continuously work the program to remain well."

"Uh-huh," I moaned.

I was so desperate that I would have paid five hundred dollars a session. I jotted down the address and told Bob that I would be at the next meeting, which was Friday night.

My only worry was what would happen to me between Brooklyn and the Upper West Side.

Thirty-Eight

Crystal kept calling, but I continued to ignore her. Right now my focus was on this room, packed tight with pretty shopping bags from boutiques from all over the city.

I looked at the clock and it said it was just past ten in the morning. I was nowhere near getting up, but a horrible nightmare nearly made me jump out of my skin. I was at LAX waiting for my Louis Vuitton overnight bag to come around the carousel, when a young girl came up to me and tugged on my hand. "I'm lost," she said. "Can you help me find my mother?"

Now, I don't usually do children. Don't really like them too tough. But I took her little hand and started walking around the airport in search of her mother.

But as I was walking, I felt like I had to shit. I told her that we needed to stop at the bathroom. We went in and I placed her by the sink, telling her to stay right there while I went into the stall to do my business.

Once inside, I squeezed out the condoms filled with drugs. No shit at all, just the drug-filled condoms. So many of them came out of me that I could no longer see the bottom of the toilet bowl, or the water.

As I gathered the condoms out of the toilet and piled them into my purse, I yelled out to the girl that I was finished and would be right out. When I finally opened the stall door, the little girl was still standing there, but she had a snarling German shepherd at her side and a DEA badge hanging from a chain around her neck!

What a nightmare, I thought as I turned over and onto my side.

It won't happen that way, I told myself as I tried in my mind to put together an outfit for dinner that night.

I had to tell them tonight if I was going to do it. And I guess I either had to do it or leave town, because I didn't have a dime left of the good-faith money Abimbola had given me.

I told myself that federal time is much easier to do. The cells are cleaner; you get more yard time than state criminals. And if I got caught it'd be my first offense, so how many years could I really get?

I was starting not to feel so bad about what I was going to do, and then I thought, What will become of my wardrobe? My shoes, boots, and coats? Can I bring them to jail, or would I have to put them in storage while I was locked up?

"Stop it, Chevy," I hissed to myself. "You don't have to worry about those things, because you're not going to get caught!"

My eyes began to grow heavy with sleep again, and just when I felt myself slipping back into dreamland, Noah clicked his television on and I was bombarded with the heavy breathing and groaning sounds of male-on-male sex!

My eyelids flew open.

The fucking I could handle—it's that goddamn background music that was going to drive me crazy!

I got up and began banging on the wall that separated our rooms and screamed, "Noah, Noah! Not all of us are sex addicts and need to hear that shit fifteen hours out of the day!"

The volume on the television went up a notch.

"Get some help!" I screamed in rebuttal before I leaped back into bed and pulled the pillow over my face.

Thirty-Nine

"Well, hello, Brooklyn—didn't think I'd be seeing your country ass so soon," I said as Crystal and I made our way down Fulton Street for the second time in two weeks.

Crystal turned around and threw me a pained look. "Brooklyn is nice. Stop putting her down."

"I just called her country, is all," I said in my best Georgia drawl.

Crystal laughed. "Brooklyn is just as cosmopolitan as Manhattan."

"Hush your mouth!" I said and swatted her on the shoulder. "How dare you insult Manhattan in that way. If that gets back to her, she might not let us back in."

We walked along, Crystal always three steps ahead of me. Even though I had my sneakers on and she was in pumps, I still couldn't keep up. Well, maybe I could have if I'd put out my cigarette and stopped topping off my fried dinners with ice cream.

We stood staring up at Noah's brownstone. It looked almost unlived in. The sidewalk outside the house was littered with debris, and the potted petunias on the stoop and down the steps were all dried up and dead.

Looking at the windows, we saw that all the shutters were closed.

Crystal and I exchanged looks and then climbed the stone steps.

We rang the bell, knocked on the door, and tapped on the parlor-floor window, and still nobody came.

I gave Crystal my "See what I mean?" look, flopped my big ass down on the top step, and lit a cigarette.

"What are you doing?"

"What does it look like I'm doing? I'm smoking a cigarette," I said and took a long puff.

After a while, Crystal came and sat down beside me.

"Some people just don't want to be helped," I said as I tilted my head back and cocked off three smoky circles.

"I guess," she said, deflated.

"I ain't coming back here again," I said matter-of-factly. "You're on your own next time."

Crystal just smirked at me.

"C'mon," I said and hoisted my body up. "Let's go home."

Crystal gave the brownstone one last sorrowful look before we descended the steps and started up the street.

Forty

Dinner at Chez Annie's, a French restaurant on the Lower East Side. Just Abimbola and me. Thank God—that Cassius woman gives me the creeps.

"You look beautiful, Chevanese," Abimbola whispered in my ear as he pulled my chair out for me.

"Thank you."

And I did look beautiful. After Noah ran me out of my bed with his porn videos, I decided to use the last bit of the money to get a wash and set, as well as a manicure. I wanted a salt scrub but was down to twenty dollars, and not even Brooklyn spas were that cheap.

"So have you thought about my offer?" he said as he unfolded his linen napkin and spread it across his lap.

"Yes, I have," I said.

"And?" He leaned forward expectantly.

"And . . . I'll do it," I said.

His face lit up and he clapped his hands together. "Waiter, a bottle of your best Merlot, please!" he boomed across the small dining establishment.

I made a face at the mention of Merlot. Red wine is not a favorite of mine.

"But," I interjected, bringing his joy to a halt, "I'll need to have double the money you promised."

I'd had a coming-to-Jesus session with myself after that nightmare, and if I was going to put my life in jeopardy, I was going to have to get more than a measly three thousand dollars.

Abimbola leaned back into his chair and folded his hands across his chest. Those bulging eyes of his studied me for a while, and then he unfolded his arms, leaned forward again, and brought his hands down onto the table. "You are a shrewd businesswoman, Chevanese," he said with a wry smile.

I nodded my head, quite proud of my business savvy.

"I will pay you another three thousand upon delivery. But," he said, holding one long index finger up, "you will get forty bags of Hades instead of twenty."

I didn't expect a "but." I stared down at the blue linen tablecloth as I considered his offer. What was the harm of swallowing twenty more bags?

"Deal," I said.

"Deal," he repeated and stuck his hand out for me to shake.

Forty-One

I expected so much more. I mean, moving men and boxes everywhere, and me trying to find space for his stuff. But there was none of that. Just Kendrick and a few suitcases filled with clothing and shoes.

"Where are all of your things?" I said when Kendrick walked in dragging two large Louis Vuitton suitcases.

I was more than prepared to spend the day unpacking and reorganizing my space. I mean, I had picked out an outfit and everything—an old blue sweatsuit complete with a blue and white kerchief for my head.

Now, as I stood there holding the door with one hand, the other came up and pulled the scarf off my head.

"Right here," he said, and then, "and three more down in my car."

"That's all? Just clothes?"

Yeah, I'd made space in my walk-in closet and in my bureau, but I'd also shifted my couch around to accommodate his favorite reading chair and had even cleared out one of the cabinets in the kitchen so he could store the Asian-inspired black ceramic plates he was so fond of.

"Yeah—what else was I supposed to bring, my leather sectional?" He laughed as he dragged his suitcases across my hardwood floors, leaving long, scraggly seams in the thick layer of polyurethane.

I cringed, bit back a nasty comment, and then made a mental note to call Joe, my floor guy, and book a date for him to come and buff the scratches out.

Following Kendrick into the bedroom, I said, "Well, no, not the sectional, but I was expecting..."

I really didn't know what I was expecting, but certainly more than what he'd come with.

"Baby," he said, "this is just a temporary situation. All of my belongings are in storage." He came and put his hands on my shoulders. "You have a big space here, yeah. But not enough to handle all of my stuff, and would it even make sense? I mean, once my apartment is finished I would be moving right back in."

I had assumed that this was the beginning of the rest of our lives together and that he would have at least brought a damn lamp or some silverware.

I had imagined that once the apartment was finished that he would have grown so used to being with me, loving me, that we would start making wedding plans and he'd put the apartment on the market.

But I now saw that those were just my silly fantasies.

He could have brought more, he should have brought more. Shit, he wasn't on vacation and I wasn't the concierge level of the Peninsula Hotel. This was a lifestyle change—this was my home!

"You could have brought more than just clothes, Kendrick," I said brightly, planting a sunny smile on my face for added effect. "You could have brought the entertainment center." I pointed toward an empty wall in the living room. "That space there would have been perfect."

Kendrick turned around and considered it for a moment, then grunted and said, "Let me get back downstairs and get the other suitcases."

"I'll help," I said as I followed behind him like an obedient puppy.

Forty-Two

I was sitting on my bed with a dozen or more pamphlets spread out around me.

WHEN GOOD GAY MEN GO STRAIGHT

CURBING YOUR CRAVINGS FOR VAGINA

HOW TO STAY STRICTLY DICKLY: THE PUSSY-FREE DIET

I'd been up all night perusing the dos and don'ts of homosexual living. One expert advised, "Try to keep your male-female friend ratio balanced. Never have too many female friends around you for more than six hours at a time. A woman's energy is very powerful, especially when she has her period. Men (hetero as well as homo) are greatly affected during this time, and the hetero instinct that is built inside us is heightened so much that a homosexual male will begin to fantasize about having sex with females, and a weaker one will actually act on it."

I guess I'm a weaker one.

Another expert explained: "While still in our mother's womb we are female until the second trimester, when our sexual organs begin to fully develop and our bodies reveal if we are to be born male or female. Because we are female first, and most females are closet lesbians, we retain that primal desire first instilled in us while we are still in our mother's womb, and so at times the homosexual male will find himself attracted to or desiring to be with women. It is a natural repercussion of being human; but we as homosexual men must fight to suppress it!"

The meeting took place in the garden-level apartment owned by "Bob," who was exactly how I'd imagined him. Tall, thin, neat, and pale. So pale that he was almost translucent.

"Welcome," he said when he opened the door. A Barbra Streisand tune sailed out from behind him. "Are you here for the meeting?" he asked through his thin pink lips.

"Yes."

"And your name?"

"Noa—I mean Wayne."

"Welcome, Wayne."

The space was tight, but Bob had managed to make it homey. There was a small overstuffed floral love seat and an old steamer trunk being used as a sofa table. Two ivory-colored wing chairs sat on either side of the trunk.

A bamboo ceiling fan whirled lazily above our heads, and in three corners of the room there were towering potted broad-leaf banana plants, giving the space a Havana-like feel.

Beyond the living room was a small hallway that led to a minuscule kitchen, and what I assumed to be the bedroom and bathroom lay beyond that.

"Please sit down," Bob said.

"Thank you." I took one of the wing chairs.

"Can I get you some iced tea, lemonade, or water?"

"Iced tea, please," I said as I crossed my legs and folded my hands in my lap.

Bob came back with a blue glass filled with iced tea and a coaster with daffodils across its face.

I sipped some, smiled, and then thought I should say something. "Nice place," I croaked.

"Thank you," Bob said as he scurried down the hallway and disappeared. On his return he carried three folding chairs.

"Can I help you with that?"

"No, no, I have it," he said as he expertly flipped the chairs open and set them out.

Afterward he looked at his watch, sighed, and then placed his hands on his hips and looked directly at me. "I'll take your payment now."

Was it fair to have to pay for a service before you were even serviced?

Suppose no one showed? Suppose everyone showed and all we did was sit around playing backgammon and singing Broadway show tunes?

"Okay," I said, standing up and pulling my wallet from my back pocket.

By seven fifteen, there were twelve of us, including Bob. After the introductions, the meeting got under way and I was astonished by the stories I heard.

"I've been having sex with women for three years now," a large, burly-looking white man named "Jerry," with a thick mustache and mouselike voice, confessed. "It all started when my lover and I went to South Beach on vacation. He can't really take the sun, you know," he said, and then his voice dropped down to a whisper. "Skin cancer runs in his family." The group moaned and nodded their heads. "Anyway, he left me on the beach because he had a massage appointment, and that's when it happened. I mean, I have always been able to admire a woman without wanting to sleep with her—you know what I mean?"

The men nodded.

"But those women down there, I mean, what the hell do they put in the water? They're just too beautiful for words, and their shapes, my Lord, it's like a cartoonist drew them!"

"It's all of those Cubans!" one man cried out.

"And don't forget the Haitians!" another one said, using his hands to make the shape of a Coca-Cola bottle.

"Well, by the time my lover's massage was over and he was tapping me on the shoulder to come to lunch, I had a full-fledged boner and there was no hiding that from him." Jerry breathed and then turned to the man closest to him, placed a finger on his knee, and said, "I'm very well endowed."

The man next to him, "George," I think his name was, pressed his index and middle fingers against his lips to conceal his smile.

"And just like that," Jerry said with a snap of his fingers, "I was lusting after women. I spent the better part of that vacation avoiding my lover's advances while I tried to get some booty from our chambermaid."

The men gasped.

Another story of female addiction was told by "Norman," a slight Hispanic man with sleek black hair and a long thin nose. He was tall and very good-looking. He reminded me of one of the Abercrombie & Fitch models I'd seen splattered across the fashion magazines.

"I have been gay since I was eight," he started. His accent was heavenly and very, very Central American. "I had been with a woman once, when I was just twelve—she was my nanny."

The men leaned back and grabbed their chests in horror.

"Although I remember the experience to have been a pleasurable one, I had already had relations with the twenty-year-old son of the gardener, so I knew what it was I wanted, and that was a man!"

A cheer went up.

"But last year, while I was traveling to Rome," Norman started, and his eyes swept the group, "first class, of course..."

"But of course," someone interjected.

"How else would you go?" another person said.

Norman continued, "I found myself sitting next to a stunning woman. Dark-haired, with green eyes. Sicilian."

"Ah, yes," someone moaned.

"Her name was—"

"Uh-uh," Bob abruptly chimed in, waving a chastising finger at Norman. "No names. Everyone deserves anonymity, even the shrews that got us into this situation."

Norman bowed his head. "Forgive me," he said. "While her name is not important, the power she exerted over me is."

Norman picked up his glass of iced tea and took a sip before continuing.

"She was a goddess and smelled like Elysian Fields after

a light rain. Her hair was as soft as spun silk. She was perfection."

He took another sip.

"Three hours in, she shared her heartbreaking story of love and loss. Some scoundrel had broken her heart and slept with her sister."

The men shook their heads in dismay.

"She cried on my shoulder and then fell asleep in my arms. Breasts like fresh-baked bread rose and fell beneath her V-neck blouse, and I found myself aroused by the nearness of her."

The men knew the feeling and moaned at the thought of it.

"Later, when the movie was playing and the cabin was dark, her hand found my knee and then climbed my thigh and grabbed a hold of my, my—"

Norman got choked up for a minute.

"You can do it," someone murmured.

"Don't be ashamed, tell it. Release yourself!" another shouted.

"We're here to listen, not to judge!" someone else yelled.

Norman recovered, wiped at his eyes, and then took another sip of his iced tea.

"Her hand found my manhood, massaging it as it had never been massaged before."

I looked at the group, and they were all on the edge of their seats.

"Before I knew it, her head was in my lap and she was giving me the best blow job I'd ever received. I had to bite the pillow to keep from screaming.

"And then she climbed over me and went to the bathroom. I wasn't going to follow—I swear I wasn't—but I couldn't help myself."

Norman dropped his head and began to weep. Bob came over and gave him a hug. "Go on, finish it—purge yourself," he urged.

"I—I slipped into the bathroom with her, and in one fell swoop I became a member of the mile-high club!" Norman blubbered and then crumbled into a weeping mess of a man.

"Women are evil!" someone screamed.

After Norman had composed himself, Bob turned to me. "Wayne, would you like to share your story?" he asked.

I looked down at my hands and then up at the faces that waited expectantly before I quietly confessed, "Beyoncé was the beginning of my homosexual end."

Our assignment was to revisit, if we could, the places that we had had our first homosexual experiences. To relive the joy and then record it in our rainbow-colored journals. "Gay porn is fine," Bob said, "but try to get out to the gay strip clubs. You need to smell the flesh, not just watch it on cable or DVD."

I left that meeting feeling charged and renewed. It was uplifting to know that I wasn't going to have to go through this alone. I would work this program and prayed to God that it would work for me.

Forty-Three

"He's a slob," Crystal whispered to me.

"What?"

"A fucking slob."

"I can't believe it."

"Geneva, I have to pick up after him like he's three years old."

"Really?"

"Socks, shoes, his shitty drawers!"

"Shitty?"

"He's been lying around here for a week, claims he's on vacation."

"Well, maybe he is."

"I don't think so. His father has called here twice, but Kendrick won't speak to him."

"What the hell is that about?"

"I don't know, but what I do know is, Kendrick ain't washed his ass in about four days."

"Stop your lying, Crystal!"

"I don't know who this man is sleeping up in my bed."

"You still sleeping in the bed with him?"

"Hell, no! I'm sleeping on my couch."

"Oh."

"Something is wrong here. I mean, I go to work and he's asleep, I come back home and he's asleep. I know he's eating because there's dishes in the sink and crumbs on the counter."

"Damn."

"And he's drunk up all my liquor."

"Say what?"

"Not that I had much, but what little I did have, he drank."

"Shit!"

"And—and I'm telling you this and no one else—the night he proposed to move in to my place . . ."

"Yeah, yeah?"

"I had to pay for the dinner! He claimed he left his wallet at home, but I swear I saw it in his back pocket when we walked out of the restaurant!"

"Get the fuck out of here!"

"Not only that, this morning he rolls over just as I was leaving for work and asks me if I could leave him a few dollars."

"No, he didn't!"

"Yes, girl."

"Something ain't right, Crystal."

"That's what I'm telling you."

"Look, when shit started going bad with Eric, I tried to hang in there for as long as I could, but it just kept getting worse. I mean, he was fucking around on me, had the women calling the house like I didn't even live there, like he didn't have a wife and son!"

"I remember."

"We were fighting like cats and dogs. Every night was a battle, and then there were the nights when all I could do was cry because he didn't even come home!"

"Hmm."

"I just finally got sick and tired of the fussing and fighting, and besides, I had Little Eric to think about. He didn't need to be growing up in a household filled with so much anger. I had to put myself second and think about the welfare of my child."

"Yeah, well—"

"Things ain't going right. And it doesn't look like it's going to get any better any time soon. You may not have a child, but you do have you, and that's a hell of a lot."

"I know—"

"Don't be putting yourself second to a man who has stopped putting you first in his life. Isn't that what you're always telling me?"

"Yeah, I guess, but—"

"No buts. Take your own advice."

"I hear you."

Forty-Four

I saw Noah for the first time in days. "Hey, Miss Thang!" he sang to me as he stood over the stove cooking an omelet.

"Hey, Miss Thang, yourself," I shot back at him. "It's been a minute," I added as I pulled out one of the kitchen chairs and took a seat.

"I been here all the time—where you been?" he said teasingly.

"Around."

"Uh-huh—got a new man?"

I smiled. "Something like that," I said and then, needing to change the subject, "What about you? How you doing?"

He looked thinner, but his eyes were sparkling.

"Oh, I'm getting better by the moment," he sang and slid the omelet out and onto a plate.

"Really? I didn't know watching massive amounts of porn could do that to you," I said slyly.

But Noah wasn't biting. He totally ignored my sarcastic comment and said, "Can I make an omelet for you too?"

"Sure, why not?" I said and then thought about what it

was I had to do in a few hours. "No, no never mind. I'll grab something later on."

After some mild chitchat, which was mostly bullshit that skirted around our real issues, I headed out and took the train up to Chelsea, to Abimbola and Cassius's loft. We were going to do a test run today, to see how much my stomach could hold. We would use sugar-filled condoms as test subjects.

"Did you give yourself the enema?" Cassius asked after she swung the door open.

"Hello to you too," I said as I breezed past her.

We'd come to understand that I didn't like her and she didn't like me. All the halfhearted attempts at civility had been thrown out the window after I received my down payment and agreed to be their mule.

I assumed that she, like most overly beautiful women, was insecure. I saw how she watched me. I wasn't no slouch: I knew how to carry myself, and I may not have had her beguiling looks, but I was gorgeous, and we both knew it!

"Good morning, Chevy," Abimbola greeted me. He was dressed in a green and gold dashiki. "My sister," he said and embraced me.

"My brother," I said and held him a bit longer, just to get under Cassius's skin.

"Whatever," she said as she brushed by us and disappeared into the bedroom.

"So are you ready for your practice run?" he said as I

followed him into the kitchen. On the table was a silver tray holding forty sugar-filled condoms.

"As ready as I'm ever going to be."

I sat down.

"Okay, now, you did give yourself a good purge last night, yes?"

I nodded my head. I was on that toilet for nearly three hours. I thought I was going to shit my guts out!

"Empty," I said.

"Good."

Abimbola pushed the tray over to me. "Okay, take your time."

I look at the condoms and then at him. "Can I have a glass of water?"

"No, no water. It will fill your stomach. The condoms are oiled, so they will slip down your throat easily. Just take your time."

"Oil?"

"Canola oil."

"Oh."

I picked up the first condom and examined it before placing it on my tongue and rolling it to the back of my throat. I swallowed, and for a moment I thought that my throat was not going to cooperate, and then it relaxed and the condom slid effortlessly down my throat.

"You see, it is simple. Next one, c'mon, next one."

"Slow your roll, Bola," I snapped as I picked up the next condom and popped it into my mouth.

Forty-Five

I was standing staring out at a beautiful Saturday morning, a cigarette in one hand and a cup of Dunkin Donuts coffee in the other, feeling quite content and musing on what it was I would do with the day.

Now that Little Eric was gone, my house remained tidy all week long and I had no pressing laundry woes. My day was free!

Just as I was about to take another long drag of my cigarette, the phone began to ring.

"Hello?"

"Geneva Holliday?"

Bill collector, I thought, and hurriedly changed my voice. "No, no, Geneva gone away. No be back till next year," I said, trying hard to disguise my voice.

"I know it's you, Geneva," the voice said.

"No speak good English—you call back next year," I said, and was about to hang up when the voice said, "This is Miriam Baxter, director of the Upper West Side division of Calorie Counters."

My mouth dropped open. "Who?"

"Miriam Baxter," the authoritative voice repeated.

"Yes?" I said stupidly.

"We met a year ago," she snapped. "I was just an enlister then, but I've worked my way up through the ranks to director. Now, I have had several conversations with your support counselor"—there was some shuffling of papers—"Nadine. And she has told me that although you've promised to return to the program, you have failed to do so. Which in my book makes you a liar."

"'Scuse me, but you have no—"

"Not only a liar, but I assume since you have not returned to the program that you're a fat liar!"

"Hey, hey, I don't have to put—"

"A blimp of a liar!"

"What the—"

"A thigh-rubbing, waddling hog of a liar!"

I was stunned mute.

"Now, my success depends on how many women I can keep in this program. Whether you lose your blubber or not is of no concern to me."

"I—I—"

"Shut up!" Miriam screamed. "Now, I have a ninety-eight percent attendance rate. Anything below that and I don't get my twenty-five-thousand-dollar bonus at Christmas time, or my trophy, and I have received a trophy every year for the past four years!"

I cowered on my couch as I pressed the phone against my ear.

"Let me tell you one thing, Miss Geneva Holliday, you will not hamper my winning streak, do you hear me! You will show up at the Upper West Side office this afternoon, pay your ten dollars, weigh your fat black ass in, listen to the encouraging stories the other fat women have to share, and then come back the following Saturday and the Saturday after that, until you've dropped a dress size or gone bankrupt, whichever comes first!"

My lips flapped helplessly, but no words came out.

"Am I clear, Ms. Holliday?"

"Yes, yes," I squeaked, finally finding my voice.

"Now if your counselor reports otherwise, you'll have to deal with me. And you don't want to deal with me, Ms. Holliday. I have ten years of military experience. Covert military experience. I will come to your place of residence, take you out, and not leave a fingerprint or a drop of your blood on your filthy carpet."

I looked down at the carpet that hadn't been cleaned in months.

"So we understand each other?"

"Uh-huh," I said, nodding my head vigorously up and down.

"Good. Have a nice day."

I heard a click and then a dial tone.

I thought of calling Crystal, but then realized how absurd I would sound. Shit, I'd just lived through it and it sounded absurd to me. No one would believe this.

Shaken, I pulled myself up and onto my quivering legs and walked into the kitchen.

Pulling open the freezer door, I retrieved a pint of Ben & Jerry's, walked it over to the microwave, popped the container in for five minutes, stirred the creamy liquid with my finger, and then guzzled it.

Forty-Six

"I'm sorry, Ms. Crystal."

I blinked at the sound of Noah's voice. "Noah?" I said unbelievingly.

"Curse me out if you have to—I won't blame you one bit. In fact, I know I probably deserve it."

I grinned. "Yeah, you know you do," I said. "What the hell is going on with you?"

"Oh, Miss Thing, if you only knew," Noah said wistfully.

"Did you break up with Zhan?"

"Oh, no, nothing like that. In fact, he's coming in on Labor Day."

"Really? That's just two days away."

Noah was quiet for a while. "Is it? I'm so behind. Where did the summer go?"

"I don't know, Noah—the older you get, the quicker time just seems to fly by."

"You said it, sweetie."

"Well, are you going to tell me what drama you've been going through, or are we going to dance around it?"

"I will, one day, but not today."

"Okay, I respect that. Just know that I love you and I'm here for you."

"I know you are, baby, and I appreciate it. And know that I'm here for you as well."

"I know you are."

We basked in the glow of our commitment as friends for a minute.

"So how's your roommate doing?"

"Chevy? Don't you know?"

"Nah, she hasn't returned any of my phone calls. Last time I saw her I was bailing her out of jail."

"Get the hell out of here!" Noah screamed, and I could hear the kitchen chair being dragged across his expensive kitchen floor tiles as he prepared himself to get comfortable while I dished the dirt. "Do tell!"

"You don't know about it, and she's living right there in your house?"

"Girl, *pleeeeeezzzze*! Ms. Chevy and I pass each other in this house like strangers in the night, like ships on the sea—"

"I get it, Noah, damn."

"So what happened?"

"She hopped the turnstile."

"Get the fuck outta here! That is a classless act, something I would never think Ms. Chevy would stoop to."

"I know, I was shocked too. But you know for yourself that she ain't working."

"Well, I figured that out when she started sleeping until noon all week long. But her not working ain't stopping her from shopping."

"What you saying?"

"I'm saying she comes in here almost every day loaded down with bags."

"What?"

"Am I speaking a foreign language?"

"No, not at all. Didn't you say you thought she had a new man?"

"Shoot, knowing Chevy's freaky ass, it could be a woman."

I had to laugh at that. "Stop it, Noah. Chevy is a card-carrying heterosexual."

"Yeah, okay—you never know what's going on behind someone's groove."

I had to think about that for a while. What Noah said was true: I was living testimony of that. I never dreamed in a million years that I would be shacking up with a man and giving him money, but here I was doing just that.

"Well, I guess you're right," I said meekly.

"So what's going on with you, Ms. Ting-a-ling?"

"Oh, nothing. Nothing at all," I lied. "Just working my ass off."

"And what about that fine man of yours?"

"Ha, ha." I laughed nervously at the mention of Kendrick. "Oh, he's still fine," I said.

"Umph, I know he is," Noah said in a lustful voice. "You better keep a tight rein on that buck, or I'll whisk him right from beneath your nose!" Noah teased.

"You do and I'll kick your ass!" I said back with a laugh.

"You'll try, at least!"

We taunted each other for a few more minutes.

"We have to get together before Labor Day," I said.

"Well, that just leaves today and tomorrow," Noah said.

"Well, let's get together on Sunday, then," I said.

"Good for me."

"I'll let Geneva know. Will you tell Chevy?"

"Well, I'll slip a note under her door."

"Better yet, stick it into one of the million pairs of shoes she owns—you know she tries them *all* on every night before she goes to sleep. It's like a bedtime prayer for her."

"Miss Crystal, you need help, girl!"

Forty-Seven

Kendrick played possum until Crystal donned her sweats and left the house for a run. She would have opted to use her treadmill had it not been for the mountain of clothes he had thrown across it.

His eyes rolled to the clock. It was just after ten, and the city was already bustling and loud.

His head was pounding, but that did not stop his progress. He pulled himself up into a sitting position and scratched at his balls.

He supposed it had been a few days since he'd last showered, but he couldn't remember just how many. The days and nights seemed to stream into each other. Even as he sat there scratching, he couldn't remember what day of the week it was.

Climbing out of bed, he stumbled to the bathroom and took a long piss. Most of which ended up on the toilet seat and the white tiled floor below.

After he turned on the faucet for the tub, he pushed the stopper down into the drain and went off to the kitchen, opened the refrigerator door, and peered inside.

There was a loaf of whole wheat bread, a half-empty

bottle of low-fat milk, a bowl of sliced watermelon, and a container of leftover egg foo young.

He removed the egg foo young, watermelon, and wheat bread and placed all of the items on the table. He then began greedily stuffing the food down his throat with his bare hands.

After he felt that his stomach was full, he left the scraps on the table, walked past the open refrigerator door, and moved into the living room, where he plopped himself down onto the couch, snatched the remote control up from the table, and turned the television on.

He'd been missing the goings-on in the world, so he flicked through the channels until he stumbled onto CNN. But soon his eyelids began to droop and he dropped off to sleep.

When he awoke due to an overly loud Nissan commercial, he jumped up from the couch, frantically looking around for the source of the noise. Finding it, he grabbed the remote and pressed the off button.

Standing there in the early-afternoon light of the living room, he tried to decipher a strange sound filling the apartment.

"Sounds like running water," he mumbled to the walls before turning into the kitchen and looking down into the bone-dry kitchen sink.

Heading off to the bathroom, he walked across the now sopping wet bedroom carpet to find that the tub was overflowing. "Shit," he muttered under his breath, but failed to turn the faucet off. Instead, he grabbed the bath towels and tossed them down onto the floor, which was covered in three inches of water.

When the towels sank helplessly to the bottom, he tossed the bath mat, washcloths, and face towels down and watched as they succumbed to the same fate.

"Fuck it," he said as he moved to the basin, where he haphazardly brushed his teeth and washed his face.

With no thought to the rest of his body or the scraggly beard that covered his face, he moved back into the bedroom and dressed himself in a pair of green chinos, a black T-shirt, and a pair of black Nike sneakers and started toward the door. Realizing he didn't have a dime on him, he backtracked to the bedroom and saw that Crystal had left a fifty-dollar bill on the dresser, which he greedily snatched up before helping himself to her jewelry chest, from which he lifted a pair of diamond and ruby earrings, a solid gold bangle, and a string of freshwater pearls.

Forty-Eight

I eased myself back into the chair and looked into Abimbola's expectant face.

"How do you feel?"

I thought about it for a minute. Besides the way my stomach bulged over the rim of my pants, I felt okay. I mean I felt full, in a strange sort of way. "Okay, I guess."

"Good!" he exclaimed, slapping his hands together. "Very, very good!"

In fact, I felt sleepy. Yes, what I wanted to do was sleep. My eyes drooped.

"I see you have niggeritis, huh?" Abimbola leaned forward and peered at me. "But you cannot lie down at this time," he said, his face turning to stone. "This whole run must be a simulation of what you will be doing on Labor Day." He abruptly stood up. "You must remain in a seated position for the next"—he stopped to consider the gold Rolex on his arm—"six hours, at least."

"Six hours?" I whined. I needed to lie down in the worst way.

"Yes, six hours—no less!"

I rolled my eyes at him and rubbed my stomach.

"No, no, you must not interfere with the packages," he said in an alarmed voice as he slapped my hand away.

"What else can't I do?" I said sarcastically.

"Look, come into the living room. You can sit in the recliner there. It's just like being in first class."

I perked up. "Will I be flying first class?" I asked.

"No," Abimbola said sternly.

I settled myself comfortably into the recliner and dropped right off to sleep.

I woke to some confusion—the loud voice of Abimbola and Cassius's screeching.

"I told you, you bitch, that we do not service clients from this location!"

"I told you not to call me that!"

"I'll call you whatever I feel like calling you!" Abimbola screamed back, and then there was the distinctive sound of a palm making contact with a cheek and then a thump as Cassius's body hit the wall.

"I hate you!" she screamed and came running from the room. I squeezed my eyes shut.

"Now that you've already told him where to come, you sell him the shit and get him out of here quick, bitch!"

The bedroom door slammed shut on Cassius's weeping.

Two minutes later the bedroom door opened again and Abimbola's voice boomed through the apartment. "I have to make a run. I'll be back in an hour," he said and then stormed out the front door.

Cassius screamed something in French that I knew wasn't "I love you, honey."

Soon after Abimbola stormed out, Cassius's cell phone rang.

"Hello? No, you have to come up. I cannot make an exchange in public. Top floor."

Cassius rushed off to the bedroom. I heard the sound of running water from the en suite and then smelled the scent of Chanel No. 5, Cassius's signature scent. No doubt she was straightening herself up after Abimbola's ass whipping.

In less than a minute a steady knocking came at the door.

"Who?" Cassius asked through the five inches of steel door.

"It's me."

I opened my eyes a bit.

Cassius pulled the door back on its hinges and said, "Come in." And when she stepped aside and I saw who it was, my heart almost stopped in my chest.

Forty-Nine

After my run, I stopped at Starbucks and bought a white chocolate caffè mocha. I didn't want to go home, so I sat myself down at one of the outside tables to people watch and think.

My conversation with Geneva flicked through my mind as I sipped the sweet coffee. She was right. Down in the deepest part of my heart, I'd already known the truth. I guess I just needed someone who loved and cared for me to say it out loud.

Not that the truth did anything to assuage the love I'd built over the years for Kendrick. In fact, it made me even more concerned about what it was he was going through and why he felt unable to share his problems with me.

It was to the point now that we hardly spoke, and when I did try to initiate a conversation, the only responses I got from him were grunts.

Maybe he was going through a midlife crisis? I mean, he was forty-two years old. Did it happen that early on? Maybe it did.

Maybe he was depressed. Maybe business wasn't going well. Lord knew the market had been going up and down like a seesaw.

Whatever it was, it was real bad.

I drained the last bits of the coffee from the cup and tossed it into a trash can as I started my short walk home.

I would try to talk to him one last time. I'd offer my help, and if he felt like I couldn't help him, then I'd offer to find someone who could.

And after that, I'd offer to help him pack, because as much as I loved him, I loved myself more.

"Hello, Mrs. Burgess," I greeted the sophisticated-looking white-haired woman who was standing outside, cradling her small poodle in her arms. Mrs. Burgess had been a resident in the apartment below me since before the building had gone co-op. And I swear, I'd never seen that dog out of her arms. I wondered if it could walk and mused even further about where and how it relieved itself.

"Ms. Atkins!" she screeched, and I almost jumped out of my skin.

"Yes?" I said, shrinking away from her.

"You have flooded my apartment!"

I just blinked at her. "What?" I said stupidly, believing that the old woman had finally lost her marbles.

"My apartment is under half a foot of water," she screamed, and then hugged her dog closer to her breast. "Coco could have drowned!"

"Mrs. Burgess, are you sure—"

"Of course I'm sure! I had to call the super. He's up in your apartment at this very moment."

I didn't wait for any more. I dashed to the elevator and jabbed frantically at the button.

"Everything is ruined, everything!" Mrs. Burgess hollered at my back. "I'm going to call my lawyer—you'll see!"

My apartment door sat wide open on its hinges. As I approached, I could hear voices inside.

"Hello? Hello?" I yelled as I gingerly stepped through the door. My sneakers made a squishing sound on the floor, and I looked down to see that I was standing in water that came nearly up to my ankles. "Shit!"

"Ms. Atkins?" The super's voice came to me from the living room.

"Yes," I said as I waded down the hall toward him. Passing the kitchen, I saw that the refrigerator door was wide open as well. I reached my hand in and pushed it shut. "Yeah, it's me," I said, my voice filled with dismay. "What happened, Henry, did a pipe break?" I asked when I was standing in front of him.

"No, Ms. Atkins, that's what I thought when I got the call. I mean, this is an old building, and things like that do happen. Like last winter, when . . ."

I stared at the hefty Puerto Rican building attendant. How long was he going to take to get to what my problem was? It could take all day, and I didn't have that much time or patience. I threw the palm of my hand up into his face. "Did a pipe break?" I said again from between clenched teeth.

Henry studied my palm for a while, and then his face went beet red. "No, Ms. Atkins. You left the faucet on."

"What!" I screamed and then shoved past him and into the bathroom. Sure enough, the water was slowly draining away.

"You see?" Henry said, using his wrench to point at the tub. "You must have forgotten."

"I didn't forget shit!" I bellowed at him. "That no-good, low-down asshole who's living with me finally decided to get up off his lazy ass and wash it!"

I lost it. My hands flailed in the air as I jumped up and down in the river of water.

Henry was horrified and began backing slowly out of the bathroom. "It's okay, Ms. Atkins. It's all right," he said in a calming voice.

"No, it's not. No, it's not all right!" I cried. "Everything is ruined, everything!"

"I'll call some of the maintenance guys to come up with the pump so we can get this water out of here," Henry said, and then he was gone, shutting the front door behind him.

I screamed until my throat hurt, and then I cried until a knock came at the door and Henry hollered, "I'm back, with José and Sanchez, and we have the pump. We going to make it all better for you."

With a pump, Henry, Sanchez, and José were going to make it all better for me? The laughter came then, spilling out of me as quickly as the water had spilled from the bathtub faucet. "Well," I yelled as I stumbled toward the front door and swung it open, "if I'd known that all I needed was a pump and you guys to make it all better for me, I would have flooded my apartment a long time ago!"

Henry and the other men exchanged glances. I'm sure I looked and sounded like a madwoman.

"Maybe we come back later, when you're—um, feeling better?" Henry said.

"No, no, I'm feeling just fine. Fine and dandy, in fact!" I said, throwing my hands up in the air with glee. "Come in, come in!"

They hesitated, but then Henry made the sign of the cross and stepped across the threshold and the others cautiously followed.

Fifty

Kendrick could see that there was someone sitting in the chair. He couldn't tell if it was a woman or a man, though. His vision was blurry, as it always was after he'd gone too long without a hit of Hades.

Kendrick squinted at the figure in the chair. "Is that Abim—" he started.

"No, it's not," Cassius said curtly and grabbed him by the hand, dragging him into the kitchen. She made a point of throwing the possum-playing Chevy a warning look as she went.

"Now, how much today?" Cassius said, once they were in the kitchen and out of Chevy's eyesight.

"Um, um," Kendrick muttered as he dug through his pockets, pulling out the fifty and the jewelry he'd stolen from Crystal.

Cassius shook her head. Kendrick was full-blown addicted. His nose was running and he could barely keep his eyes open. His beard had grown out full and bushy, he was in desperate need of a haircut, and as far as Cassius could see, Kendrick hadn't even taken the time to pull a comb through his hair, which was now a matted Afro.

What a shame, Cassius thought to herself. He'd been such a good-looking man. And a good fuck at that.

"I got this," Kendrick said as he weaved and bobbed in place.

Cassius looked down at his meager offering. "What the hell am I supposed to do with this?" she said, her voice filled with revulsion.

"Take it and give me a vial," Kendrick said, sounding offended.

"This wouldn't even pay for a quarter of a vial," Cassius spat. "You're wasting my time."

Kendrick looked down at the money and jewelry. He tightened his fingers around it and pushed it toward Cassius. "Please, c'mon now—you know we been doing business for a long time. Can't you just help me out this one time?"

Cassius shook her head pitifully. "No. I'm sorry, Kendrick, I can't."

The first rule of the game was never to give in. No one gets a break or a handout, because that is like feeding a stray cat. Everybody knows that once you feed a stray it comes back every day.

"C'mon now, Cassius, c'mon," Kendrick pleaded, hopping back and forth on his feet like a two-year-old.

Chevy couldn't believe what she was hearing. Kendrick Greene, an addict! Look at that, she thought to herself. Crystal always coming down on her, telling her the right way to live, and here she was, dating a junkie.

Wait until she saw her again. She was going to smear it all across her pretty little face!

"I can't, Kendrick, really," Cassius said, shaking her head. "Now you have to go."

Kendrick just stood there staring at her for a while before calmly placing the money and jewelry back into his pocket. "Okay, okay, then. What do you want me to do for it?"

Cassius gave him a strained look. "Only thing I want you to do is leave."

"You want to fuck me, don't you?" Kendrick sneered and pulled his shirt over his head. "Fine. I'll fuck you for a vial!"

Cassius made a face at him and then stifled a laugh behind her hand. "I don't want to fuck you. Look at you. You're disgusting!" she spat.

"Oh, now you wanna act like you don't want it?" Kendrick said as he unzipped his pants.

"Stop," Cassius said. Her voice was beginning to shake. Kendrick was frightening her. "You're embarrassing yourself."

Kendrick dropped his pants and stepped out of them. He had no underwear on, and his dick hung limp between his legs.

"So you want me to eat you out? That's what you want!" Kendrick took a step toward Cassius.

Cassius tried to remain cool, but she was scared to death. She thought of calling out to Chevy for help, but that would probably be futile. Chevy wouldn't raise a finger to help her, even if Kendrick tried to rape her or, worse yet, kill her.

"Look, Kendrick, Abimbola will be back any second

now, and if he walks in here and finds you naked, he's going to kill you."

Kendrick balled his fists and placed them on his hips. He was beaten. He chewed at his bottom lip and bounced his head up and down. "All right, all right," he sputtered. Turning his back to Cassius, he bent over to retrieve his pants, mooning her.

Cassius turned her head away, embarrassed for him.

Pulling his pants up, he then reached for his shirt and pulled that on too. Turning back to Cassius, he offered her a boyish grin. "I'm sorry," he whispered.

Cassius was taken off-guard. "What?"

"I behaved horribly. You're right. I should be embarrassed, and I am," he said as he extended his hand to her. "No hard feelings?" he said, smiling sweetly.

Cassius looked down at his hand. She was confused, but mood swings were common in people who used Hades.

"None," Cassius said and placed her hand in Kendrick's.

They shook, and then the smile suddenly slipped from Kendrick's face as he roughly jerked Cassius toward him and promptly butted her in the head.

Cassius's eyes registered fleeting surprise before they rolled up and into her head and she fell unconscious to the floor.

Kendrick wasted no time. He shot out of the kitchen and nearly fell as he scurried across the hall and into the bedroom, which contained only a bed and a nightstand. He ripped the drawer open. Empty. He tugged it out and looked beneath it. Nothing.

Throwing it to the floor, he turned to the bed. Like a wild man he ripped the linens off the mattress. Then he tore the mattress from the bed. Still nothing.

He went through the closets, tearing the clothes from the hangers and tossing them to the floor. Nothing. He peered into the dark crevices of shoes. Still he came up empty.

Kendrick ran out of the room and back into the kitchen, where he tripped over the still-unconscious Cassius. His head struck the edge of the counter. He hardly felt the pain, but he was annoyed by the blood that was trickling into his eyes, and he levied a kick on Cassius because of it. "Bitch!" he bellowed when the toe of his sneaker made contact with her thigh.

Cassius grunted but her eyes remained closed.

Kendrick opened all of the kitchen cabinets, but all were empty except for a tin of coffee. That he opened, shaking the contents out and into the sink.

"It's got to be here somewhere!" he screamed and then bent over Cassius. "Where is it, bitch, where!"

Cassius didn't flinch.

"Think, Ken, think. Now, you're a smart man—where would you hide your drugs?"

Kendrick pounded his fists into his head.

"Where, where!" he screamed, and his voice bounced off the walls and back at him.

After some time, Kendrick's head popped up and a broad smile spread across his face. "Ah, you smart bitch," he said as he knelt down beside Cassius and turned her over and onto her back.

He tore her blouse open, revealing a black lace bra. He studied her 38-Cs for a moment and then gingerly removed her breasts from the bra cups. Nothing.

"Okay, okay," he said and then pinched his lips together as he tried to slip his hand down inside the waistband of her skirt. He couldn't get his hand down far enough.

Frustrated, he yanked his hand out and then, as if suddenly slapped with the smart stick, he pushed up the hem of her skirt.

"Voilà!" Kendrick bellowed.

There, beneath her skirt and in a custom-made thigh holster, were forty vials of Hades.

"Eureka!"

Fifty-One

He wasn't going to kill me too! No, man, not me! When he ran into the bedroom and started rifling through and turning over shit, I made a break for it. Slipped right past him and out the door.

I couldn't even believe what I'd heard. Kendrick was a stone-cold addict! Damn, what it must be like to be addicted to something so hard, you're willing to degrade yourself like that. Begging and pleading and offering up your body!

I should really call the police, I thought. I mean, Cassius was a bitch and all, but she didn't deserve to die. She had to be dead. I mean, I saw her sprawled out on the floor. She looked dead, anyway. It wasn't like I had any time to stop and check her pulse or anything.

But sometimes people ain't dead—they're just unconscious. If I called the cops now, maybe they could save her.

Yeah, yeah, I'd call the cops. I didn't have to give my name—I knew that much.

But wait, my fingerprints were there. They'd dust for

fingerprints. That's what they did at crime scenes, right? I didn't need any more blemishes on my record!

Damn, she was just gonna have to die, 'cause I ain't done nothing but swallowed some sugar.

Sugar? Oh, shit—I had to get me some Ex-Lax and get this mess out of me.

Fifty-Two

When the phone rang, I almost jumped out of my skin. I looked at the door. It was pretty well barricaded. I'd dragged the couch over and pushed it up against it, and then for good measure I'd piled the kitchen chairs on top of the couch.

I wasn't taking any chances.

"Hello?" I whispered into the phone.

"Well, I'm sitting here in five inches of water," Crystal said.

I was relieved that it was Crystal and not the Calorie Counters militia.

"What?" I said, my eyes watching the front door.

"That bastard left the tub running and flooded my apartment," she said in a voice that was so calm, it almost sounded crazed.

"Um, are you okay, Crystal?" I asked as I walked over to the window and peered down into the courtyard.

"Sure, fine," she said calmly. "I have thousands of dollars' worth of damage and loss, and I'm just fine."

I walked to the other window and looked down at the sidewalk.

"So did he fall asleep or something?"

"No, nothing like that. He just turned it on and walked out."

"What—he did what?"

"He turned on the water and walked the fuck out and flooded my apartment. Of course, all his shit is in storage. The only thing of his that's ruined are his 'dry clean only' clothes," Crystal said, and then let out a crazed laugh.

I looked at the phone. "Do you need me to come over?" I asked, even though I was petrified of leaving the apartment.

"No, I'll come to you," she said and then hung up.

I looked at the phone again and then pressed end.

Two minutes later the phone rang again. I snatched it up and said, "Crystal, can you bring some potato chips when you come?"

"I'll be bringing my foot to put up your ass!" Miriam screamed from the other end.

That was it for me. I threw the phone down, snatched my pocketbook up from the kitchen table, and bolted.

It took me no time to throw the chairs off and push the couch to one side. So before you could say boo—I was out the door.

Fifty-Three

"What are you doing down here?" I said as I approached Geneva, who was shifting nervously from foot to foot as she lit a fresh cigarette with the butt of another.

She turned on me; her eyes were wild and darting all over the place.

"Let's go, Crystal," Geneva said and grabbed at my arm.

"Hey," I cried and tried to snatch my arm away from her, but she held tight. "What the hell is wrong with you?"

Geneva kept walking. "I can't be standing on this corner out in the open," she barked. "It's not safe for me." She began walking quickly away.

"What are you talking about?" I asked, finally freeing myself from her death grip.

Geneva turned on me. "If I tell you what I've been going through over the past few weeks, you're not going to believe me. You're going to say it's my guilt eating at me and playing tricks on my mind, but I know it's not!" Geneva said, and her index finger shot up in the air for emphasis. "Now, if I say it's not safe to stand here, it's not safe to stand here." Geneva's tone was stern and serious.

"Okay, okay," I said and looked cautiously around me.

Shoot, she had me feeling paranoid now. "Well, why don't we just go upstairs to your place," I suggested as I moved alongside her.

"Uh-uh, I can't be there right now."

"So where are we going to go?" I said, coming to a full stop and placing my hands on my hips.

Geneva stopped walking, tossed her cigarette butt to the ground, and then shook another one from the pack before turning around to face me. "I don't know," she said as she popped it between her lips and lit it.

"Geneva, what's going on?" I asked again, but all I got for a response was a shake of her head before she turned around and started walking again. "Well, we can go to one of the restaurants, sit outside and have something to eat. It's a beautiful day and—"

Geneva turned on me. Something primal had been released in her eyes. "Have you not been listening to me? I cannot be out in the open." She spoke slowly and carefully, as if I were learning disabled.

"Well, we don't have to eat outside. We can get a table inside."

"It's just not safe for me to be anywhere in the city right now," she huffed, and then her head snapped around suddenly.

"What?" I asked, terrified.

"Did you hear that?"

"Hear what?" I said, looking frantically around.

Geneva started walking again and mumbling something like "I thought I heard nunchucks."

"What?"

"Nothing, nothing," she said and broke into a run.
"Where are we going!"
"Brooklyn!" she yelled back over her shoulder before turning right and breaking hard for the subway station.
"Brooklyn?" I said, coming to a halt again.
The last thing I could hear her say before she disappeared down the steps was "Call Noah—tell him we're coming."

Fifty-Four

Chaka Khan was blowing my walls down from my hi-fi as I lay stretched out on my couch, snapping my fingers to the music while my other hand ushered my glass of wine to and from my lips.

Who knew just talking about my problem could make me feel almost normal again? That's not to say that my mind hadn't wandered. Not to say that I hadn't had a craving or two, because I had.

The first step to recovery is admitting you have a problem. So I'd openly admitted it, and that first step really felt wonderful, and that's why I was lying there, basking in Chaka and Pinot Noir.

Zhan would be there in just two more days. I could hardly wait. Just having him there would help to get this monkey off my back. I'd have to tell him, of course, but he loved me and I was sure he'd understand, and . . .

Ring, ring, ring.

"Hello?"

"Noah? I can hardly hear you. Can you turn the music down, please!"

"Stop your screaming, Chevy." Rolling my eyes, I plucked up the remote for the hi-fi and lowered the volume. "Sorry, Ms. Chaka, Ms. Drama is on the phone," I said, loud enough for Chevy to hear. "Now what's the problem?"

"The problem is, I think Kendrick just killed this woman."

I yawned. "I thought you stopped watching the soaps?"

"You're so funny," she said calmly before screaming, "I'm serious, Noah!"

"Okay, you're serious." I lifted my hand and literally wiped the grin off my face. "Now I am too. Now, who is Kendrick?"

"Kendrick Greene, Crystal's boyfriend."

I just smirked. "You been smoking again?"

"I ain't high, Noah. I'm serious. I saw him do it!"

The call-waiting signal beeped in my ear, but Ms. Drama did sound serious, so whoever it was would have to wait.

"Where?" I asked.

"In this apartment in Chelsea."

"What were you doing there?"

"I was . . ."

Uh-huh. Chevy was someplace she had no business being, I thought after she took an eternity to answer.

"I-I was visiting my friend," she stammered, "the one he killed."

"Are you shitting me?"

"No," she whined.

"Did you call the police?" I was up and pacing the floor now, near hysterics. "Are you hurt? Did that bastard hurt you?"

"No, no," she stammered. "But she's lying dead right on the kitchen floor!"

"Okay, okay. You have to call the police, Chevy."

"I-I can't."

"What? Why?"

"Please deposit twenty-five cents to continue this call," the recorded voice instructed, but I knew she wouldn't. Miss Chevy didn't have a dime to her name, never mind a quarter.

Fifty-Five

Geneva and I had been on the train for about twenty minutes when we pulled into the 14th Street station. Saturday commuters piled in, loaded down with Loehmann's, Banana Republic, and Gap shopping bags filled with new fall merchandise and the ragtag, half-priced last bits of summer attire.

I felt uncomfortable. My feet were wet, and since I hadn't had a chance to change out of my jogging gear, the sweat I'd worked up during my run had dried sticky around my neck and deep inside my armpits. I kept my upper arms pressed tightly to my body as I prayed that my deodorant would hold out for at least another half hour until we got to Brooklyn. There I could take a shower and throw on something of Noah's.

My eyes flitted over the faces that either looked back at me or studied the advertisements overhead. Some people were engrossed in paperback best sellers, while others bopped their heads to the music streaming from their Discmans.

I leaned back a little further into the seat, and that's when I saw Chevy. Or at least it looked like Chevy. Standing at the far end of the car, back pressed up against the door, she wore an expression on her face that seemed strained. I squinted and then nudged Geneva.

Geneva nearly jumped out of her seat, and when she turned to look at me her eyes were as wide as saucers. "What?" she said breathlessly as she grabbed at her chest.

"What is wrong with you?"

"You just startled me," she said, wiping the perspiration from her forehead.

"Doesn't that look like Chevy standing over there?" I said, nodding my head in her direction. Geneva strained her neck this way and that and then shouted, "Chevy!" And a dozen eyes fell on us.

Geneva could be so uncouth at times.

"Shh," I pleaded and nudged her again. "Do you have to be so loud?"

Chevy looked around quickly and I noticed that she had the same haunted look on her face that Geneva was sporting.

"Over here, Chevy!" Geneva shouted out again and shot her hand up into the air and began waving.

More eyes turned in our direction.

Chevy finally spotted us and started making her way over.

When she broke through the crowd and was standing in front of us, all Geneva and I could do was sit there with our mouths hanging open.

"Where y'all headed?" Chevy asked, offering us a nervous smile.

We couldn't say a thing; our eyes were locked on

Chevy's belly, which was bulging out of her size-six pants like she was five months pregnant.

Chevy's eyes followed ours, and then she quickly brought one hand up to rest on the protuberance. "I'm just bloated," she said before we could compose ourselves to ask.

"Bloated?" Geneva said, reaching out and slowly pushing Chevy's hand aside. "That looks more like a *baby* to me."

Chevy slapped her hand away. "I ain't pregnant. You crazy?" She laughed nervously. "Just retaining water." She tried in vain to tug her waist-long shirt down over the swell of her belly.

"Really?" I asked. I wasn't sure about that. Maybe this was why she had been AWOL.

"Yes, really," she snapped back. Then she gave me a strange look.

"Why are you looking at me like that?" I asked.

"Nothing," she said quickly and shifted her eyes to Geneva. "So where are you all going?"

"Brooklyn." Geneva's answer was curt as she continued to stare at Chevy's belly.

"Brooklyn? For what?" Chevy was taken aback. "Y'all don't ever go to Brooklyn."

"Well, my apartment got flooded and—"

In the middle of my explanation we pulled into the Spring Street station and I looked up to see Chevy's attention snatched away by boarding passengers. I looked over and saw that Geneva was distracted as well.

"What is going on with you two?" I bellowed. "What y'all got, the mob after you or something?"

Chevy's eyes popped in their sockets. "Shh, don't be saying shit like that."

"Yeah, you don't know who's around," Geneva said in a conspiratorial tone.

Utica Avenue couldn't come soon enough.

Noah swung the door open and we were greeted by the scent of simmering oil and the mellow sounds of Luther Vandross.

"Hey!" he squealed when he saw all of us. "What a surprise!" He pressed quick kisses onto our cheeks. "What did I do to deserve this honor?" He beamed.

Chevy stepped quickly around me and came face-to-face with Noah. Her eyes swung angrily between the glass of wine he held and his face. "What's wrong with you, Ms. Drama?" he asked.

"Have you forgotten what I called and told you on the phone?" she said from between clenched teeth.

The brightness in Noah's face went dark. "Oh—oh my God, yes," he said and hurriedly stepped around Chevy and came to me. "Oh, Ms. Crystal, you must be beside yourself." He wrapped one arm around me and guided me to the living room.

"Well, yes, I mean, all of my stuff is ruined—" I began but then remembered that I hadn't been able to reach Noah on my cell phone before I went down into the subway station, so how could he know about my apartment catastrophe?

"Stuff?" Noah said, his head jerking back.

Noah's head swiveled to Chevy, whose mouth opened and closed like that of a fish out of water. "Ms. Drama said that Kendrick—" Noah began and then stopped and turned back to me. "Do you know about what Kendrick did?"

Yeah, I knew what he did. He flooded my apartment, and I was just about to voice that outwardly when Geneva, who was peering out the front window, spouted, "He flooded her damn apartment, that's what he did."

"Flooded your apartment!" Noah and Chevy cried out together, and then exchanged strange looks.

"Yeah," I said slowly, feeling more and more like I had landed in the Twilight Zone.

Noah grimaced and threw Chevy a long, wicked look. "You see, Ms. Drama, you always starting some shit. Now, why you wanna lie—"

"I didn't lie!" Chevy screamed. "I was there when he did it!"

"You were in my apartment?" I said stupidly.

"Not in your apartment. Down on Seventeenth Street at the loft—"

"What loft?"

"Ms. Drama called me up a wreck, saying she had just witnessed a murder—"

"What!" Geneva and I shouted together, and Geneva came running over and flopped down on the couch beside me.

"Who'd you see get murdered?" Geneva probed, her eyes wide.

Chevy took a breath. "This girl named Cassius," she said slowly, all the while looking at me.

"What does that have to do with Kendrick?" I asked, confused.

"He's the one that did it," Chevy said.

Fifty-Six

First Crystal's face went blank, and then she began to laugh hysterically.

Geneva laughed too, but she stopped when she saw that my lips hadn't cracked a smile.

Noah's face registered about twenty different emotions in just as many seconds; I knew he didn't know what to believe.

"Your pregnancy must have you seeing things," Crystal declared after she'd wiped the tears from her face.

"Pregnancy?" Noah piped, and his eyes fell on my swollen stomach. "No, you didn't go and get yourself knocked up, Ms. Drama!" he shrieked and threw his hands over his mouth.

"I am not pregnant!" I screamed and marched over and snatched up Noah's half-finished glass of wine and guzzled it.

Turning to Crystal, I said, "I know what I saw." And then I turned my back on all three of their blank faces and stormed dramatically out of the living room and into the kitchen.

When I returned, wine bottle in hand, I tilted it to my

mouth and drank deeply before I looked them in their eyes and said in my best "I see dead people" voice, "I saw her. She was dead, and Kendrick was the one that killed her!"

They looked at each other and then back at me before Crystal calmly said, "Okay, Chevy, sit down and start from the beginning."

I told as much as I could without incriminating myself. I explained that Cassius and I were casual friends. That we'd worked together and she'd introduced me to her brother, who was visiting from Nigeria. I explained that I was at her loft for brunch and that her brother, Abimbola, had stepped out to get some eggs and that she and I were sitting in the kitchen drinking coffee when the knock came at the door.

When she opened it, Kendrick stormed in looking like a madman and demanding drugs.

"Drugs?" Crystal said, and even though she sounded as if she didn't believe it, I could see by the look on her face that she kind of did.

"She was a drug dealer?" Noah asked, in awe.

"Well, I didn't know that until then," I lied.

I went on to say that Cassius told him that she didn't have any in the house, and that he'd better leave before her brother came back.

"And what were you doing all of this time?" Geneva said.

"Didn't Kendrick recognize you?" Noah added, and

Geneva, Crystal, and I looked at him like he had three heads.

"C'mon, Noah, Kendrick had met Chevy only three or four times to begin with," Crystal said.

"And you know Chevy looks like someone different each time you see her," Geneva added.

"True," Noah said, nodding his head.

"So what were you doing while all of this was going on?" Geneva asked again.

"Well, like I said, I was in the kitchen, and when they took their little discussion into the living room, I ran out the front door."

I'd fucked up somewhere. I could tell by the way they were looking at me. But I'd been talking so fast, I didn't know where I'd made the wrong turn.

"So if you left, then how do you know that he killed her?" Crystal asked.

I turned the bottle up to my mouth again and drained it.

"What I meant to say was I left *after* he knocked her down."

"In the living room?" Geneva said.

"Yeah," I answered quickly and then said to Noah, "You got any more wine?"

"No, but there's some Grey Goose in the freezer," he said, and I was gone before he could hardly get all of the words out of his mouth.

I returned with a glass filled with vodka and ice.

Noah scratched at his chin and said, "On the phone you told me she was sprawled out on the kitchen floor."

"Did I?" I took a long sip of my drink, swallowed, and made a face before speaking again. "I was nervous, Noah! Kitchen, living room, what does it matter—she was dead!" I shrieked and got up and started walking circles.

"Did you call the police?" Crystal asked, total belief blanketing her face.

"Hell, no!" I said.

"I told her to," Noah said. "But you know she's hardheaded."

"Well, I'm going to call the police," Crystal said and jumped up and started toward the kitchen. I scrambled in front of her and pressed one unsteady hand against her shoulder. "I don't think you should."

Crystal eyed me. "Wasn't this Cassius a friend of yours?" Crystal cocked her head to one side. "Are you that coldhearted? Would you do one of us like that, Chevy?"

I looked around at the expectant faces, took another swig of my drink, and then said in a slurring voice, "She was just an acquaintance."

Crystal sucked her teeth and shoved past me.

"What's the address, Chevy?" Crystal yelled at me from the kitchen.

I looked stupidly around as if the answer was somewhere in the air. "What's the address?" Noah pushed.

I could hear Crystal in the kitchen, saying, "Yes, I'd like to report a murder."

"What's the goddamn address!" Geneva screamed at me.

That finally snatched me out of my daze, and I answered: "Three hundred West Seventeenth Street, top-floor loft."

Crystal was repeating the address when a pain suddenly cut through my stomach. I doubled over and fell to my knees.

"Ugh, I don't feel so good," I said before I started puking wine and vodka all over Noah's shiny hardwood floors.

Fifty-Seven

Needless to say, we had to rush Chevy to the emergency room at Brooklyn Hospital. We were all convinced that she was pregnant and just in denial, because if you opened up the dictionary and looked up the word *denial*, you were sure to find her picture right next to it.

When they rolled her into the examination room, we followed—yes, all three of us—refusing to let Chevy out of our sight.

Chevy was green, and each time the doctor pressed down on her stomach she spewed more vodka and wine.

Dr. Chin was the attending physician's name. He was a handsome, deeply sun-kissed Trinidadian with slanted eyes and a long silky ponytail. If Chevy weren't on her dying bed, she would have been pushing up on him.

Dr. Chin pressed some more and then asked Chevy, who seemed to be swinging in and out of consciousness, if she had fibroids.

Chevy just groaned and threw up. So he turned his attention to us. "Do you know if your friend has fibroids?"

Noah made a face and turned away. I shrugged: who knew what Chevy had? She was so secretive about shit.

Crystal was the one who said, "I don't think so."

The doctor considered us for a moment and then went back to examining Chevy. "Well, there are a lot of small lumps in her lower abdomen that could be fibroids, but the problem is that the lumps are also prevalent in her upper abdomen," he said thoughtfully. "I'm going to have to send her down for X-rays."

"You don't think she's pregnant?" Crystal asked.

The doctor snapped the gloves off his hands and discarded them into a nearby receptacle. "If she is, that will come up in the blood test."

We were all then hustled out of the examining room and into the waiting area. "She should be done with the X-rays in about a half hour," the doctor said before he disappeared behind the green curtain of another exam area.

We just sat there, quiet, for a while, watching people come and go, until finally Noah looked over at Crystal and me and said, "Miss Girls, I have a confession to make."

It's amazing what being around sickness and approaching death can do to a person. Noah spilled his guts about his heterosexual escapades.

At first we thought Noah was just being humorous, trying to shed some comedy on an otherwise dismal situation, but when we saw the tears in his eyes, we knew he was telling the truth.

"Why didn't you tell us this before?" Crystal said, digging into the pockets of her tracksuit in search of a tissue.

"How could I tell my girls something like that? It's so embarrassing." He sniffed.

"You should never feel embarrassed about telling us anything," I said, and I meant it.

"You shouldn't have had to go through something like that alone," Crystal said, trying hard to keep a straight face.

Noah peered at her through his tears. "What's so funny?"

Crystal's face was twitching uncontrollably. She was fighting hard to remain serious. "What is so funny!" Noah demanded, his voice filling with anger.

"I'm sorry, Noah," Crystal blurted out behind a roll of laughter. "I just can't imagine you and a woman . . . you know, getting it on!"

Now I was laughing too—it was a funny mental picture.

"Well, I did," Noah said, snapping his fingers and twirling his head on his neck. "And I was good!" he said before joining in on our laughter.

After we'd composed ourselves, Crystal turned her attention to me. "Now that we're confessing here, do you have anything you want to clear your soul of?"

Noah's eyebrows climbed his forehead. "What you hiding?"

"Nothing," I said, a little too quickly.

"Earlier today she was walking down the street like an escaped convict."

"*Whaaaaaaat!*" Noah shouted. "Who you hiding from, Miss Girl?"

I really didn't want to get into this. I mean, as fucked up as Noah's situation was, mine was simply unbelievable.

I took a deep breath and said, "I got the head honcho of my weight-loss program chapter out to kill me."

Noah and Crystal looked at me, back at each other, and then they doubled over with laughter.

"I'm serious," I said, folding my arms across my chest and turning away from them.

Crystal wiped at her eyes and looked at me. "C'mon now, Geneva. I know you have a wild imagination, but out to *kill* you?" she said, and the giggles started up again.

"I think those brain freezes from all of that goddamn ice cream you've eaten have affected the part of your mind that separates fantasy from reality," Noah whispered through a grin.

"Okay, don't believe me," I said and dug into my pocketbook for my pack of Newports. "I'm going outside to have a smoke." I stormed off, leaving my snickering, insensitive friends behind me.

Three cigarettes later, I had resigned myself to the fact that Noah and Crystal were not insensitive. I mean, what I said did sound ridiculous. I laughed at my reaction, tossed the butt of the cigarette to the ground, and turned and started back toward the glass hospital doors.

As I stood waiting for the elevator, two large white men dressed in navy blue from head to toe suddenly appeared beside me.

The elevator doors opened and we stepped aside to allow an elderly man being pushed in a wheelchair by a young woman to pass.

"After you," one of the men said to me.

I mumbled a word of thanks as I stepped into the elevator and moved to the back wall.

The men stepped in and took up the space in front of me. They stood at attention, their shoulders touching.

"Floor?" one said to the other.

"Five," the other responded and then turned around a bit and looked at me. "Ma'am?"

"Um, I'm going to five too," I said.

The doors slid closed and the elevator began to climb.

Once we got to the fifth floor and the elevator doors opened again, the two men turned to face each other, leaving a wide gap for me to pass through.

"After you, ma'am."

This day just keeps getting weirder, I thought as I stepped between them. As I passed, my eyes caught hold of the shiny brass badges that hung from chains around their necks. The badges had big blue letters pressed into their center that said DEA.

I heard the little girl in me moan, *Oooooohh, you're in troubbbbbbble!*

I walked toward Noah and Crystal, but my eyes were on the DEA agents, who were marching past the nurses' station and back toward the exam rooms.

"Are you okay?" Crystal said, a wisp of a smile still on her lips.

I shook my head yes, my eyes still on the men, even though I couldn't understand why I was so bothered by them.

"Miss Girl, can you tell me again about someone trying to kill—" Noah had started to chide me, but I put my hand up when one of the DEA agents reappeared, asked the nurse something, and then turned and looked directly at us.

"Oh, shit," I said.

The agent marched over to us and said, "Are you with Chevanese Cambridge?"

Noah's and Crystal's eyes were pinned on his badge. They nodded their heads slowly up and down, and then I knew that they were feeling that same uneasiness that I was experiencing.

"Come with me, please," he said and turned on his heel and marched away.

We followed him into an empty examination room, where he told us to have a seat; he then left, pulling the green curtain closed behind him.

We all exchanged looks and did exactly what we were told. There were only two chairs in the room. Crystal took one and let Noah take the other, because it looked as if his legs had turned to rubber.

"What the hell has Ms. Drama gotten us into!" Noah snarled.

Crystal looked at the curtain and then back at Noah. "Shhhh," she hissed at him.

We were separated from the next room by a soft retractable wall, which offered about as much privacy as the hospital curtain that enclosed us, so we were able to hear the entire conversation going on between Dr. Chin and the agents.

"The X-ray revealed foreign matter in her stomach. Looking closer, I realized what it was, and that's why I called you guys."

"You did the right thing," one of the agents said.

"How much longer?" the other inquired.

"Shouldn't be too much longer now. We gave her a double-strength enema," Dr. Chin said.

We all shook our heads in disbelief.

"Am I hearing what I think I'm hearing?" Noah whispered. Crystal and I just nodded.

"Why are they holding us, though?" he said.

"They're probably going to say we were her accomplices," I blurted out.

Noah's eyes bulged. "I can't do no time! I am too pretty, and you girls know what happens to pretty boys in prison!"

"We haven't done a thing. We're innocent," Crystal said, and I was surprised at the calmness in her voice. "If Chevy has done what they're suspecting she has, it is all on her."

A moment later we heard another voice say, "We've extracted all of the foreign matter, Dr. Chin."

"Put the bowl down here," Dr. Chin said. "Hmm, just as I thought. Condoms."

Noah made the sign of the cross on his chest, squeezed his eyes shut, and began silently to pray.

It was eerily quiet for a few minutes on that side of the wall, and then one of the agents announced, with great disappointment, "It's sugar."

Noah, Crystal, and I looked at each other in disbelief and said, "Sugar?"

After an odd moment of silence that was followed by some embarrassed clearing of throats, the curtain enclosing us was snatched open.

"I don't know what your friend was planning to do,"

the agent started, blanketing us with an icy stare, "but whatever it was, I suggest you all think better of it."

We all exchanged looks.

"You're free to go for the moment, but know that Big Brother is watching all of you," he said as he tapped his left eye with his index finger.

Noah was the first to scamper nervously past the DEA agent, and Crystal and I followed close behind.

Dr. Chin was standing in the hallway, watching the agents march toward the elevators. He had a dumbfounded look on his face, and when he looked up and saw us approaching he turned and started to walk quickly in the other direction. "Your friend is in room 203," he mumbled, before snatching a clipboard from a passing nurse and demanding that she follow him.

"Punk," Crystal said.

We took the stairs down three flights and after some time found ourselves standing in front of room 203.

Chevy was propped up in a hospital bed, snoring, a Tide commercial blaring from the wall television.

I picked the remote up from the nightstand and turned the volume down.

"Wake up, heffa," Noah yelled as he gave Chevy's arm a nasty jab.

Chevy's eyes rolled and her lids fluttered open. "Hey," she said, giving us a sleepy smile.

"Hey, nothing. Do you know what—" Noah started to screech, but Crystal pulled him away from the bed.

"None of that matters now," she said in a soft voice, then turned her attention to Chevy. "How are you feeling?"

"Well," Chevy said, smacking her mouth like a geriatric patient, "I did feel like someone had stuck their hand up my ass and pulled a grown person out of my stomach, but after the Percocet, I feel *fiiiiiiiiiiiiiiiinnnnnnnnnnne* as wine," she half slurred, half laughed.

"I bet you do," Noah huffed.

"Tell me something, Chevy?" I asked, coming to stand beside her. "How many of those condoms did you swallow?"

Chevy's face strained with concentration as she fought with the wall the Percocet had put up in her mind. "Oh, oh yeah, I remember," she said, trying to raise her head, "forty!"

"Forty!" Crystal yelled.

"Damn fool," Noah mumbled as he shook his head.

"Well, what the hell did you tell them when they asked you why in the world you'd swallowed them in the first place?"

A stupid grin spread across Chevy's face and she blurted, "I said, 'Haven't you heard? It's the newest craze in appetite suppression!'"

That was Chevy for you—always thinking on her feet!

Fifty-Eight

Chevy rolled in and out of her Percocet-induced haze, sometimes muttering obscenities, other times laughing out loud, but mostly snoring like a black man after a long day and a fifth of Thunderbird.

Dr. Chin strolled in and was visibly stunned to see us. He quickly moved his eyes to the clipboard he was carrying and said, "We're just going to keep her overnight for observation. She'll be released tomorrow morning at about eleven." He then turned and rushed out.

I just shook my head, stood up, stretched, and was about to suggest that we leave when Noah snatched the remote control from my hand, frantically pressing the volume button as he said, "Isn't that Kendrick, Crystal?"

We all looked up at the television to see a ragged-looking Kendrick peering menacingly into the camera. He was handcuffed and being shoved into the back of a police cruiser by two officers.

Roz Abrams was at the scene:

Police said they'd received an anonymous tip earlier that day and sent detectives here, three hundred West

Seventeenth Street, a luxury loft apartment building in the Chelsea section of Manhattan.

Authorities walked in to find two men fighting. One man was Kendrick Greene. The other man has been identified as Abimbola Lenguele of the Nigerian Doshi drug cartel.

There were more than eighty vials of the highly addictive drug Hades in the apartment, as well as assault weapons.

Police are still searching for another member of the Doshi cartel, a woman, one Cassius Maynard.

The studio floated a glamorous picture of Cassius in the upper right-hand corner of the screen.

Noah and I looked at Crystal, our mouths hanging open.

Crystal couldn't seem to stop her eyelids from blinking.

"Are you okay?" I ventured, walking over to Crystal and throwing my arms around her and embracing her in a warm hug.

"I'm fine," she said, hugging me back. "To tell you the truth, I think I feel relieved. Is that wrong?"

"Of course it's not," I said.

"So I guess Ms. Drama was telling the truth?" Noah said, pointing down at the snoring Chevy.

"Yeah, I guess she was," Crystal said, bending and giving Chevy a loving kiss on the cheek.

"Damn," Noah breathed as he shook his head at the

television screen. "You never know what's going on behind someone's groove, huh?"

"Ain't that the truth," I said.

Crystal nodded in agreement, and then her face broke into a sunny smile and she said, "I think I need a drink—what about y'all?"

Fifty-Nine

So that's the story of how we ended up in the Brooklyn Hospital emergency room two days before Labor Day.

Oh, sure, I could have given you the short version, but then you would have missed out on all the good stuff in between!

Little Eric came back from basketball camp the next day. I swear he looked as if he'd grown six inches!

We all spent Labor Day with Noah and his lover, Zhan. They look good together and seem to be very much in love. And he's a good guy; he totally understood when Noah shared his "little problem" with him.

A month later and after some prodding, we finally got the entire version of Chevy's involvement with Abimbola and Cassius. She claims that she's learned her lesson and is working on changing her selfish, senseless, money-worshipping ways. I guess having to sit on a rubber doughnut for three weeks will do that to you. But I'm not quite sure she's totally sincere; why, just the other day when we were strolling through the Village I caught her ogling a Pucci scarf in the window of a high-end boutique.

She has to appear in court next week in order to clear up her warrant situation. Crystal got the attorney who works with AIW to represent her pro bono, and he feels that he can get her off with just a slap on the wrist and a year or so of probation.

In the meantime, she's still living with Noah, but he's barely there and, in fact, seriously thinking about selling the house and moving to England with Zhan. He'll be missed, but that'll give me a reason to finally get my fat ass on a plane!

Crystal is still beautiful and successful. The insurance money she received from the flood and the little she borrowed from her bank account allowed her to renovate the entire apartment, and it looks even more fabulous than before.

She gets lonely sometimes and has confided in me that she doesn't know when or if she'll ever be able to let someone get as close to her as Kendrick did.

I told her that her Prince Charming is out there, the two of them just haven't found each other yet. She knows it's true; she just likes to hear someone say it every now and then. In the meantime she's decided to train for the New York Marathon, which brings things around to me.

The Wednesday after Labor Day I received a call from the weight czar Miriam. Right off she began ranting, raving, and belittling me, and once again I found myself sitting there like an obedient, emotionally abused child, just taking it.

I looked around and saw the place I had made into a home. Turned and looked at my big beautiful son, who was standing at the stove frying franks. Thought about where I had come from and where I was going and realized that this bitch didn't fit into my life—past, present, or future. I calmly said, "Miriam, if you call my home again, I'm going to come up to your office and put my foot so far up your ass, you'll be able to taste the sole of my aerobic sneaker in your mouth."

And, with that, I hung up the phone.

Not too long after that, I saw on the news that someone had finally blown the whistle on Calorie Counters, hitting the company with a ten-million-dollar harassment lawsuit.

I was watching with glee as they brought Miriam Baxter out in handcuffs. She looked exactly the way I pictured her. Built like a man, face like a bulldog, and a military haircut. She growled at the cameraperson and head-butted the reporter who kept pushing his microphone in her face.

I've since joined Jenny Craig and have lost two pounds!

Little Eric and I spend a lot of time looking through college brochures. He's excited that we'll be attending college at the same time. He tells me how proud he is of me for making the decision to continue my education and even throws in an "I love you" every now and again.

His father is coming around more often to be with Little Eric. It's slow going, but they're starting to warm up to each other, and I'm glad for that.

I'd been hinting around to Crystal that I was beginning to feel guilty about sleeping with Eric and was thinking about cutting him off, so to get me to go the extra mile, she gave me a gift.

A nine-inch-long, candy-striped vibrator!

The first night I used it, I came so hard and screamed

so loud, the neighbor above me banged on the floor and screamed, "Keep it down! Damn!"

After that night I named the vibrator Mandingo and knew that Eric would never get another drop of my loving again!

Anyway, it was time to stop fooling around with him. I realized that we were tempting fate each and every time we'd been together, because the last time we had sex, the condom broke. Now if that's not a sign from God, I don't know what is.

My period's not due for another week, but I'm not worried. Really, I'm not . . .

About the Author

Bernice L. McFadden is an associate professor of English at Tulane University and the author most recently of the memoir *Firstborn Girls*, and of several critically acclaimed novels, including *Sugar*, *The Warmest December*, *Loving Donovan*, *Nowhere Is a Place*, *Glorious*, *Gathering of Waters* (a *New York Times* Editors' Choice and one of the 100 Notable Books of 2012), *The Book of Harlan* (winner of a 2017 American Book Award and the NAACP Image Award for Outstanding Literary Work, Fiction), and *Praise Song for the Butterflies* (longlisted for the 2019 Women's Prize for Fiction). She is a five-time Hurston/Wright Legacy Award finalist, as well as the recipient of three awards from the Black Caucus of the American Library Association.